PRAISE FOR LISA RENEE JONES

"Jones's suspense truly sizzles with an energy similar to FBI tales with a paranormal twist by Julie Garwood or Suzanne Brockmann."

—*Booklist*

"Intoxicating, intense, and deeply seductive."

—*RT Book Reviews* (Top Pick) on *Escaping Reality* (*RT Book Reviews* Award for Best Romantic Suspense, 2015)

"Darkly intense and deeply erotic, each new reveal involving Chris and Sara leaves you raw and restless, emotions running high as you wait for the next obstacle. These books are an addiction!"

—*RT Book Reviews* (Top Pick) on *No In Between*

"Passionate, all-consuming."

—POPSUGAR

MURDER
GIRL

OTHER TITLES BY LISA RENEE JONES

CARELESS WHISPERS

Denial

Demand

Surrender

THE SECRET LIFE OF AMY BENSEN

Escaping Reality

Infinite Possibilities

Forsaken

Unbroken

INSIDE OUT

If I Were You

Being Me

Revealing Us

His Secrets

Rebecca's Lost Journals

The Master Undone

My Hunger

No In Between

My Control

I Belong to You

All of Me

ZODIUS

Michael

Sterling

Kel

Damion

VAMPIRE WARDENS

Hot Vampire Kiss
Hot Vampire Seduction
Hot Vampire Touch

WEREWOLF SOCIETY

Wicked Werewolf Night
Wicked Werewolf Secret
Wicked Werewolf Passion

THE KNIGHTS OF WHITE

The Beast Within
Beast of Desire
Return of the Beast
Beast of Darkness
Demon's Seduction
Captive of the Beast
Beast of Fire

MURDER GIRL

LISA RENEE JONES

Montlake
Romance

Text copyright © 2018 by Julie Patra Publishing
All rights reserved.

Published by Montlake Romance, Seattle

www.apub.com

Amazon, the Amazon logo, and Montlake Romance are trademarks of Amazon.com, Inc., or its affiliates.

ISBN-13: 9781503902619
ISBN-10: 1503902617

Cover design by Caroline T. Johnson

Printed in the United States of America

MURDER GIRL

CHARACTERS

Lilah Love (28)—dark-brown hair, brown eyes, curvy figure. An FBI profiler working in Los Angeles, she grew up in the Hamptons. Her mother was a famous movie star who died tragically in a plane crash, which caused Lilah to leave law school prematurely and eventually pursue a career in law enforcement. Lilah's father is the mayor in East Hampton; her brother is the Hamptons' chief of police. She dated Kane Mendez against her father's wishes. She was brutally attacked one night, and Kane came to her rescue, somewhat, and what unfolded that night created a secret between the two they can never share with anyone else. This eventually causes Lilah to leave and take the job in LA, away from her family, Kane, and that secret.

Kane Mendez (32)—brown hair, dark-brown eyes, leanly muscled body. He's the CEO of Mendez Enterprises and thought to be the leader of the cartel that his father left behind when he was killed. But Kane claims his uncle runs the operations, while he runs the legitimate side of the business. Lilah's ex from before she left for LA. He found her the night of her attack and shares that secret with her.

Director Murphy (50s)—gray hair, perfectly groomed. Former military. Lilah's boss. The head of the LA branch of the FBI. Sent Lilah to the Hamptons to follow the assassin case.

Rich Moore—blond surfer-dude looks, blue eyes. Works with Lilah. He and Lilah were sleeping together until Rich wanted more and Lilah called it off.

Jeff "Tic Tac" Landers—Lilah's go-to tech guy at the FBI.

Grant Love (57)—blue eyes, graying hair. Lilah's father, the mayor, and retired police chief of East Hampton. A perfect politician. Charming. He's being groomed by Ted Pocher to run for New York governor.

Andrew Love (34)—blond hair, blue eyes. Lilah's brother and the East Hampton police chief. Andrew is protective and seems to be the perfect brother. The problem is that he's perfect at everything, including being as macho and as bossy as their father. There's more to Andrew than meets the eye.

Alexandra Harris-Rivera (29)—brown hair, pretty. Assistant District Attorney of Suffolk County; Lilah's ex–best friend. They didn't go to school together but grew up hanging out on the local beaches with each other. Lilah has her reasons for cutting off all communication with Alexandra, but she has yet to share them with her. Alexandra is now married to Eddie Rivera.

Eddie Rivera (30)—buzzed brown hair. A detective who had a chip on his shoulder growing up. He knows Lilah from their youth and was ever present at their family dinners around the time Lilah left the Hamptons. He went through some hard times, and Lilah's dad took him under his wing. He had a thing for Lilah, but she was all about Kane. His own father was an ass, and her dad has become a father figure to him. He's also married to Alexandra Harris, who was Lilah's best friend during her college years.

Samantha Young (27)—blonde, gorgeous. A powerful socialite in the Hamptons. She had a "relationship" of convenience with Kane prior to his dating Lilah, and they have struck it up again in the years since Lilah left the Hamptons, even though Samantha is supposed to be dating Andrew Love, Lilah's brother.

Lucas Davenport—tall, looks like a preppy version of Tarzan. A very successful and good-looking investment banker, he has taken to hacking in his spare time. He is a cousin of sorts to Lilah and Andrew. His father was the stepbrother to Lilah's father. His father was also known to be with Lilah's mother, Laura, on the night they both disappeared in the plane crash. He flirts mercilessly with Lilah, seeing as they're not blood related, but she always shoots him down.

Greg Harrison—Lilah's old partner from the New York Police Department. Currently in a lot of hot water with Internal Affairs over an incident that may or may not be of his own making. He was partnered with Nelson Moser prior to being put on leave by IA pending further investigation but has been working independent security with Moser in the meantime.

Nelson Moser—a lowlife police detective who offended Lilah on numerous occasions before she moved to Los Angeles. She is not very fond of him, and the rumor circulating about him is that he's a dirty cop.

Laura Love—Lilah's mother. Famous actress. Died four years ago in a horrific plane crash. She infamously portrayed Marilyn Monroe in an Oscar-winning performance. Much mystery still surrounds her death, and will be a recurring issue throughout the series.

Ted Pocher—billionaire CEO of the world's fifth-largest privately held conglomerate, Pocher Industries. Has taken a liking to Lilah's father in hopes of furthering her father's political career. He tried to do business with Kane and Mendez Enterprises but was turned down because of his rep for shady business deals.

Beth Smith—blonde, tall, thin. New medical examiner in Suffolk County. Lilah's friend from back in the day. Beth is working one of the assassin murder cases.

DEAR READERS:

Thank you so much for picking up the next book in the Lilah Love series! If you haven't read Book 1, *Murder Notes*, please don't read any further! I'm about to recap Book 1, which will contain spoilers. In Book 1, you met Lilah Love, a brash and intensely dedicated FBI agent, as she is called to a crime scene on the Santa Monica Pier. As she gets ready to dispatch to the scene, we witness a quarrel between her and her bed partner, Rich Moore, who she works with at the FBI. This is obviously an ongoing relationship, but Lilah is trying to put on the brakes once Rich yet again mentions their moving in together. The relationship was never that serious for Lilah, and she wants to put space between them now. They leave things with Lilah saying he deserves more and him saying they'll talk about it later.

Back to this murder case on the Santa Monica Pier that will set into motion the case that unfolds over the first two books in this series: a naked male body has been discovered on the beach, much like a crime scene Lilah and the locals worked two days prior. But what is different is the tattoo on the body, which harkens Lilah back to her attack two years ago in the Hamptons where she grew up. And through that flashback we learn the attack was sinister and definitely had an impact on Lilah's future. As Lilah is consorting with the locals on this latest case, her boss, Director Murphy, shows up and tells her of a similar case in New York. With both cases spanning more than one state and the body count rising, Murphy wants Lilah out there. This is when she tells him she's seen that tattoo before but refrains from divulging in what capacity.

Murphy sends Lilah to the Hamptons to get a read on the situation. But as she lands, she's called to another crime scene: a murder identical to the two in LA and the one in New York. From the looks of all the murders, everyone assumes the perp is a serial killer, but Lilah is convinced they're dealing with an assassin, someone who has a hit list they're marking off one by one on orders from someone else. Who is calling the shots is a mystery for Lilah to figure out.

The case in the Hamptons has her back in the web of her ex-boyfriend, Kane Mendez, in two seconds flat. It's his rental property the body was found at and his employee who was murdered. This doesn't look good for Kane, but Lilah knows him, and despite the murmurings of his running the local cartel that his father once ran prior to his death, she knows this isn't Kane's doing. Of course, that doesn't stop Kane from showing up and taunting Lilah in an attempt to get her back in his bed, which fails to work . . . this time. Lilah refuses Kane. He's too much of a reminder of the night she was attacked, and too much of a risk to her reputation.

As Lilah deals with the locals on the Hamptons case, she runs into Beth Smith, now the medical examiner and who she once knew in school, and Eddie Rivera, a smart-ass cop, now detective, who was always trying to steal her father's affection and attention growing up.

Lilah is still going through the scenarios of the murders as she pulls up to her beach house, where she was attacked on that night two years ago. And of course, being Lilah, she decides to face those memories head-on. Prior to going inside, she goes out to the beach where the attack took place, reliving those horrific moments. After Lilah regains her composure from that memory and heads back to the beach house to get to work on the cases, there's a message waiting for her in fake blood on the side of the house:

A is for the Apple a day that keeps the doctor away. But a doctor couldn't help him, could he?
I KNOW.

The author of this message is a person Lilah begins to think of as "Junior," and the message is the first of what she calls "murder notes." So now Lilah has two mysteries to solve: Who is the assassin, and who else was there the night of her attack who knows her and Kane's secret? Lilah sets up shop in Purgatory—the name for the room in the cottage where she organizes her cases and does her best work—and then makes lists on top of lists of who could be responsible for any and all of this. She reminds herself of the nickname people have for her: Murder Girl. It describes how she's so good at what she's done to solve cases: she can be more in tune with a dead body than a live one. She lives and breathes murder scenes and gets inside the perp's head.

While she's in Purgatory, Rich and Kane both call, Rich wanting to be the one Lilah depends on, which doesn't work for her right then and there, and Kane trying to get under Lilah's skin, where he's always been, and also to give her his solid alibi: he was with his friends-with-benefits buddy, Samantha, which rubs Lilah the wrong way considering they were an FWB pair prior to Lilah and Kane being together years ago. Kane signs off with a reminder that he knows Lilah's demons and he can help ease them if she'll let him. Which, of course, she won't.

Following that little chat, none other than the East Hampton chief of police shows up at Lilah's door, her brother, Andrew. They banter back and forth about jurisdiction, their father, who Andrew even calls so he can talk to Lilah, and an upcoming press conference on the murder. The conversation ends with Andrew telling Lilah that he's in a relationship with Samantha Young, *the* Samantha Young who just happens to be Kane's alibi for the time of the murder . . .

Once Lilah is alone again and back at her drawing boards, she can't shake one thought: she's the common denominator in all of this. The murders. The notes. The tattoos. Samantha and her brother and Kane. New York and California. But there could be a multitude of connections that just haven't been realized yet. And with that conclusion, Lilah is making lists of things and people she needs to look into. This effort fades into a nightmare-laden sleep with Lilah remembering more of *that night*: her and Kane bloodied, her sans clothing, and an eerie feeling to the memory that is still not fully realized.

Lilah sends a set of fingerprints from her house to be tested by Tic Tac, her go-to FBI tech guy back in California, in hopes that the prints will match someone out of the ordinary. In the meantime, she pays a visit to Kane at his office and grills him about his whereabouts last night, and about Samantha and Andrew. She learns that her father is running for New York governor, and that Andrew and Samantha aren't necessarily as squeaky-clean as they'd like everyone to believe they are. And that, along with his bid for governor, her father has gotten wrapped up in favors owed to a rival of the Mendez family/cartel, the Romanos. As Lilah leaves in a rage over the things Kane is keeping from her, she finds another note on her car:

T is for TRUST.
You TRUSTED him.
F is for FOOL.
That's YOU.

Lilah then heads off to question Samantha, which ultimately amounts to nothing but more questions and the refusal by Samantha to back up Kane's alibi.

Lilah needs answers, so she contacts Beth, the medical examiner, and asks to meet her at the local diner. Before Beth arrives, Lilah runs into her ex–best friend, Alexandra, who is the assistant district attorney and married to Eddie Rivera, now a detective, who has always competed for her father's attention and been a general asshole. Alexandra's presence throws Lilah back into a flashback of *that night*; Alexandra was with her at a bar prior to her attack. They'd seen the movie star Jensen Michaels at the bar, and even though they were celebrating Lilah's birthday, Lilah convinced Alexandra to go talk with him as she'd been lusting after him for quite a while. All through this Lilah had been texting with Kane, who was in New York but getting on a chopper to come back to the Hamptons. When Lilah got up to leave the bar, it became very evident that she'd been drugged somehow. But by who? As Lilah comes back to the present, it's divulged that after that night, Lilah cut Alexandra out of her life for good—thus the *ex*–best friend title.

Alexandra now spots Lilah in the diner, and they have an almost inane conversation about the potential reasons Lilah may be in town; she sticks with "it's personal" and other cursory shoptalk. As Alexandra leaves to take a phone call, Beth arrives, and Lilah digs in deep about the current murder case. Before they can get any further, Eddie shows up and intervenes, demanding that Lilah back off and even claiming he has a suspect: Kevin Woods, who seems to have had a violent history with the victim. But as Beth is leaving, she confides to Lilah that Kevin Woods shouldn't take the hit for this murder. She knows he's not a killer.

Lilah asks Tic Tac for background on Woods. The locals are just trying to get him for their one case and not the rest of the murders, a strategy that is already making Lilah suspicious of their motives. Eddie seems to be very adamant that Lilah leave town and not get involved. And Kane is very adamant that Lilah leave the tattoo connection alone. So who's playing who?

Lilah calls up Lucas Davenport, her "cousin" (really, her step cousin—his father was her father's stepbrother, but Lucas is family all the same to her). Her endgame is to get him to help her hook up a security-camera system for her house. If someone vandalizes it again or leaves her another note, she'll have it on tape. There's a brief mention of her mother's death: she was with Lucas's father in the plane that went down. No one knows why they were together or what may have really happened on that flight.

Once Lilah is home and has the cameras set up, she dials Kane to ask for video proof of his alibi since Samantha didn't corroborate his story. But it's also an excuse to ask for footage from his office to see if she can discover who left the note. Of course, Kane calls her on her falsities but still confirms he'll get all the information over to her the next day.

Lilah, in the meantime, has been invited to a family dinner at her father's house that night. When she arrives, she notices a fancy car that doesn't belong to either her father or brother but learns soon enough that it belongs to Ted Pocher, the billionaire CEO of the world's fifth-largest privately held conglomerate. Pocher tried to partner with Kane in their oil businesses, but Kane refused, causing bad blood between the two. Pocher is the driving force behind Lilah's father's political agenda.

Lilah is greeted by her father, and as she's led to the dining room she's accosted by her brother, Eddie, and Alexandra at the table, who seem to have become regulars in her father's house in her absence. They fight. Lilah's pissed about their presence, Alexandra baiting her for information at the diner earlier, and Eddie in general. Eddie, likewise, is pissed about Lilah's potential jurisdictional claim, and Andrew insists he will "deal with Lilah," which of course does not sit well with her. Lilah challenges their supposed proof of Woods's guilt, and Alexandra says he called her and confessed in a voice mail while rambling like a crazy person. Once Lilah secures a promise that she will receive a copy of the "confession," she leaves her father's house. There is no doubt in her mind that the locals, her family especially, want this case closed immediately so as not to mar her father's bid to become the next governor of New York.

Lilah hits up Tic Tac for more information on Woods, of which he doesn't have much other than a few flimsy connections between Woods's clientele and the places of the murders. Lilah then updates her boss, Murphy, on the situation. They discuss how to go about claiming jurisdiction and if they have enough evidence to do so. But they need to find Woods first.

Lilah concludes that she needs any information she doesn't already have from Kane and has him meet her at "their spot" at the Cove. It was the spot where they first met, and where they would always meet thereafter. While there, she questions him about the cartel, and he insists that he did not follow in his father's footsteps and take control. Kane divulges that he doesn't know anything else about the murder, that he's looking into it as well, and that there is a singular for-hire killer who kills the same way that the assassin has been killing. After Kane refuses to tell her more about the assassin because she might drive him underground, she gives him forty-eight hours to get her the name of the assassin or something else she can go off.

Of course, Kane reviewed the tapes he promised her and noticed someone slipping a note on Lilah's car. Kane tells her that the person had their face covered, so there was no way to ID the person. When he questions her on it, Lilah avoids answering and leaves him with his deadline to deliver information.

At home, Lilah calls Lucas to discuss the security cameras they've put in place, and he informs her he needs a date on Saturday night to a charity event her father and Pocher are hosting. She agrees so she can get an inside look at some people who are ending up potential key players in the case. Junior leaves another note for Lilah on her chair:

D is for Deception.

While waiting for a few key points to manifest, Lilah decides to approach the New York murder by speaking with the detective who handled the case. Said detective, Marcus Rick, is out on leave, and now Nelson Moser has the case. Moser is an ex-colleague of Lilah's who she shares a bitter past with. She also tries to get in touch with her ex-partner, Greg Harrison, but he's out as well, leaving Lilah no choice but to track him down and see what he knows.

Arriving at the train station, Lilah is bombarded by the media, and Kane shows up as a saving grace and ends up choppering her into the city for her errands. It's here where Kane and Lilah divulge more details of what went down *that night*. Lilah was drugged, and whatever she did would have caused her to lose her badge if Kane hadn't helped hide the body. Though the true events are still a little hazy, as are the long-lasting impacts of it.

In the city, Lilah touches base with Tic Tac, and Kane lets her know what really happened with Marcus Rick—he was at a corner store when a robbery took place and tried to help, only to end up with a bullet in his gut and on leave. Thus Nelson took over the case, and word is he's about as dirty as a snake. Lilah calls Greg after hearing this and tells him not to look into the New York case for fear he might get caught in the crosshairs.

When Lilah meets up with Greg, he's a drunken mess on forced leave from the department due to an Internal Affairs probe. Given that Moser is his partner now, since his old one died a few weeks ago, and he's being set up for taking bribes, there is a lot that doesn't match up right now. But Moser is giving him extra work in private security, which he doesn't like but he has to do to pay bills. Lilah promises to help Greg and leaves, now on the hunt for more answers about the tattoo.

Eventually cornered in an alleyway by an old man, Lilah learns that: "It's a blood tattoo. It bleeds because you bleed."

With that quote ingrained in her memory, Lilah heads home. On the trip back, she's accosted by the flashbacks of her attack in more vivid details and Kane's presence. The truth finally comes to light. Lilah was raped two years ago on the beach, and the minute Kane showed up to save her, she grabbed a knife and murdered her attacker, shoving the knife into him again and again and again. Kane buried the body, both of them having committed the perfect crime after a heinous one had been exacted on Lilah. Back to the present: Kane is pushing her to talk about the past and present. Their passion explodes into a one-off sexual encounter, after which Lilah brushes him off and sends him on his way.

The next morning, Lilah catches up with Tic Tac, who found a connection between Moser and the Romano family—the rival cartel to the Mendez cartel. The niece of one of the big Romano players has catered three of the last six events that Blink Security worked. Blink Security happens to be the company that Moser works for in his off-duty hours, and the one that he got Greg work with as well.

With that in mind, Lilah tracks down Moser, asking him for the case file on the New York murder. After Lilah catches Murphy up on the case, he mentions an army sniper who had the signature of the assassin. They called him Ghost. This is who Kane had to be talking about, so Lilah brings it up again, even threatening to go as far as approaching Romano about it.

Afterward, Lilah searches the words the old man in the alley said to her and comes up with a quote from a movie, *Take Me to Church*, that starred none other than Jensen Michaels—the movie star Alexandra hooked up with the night of Lilah's attack. Lilah's wheels start to churn. Did Alexandra help set her up to be attacked?

As more pieces start falling into place, Lilah gets yet another note, and with each one they become less and less effective in scaring her. This one reads:

B is for Body.
B is for Buried.
And I know where.
Do you?

She throws this note in her back seat.

As Lilah is leaving the bagel shop after having had quite the conversation with Andrew, Alexandra, and Eddie, she comes out to a flat tire and another note reading:

W is for Warning.
I don't like to be taunted.

Just then, Greg shows up. He's been called into town to work security for the charity event Lilah is attending that evening that her father and Pocher are hosting.

As Lilah is going through all her case files, she finds a familiar face staring back at her on the TV as she's watching *Take Me to Church*: Laney Suthers, a high-end call girl/actress who had a world-class client list that both the NYPD and Lilah were trying to get her to give up. They were close to turning her when they found she had committed suicide, though Lilah never believed that was the cause of death.

Lilah is now on the hunt to see if there is a connection between any of the film executives or funding companies. Tic Tac finds a Chinese production company that could be a lead, since Laney did two other movies under an alias with their backing, but nothing concrete turns up before Lilah has to attend the charity event.

Leaving the event, Lilah sees Greg getting quite close with none other than the previously mentioned niece of one of the big Romano cartel members. And as if that weren't enough, when Kane catches up with her, insisting on escorting her out, none other than Rich shows up. Lilah, afraid of how Kane will react, turns Rich away and tells him to go home.

Of course nothing can be that simple, but as promised Lilah takes a break from the intensity of the investigation and meets with Andrew at their mother's grave in the cemetery. And as they're discussing the likelihood of their mother having had an affair with their father's stepbrother—Lucas's father—who was also aboard the plane, though no one knows why, Andrew gets a call that there's been a decapitation murder in Manhattan. Decapitation. The calling card marker of a Mendez murder. Someone is trying to pin this on Kane. When Lilah gets to the gruesome scene with Andrew, there's a little-known message waiting for her. Something no one else would see as a message. The movie *Take Me to Church* is sticking out of the DVD player.

Lilah is convinced Kane has nothing to do with this. Back at her house, she orders a pizza only to have another message taped inside, this one reading *M is for Murder. Murder. Murder. Murder. Murder.* on one side and *K is for Kane. Kane. Kane. Kane. Kane.* on the other side. Lilah rushes off to see Kane. She needs answers and now.

But when she arrives at Kane's house and he ushers her into the garage, imagine her surprise when she finds the old man who gave her the clue bound and gagged there . . . And even more surprised when Kane informs her that this old man is the patriarch of the Romano cartel . . .

And that is where we left off. And that's exactly where we'll pick back up again . . .

CHAPTER ONE

It's Sunday night, and like many people, that means catching up on dirty laundry. Unlike most people, however, my list rarely includes jeans, shirts, and socks, though some might say it probably should. And it would if my list wasn't consumed by blood, bodies, and random crime scene nastiness. Tonight, that list includes Kane Mendez, my ex-lover, who swears he's clean when we both know he's dirty—as in the-head-of-the-Mendez-cartel dirty. A complicated piece of the puzzle that is my life. Kane runs a powerful legit business as well, I'm an FBI profiler, and at one point he and I have killed and hidden a body together, or rather in some combination of "together." I did the killing. He did the hiding.

Even more complicated is the fact that despite that secret, I'm presently standing in his garage pointing a gun at him, while the patriarch of the Romano family, who doesn't exactly get invited to the Mendez family outings, is tied to a chair and gagged several feet away. Of course, he's not the man we in law enforcement believe to be the patriarch, but Kane would know. And now I know, which is a weapon Kane has handed me, and not by accident. Kane does nothing by accident.

I give this newly discovered patriarch a quick once-over, confirming that he's the same sunbaked old man in jeans and a T-shirt, gray hair braided down his back, I remember cornering me at the tattoo shop in the city. He'd given me a lead I'd like to know more about, which means I need him alive, thus it's one of the reasons I confirm he's not dead, which isn't hard, since he's presently fast-blinking at me. That's enough for me to know he's not feeling really warm and fuzzy right now, and also enough for me to dismiss him, at least for the moment, and for the obvious reason: he's tied up and Kane is not.

I eye Kane, who is now two feet away and between me and the door, my gaze dropping to the silver cuff dangling from his wrist where I'd latched it the minute he opened the door. I part my lips to command him to cuff his second wrist, but in my mind, I play out exactly how that scene might be enacted:

I'd give him the same once-over I'd given the old man, as I do now, taking in his casual wear that's replaced his business suit: his black jeans and snug black T-shirt that reads MENDEZ ENTERPRISES, which we both know translates to Mendez cartel, and that would piss me off. I'd lift my gaze, look right into those dark-brown eyes, and issue my command. "Finish cuffing yourself."

He'd say, "I'm not going to do that."

I'd then say, "I won't kill you, Kane, but I will make you bleed, and at least two of the three of us will enjoy it. Cuff your wrist."

"No," he'd say, offering me nothing more as an explanation because that's Kane. A man of few words because he means every damn one he speaks. But then he'd ask, "Would you like to have a private conversation in the kitchen?"

And I'd consider shooting him, but then I'd remember what my mother, of all people, had once told me when she was speaking of Hollywood: "When you are swimming with sharks," she'd said, "and one of them wants you alive, you feed that shark and defang the others." And so I would say, "Yes, Kane. I would like to have a private conversation in the kitchen." And if it went down like that, Old Man Romano would know the dynamics of our push-and-pull, right-and-wrong connection that I won't call a relationship, which he would most certainly exploit. And I can't let that happen, especially since, as Kane's enemy, he should have long ago been considered in my attack.

And so my gaze collides with Kane's, and the arch of his brow dares to challenge me to be stupid enough to act on the fantasy scene in my head, while the glint in his eyes says he knows exactly what I've been thinking. He does. He knows me too well. He understands me in a way no criminal should understand a law enforcement officer. And I usually like it, which really fucking pisses me off, but this moment isn't about my anger issues with Kane. It's about what my gut says Romano should be allowed to see and hear, which is not division between Kane and me.

And thus, I act out another scene.

I holster my weapon and remove the key to the cuff, dangling it in the air. "You were right," I say. "Sadly, now isn't the time for these types of games." I walk to him and lift his hand, removing the cuff before returning them both to my pocket with the key.

Kane smartly doesn't push his luck and touch me but instead says exactly what he said in my fantasy scene. "Would you like to have a private conversation in the kitchen?"

So I say what I said in my fantasy scene. "Yes, Kane. I would like to have a private conversation in the kitchen." I sound sticky-sweet and sarcastic, but I figure that isn't really a misstep. Ask around and you'll know. I'm not exactly the agreeable type, even if I like you. Okay. Accept you. I don't really like people. Any of them. Which is perhaps the answer to why I'm so comfortable with dead bodies.

I don't wait for him to motion me forward; I'm already walking toward the kitchen, which is another one of those push-and-pull things between Kane and me that I make obvious. I'm not in his control, but I dare to give him my back, actions that tell Romano the story I want him to believe: I trust Kane. I'm intimate with Kane, but he doesn't own me. *Lies.* I don't like lies, but they can sometimes keep you alive and catch the bigger liars, the perps. That I have fucked one of the two perps at my back right now too many times to count and enjoyed every moment . . . well, at least I know what makes him tick: me. I do. I'm his weakness, but he's not mine. I'm my own weakness. I let a man who is not only off-limits but should be my target get to me, and that's a problem I need to fix.

We enter the kitchen, dark wood beneath my feet with lighter shades, even a hint of blue, streaked here and there, but it's still dark. Everything about Kane is dark, which is exactly one of about ten reasons I am certain I could list to put space between myself and him, now and always. But my intent to place myself at the end of the heavy wooden island, my gun on the surface of the navy-blue marble countertop, ready to aim, falls as lame as my denial that I understand Kane, because I am like Kane in too many ways for comfort. The door shuts almost the moment I've passed through it, and Kane is on my heels.

I whirl around to face him. "Consider this official business. I have two dead bodies sitting with their heads in their laps, Kane. Romano's people, and now you have him in your garage."

"Exactly why he's in my garage, *Agent Love*," he says, as if that should absolutely make it all right. "He followed you. That was a threat, and I wasn't going to give him time to act on those murders and go after you."

My eyes go wide. "Did you kill his men, *behead* his men, because he followed me?"

"No," he says without so much as a blink. "But I should have. Our women are off-limits. Always."

"I'm not your woman, Kane. Not for two years. And I thought you didn't chop off heads like your father?"

"Beautiful, I can still smell you on my skin. Taste you on my lips if I try hard enough."

"I fucked you, Kane. You owed me that after showing up on the beach where *it* happened. But it was just a fuck and an escape. If that makes me yours, then I'd say Samantha, my brother's woman who you fucked, is yours and his, too." His eyes glint with anger, and I seize it, pushing him for an admission of guilt, repeating, "And I thought you didn't chop off heads like your father?"

"I didn't kill Romano's people or order them killed," he bites out, "and I wouldn't be surprised if Romano did it himself."

"Why would he do it himself?" I ask, aware that he's avoided the entire topic of chopping off heads.

"To turn the attention on to me. And it worked," he says.

"And his motivation?" I ask. "Outside of the everyday conflict between two patriarchs?"

"There's the question," he says, ignoring my inference that he is the old man's equal when he claims it's his uncle. "Is it to distract everyone, us included, from something else? Or is it to try to tie my hands, weaken me before a blow?"

It could be either or both, I think, because he's right. The attention is on him. My brother, the police chief, is breathing down his neck and no doubt rallying my father, the mayor, behind him. Rich, my other ex and fellow FBI agent, who was already in a damn cockfight with Kane, sees the *X* on the target that is my other ex. And the list goes on. But if any of them thinks that Kane's hands are tied, they're wrong, and so I circle back to what feels important right now, to a question asked and answered but I need answered again. "I waded through blood to examine those bodies, Kane," I say. "They sat in chairs facing the TV, their heads in their laps."

His eyes narrow. "What was playing on the TV?" he asks.

And there's the contradiction that is Kane, the man who would kill for me but accepts what no one else in my life accepts: dead bodies don't freak me out. The problem is that he understands this because they don't freak him out. Which is exactly why the Yale graduate attorney and criminal businessman in him has analyzed the scene the way I did and asked the same question I would ask—did ask.

In other words—was there a message left for him or me, on or near that TV? And there was: a DVD that ties back to the case I was working the night I was raped. But even if I were at liberty to share that information, which I'm not, I don't like that Kane Mendez gets that about me. So for right now, I go to my question that I still need answered. "Did you kill, or order the killing of, those people?"

"You're dodging my question about what was on the TV."

"Crime scene details of any type are confidential law enforcement information," I say.

"You've already shared details," he points out.

"And that's the last time you're getting lucky tonight. Back to my question—the one you seem to be dodging."

"Your question has been asked and answered," he says, repeating my thoughts, "but I'll answer again. No. I did not kill them, nor did I order those people beheaded. You know me. I'd hit closer to his home. And you didn't have to ask two times, let alone three. I don't lie to you, Lilah."

I know him. He'd hit closer to home.

In other words, he believes that no matter how many times he tells me that he's not his father, I know he's got his father in him. I set that bitter pill aside, not ready to swallow it, but because I'm apparently a masochist, I decide to choose another. "No lies?" I challenge. "The tattoos, Kane. I saw your face when I showed you the photo in the chopper of the victim's tattoo. I know you know more than you're telling me."

"*About the tattoos*, Lilah *fucking* Love." He steps closer to me, and I have that same urge to back up as I had in his office the other night. But this time, there isn't an opposing urge to kiss him before I bite the fuck out of his tongue. The scent of blood from my crime scene still lingering in my nostrils, and the head of a crime family tied up one room over, tamps down at least some of my urges. "I told you," he bites out, "to leave them the fuck alone."

"That doesn't work for me anymore," I say. "The tattoo artist—"

"You think that I haven't been to every tattoo parlor in the area and beyond, Lilah? Do you really think that I don't relive seeing that man on top of you and need vengeance for you?"

"And yet you were silent for two years," I say. "You didn't find answers. That's too long. That artist—"

"Says he's religious and the Virgin Mary inspires him, thus the tattoos," he says. "I spoke to him personally, in depth. I have that parlor being watched. I have him being watched. It's time for you to leave now."

"Leave? You have a man tied up in your garage who you think killed your father. I'm not leaving while you kill him."

"Despite the fact that the world would be a better place without that bastard, I have an alliance with him, a truce that invokes peace in my territory that I intend to keep in place. I won't kill him unless he leaves me no other option."

"That's how you treat people who you have truces with?"

"He killed my father and he followed you, Lilah, which, I repeat, *was a threat*. You bet the fuck that's how I treat him."

"You *think* he killed your father, and I don't think him following me was a threat. He gave me a clue that led me someplace that I don't quite understand. But there's an answer there. I need to talk to him."

"What clue? What answer and what question?"

"I'll talk to him," I insist.

"Is that how you want to play this? You want to be complicit in his kidnapping and whatever comes next?"

"Now you're protecting my honor? I just made that man think that I came over here to play a sex game with you."

"Because it was the right decision. No matter who or what we are in private, to that man you're my woman, and if he touches you, he dies. That's the message you needed to send."

"No. What I needed to do was arrest you both."

"On what charges, Lilah?"

"Kidnapping for you," I say.

"He wouldn't press charges. There's no crime here. Walk away."

Now I step back, my badge the invisible line between us. "If he ends up dead, I will arrest you. Do you understand? I'll have to."

"I told you. I won't kill him unless I have to."

"Spoken like the true patriarch of the Mendez cartel."

"I am who I have to be for reasons I hope you never have to understand. And as for arresting me, everything we're saying is being recorded, *Agent Love.*"

"Now you're threatening me?"

"I'm still protecting you," he says. "I'm setting you free. Now you don't have to question your decision to walk away. I made it for you."

"Fuck you, Kane."

"Later, Lilah. What did the old man tell you?"

"I'll talk to him myself. You're recording me. I have nothing else to lose by staying."

"You're leaving, and when you wake up tomorrow morning, remember two things: you were never here, and I did what I had to do to protect you."

The way he says those words, cold and calculated, sends a chill down my spine. "What does that mean, Kane?"

"You're going to leave now, Lilah."

Those words are the proverbial slammed door. He's shut me out. I see it. I feel it, and since I'm the only person on this planet who has ever influenced him, that's dangerous for everyone he intends to punish. "On one condition," I barter.

"Sorry, beautiful. As much as I enjoy the challenge of your conditions, not this time." His hand comes down on mine on the counter. I pull back, but not before I feel the pinprick, which might be nothing, except that this is Kane, and just as he says nothing without purpose, his actions follow the same rules.

"Holy fuck," I hiss as the room starts to spin. "What did you just do to me?"

"Gave you the gift of deniability."

I sway and he catches me, and my fingers close around his shirt, anger surviving the haze overwhelming me. "I'm going to . . . *Fuck you,* Kane." The stupidity of how those words have come together is the last thing I remember before everything goes dark.

CHAPTER TWO

I blink into a bright light, focusing on flat white space that resembles a ceiling, and holy hell, I can't seem to move. No. I can't seem to *want* to move. My body is heavy, my mouth cottony. And just for kicks and laughs, someone seems to have added Orajel to the mix, or some kind of numbing agent, because despite the bitter taste tormenting me right now, I can't seem to find my tongue. *Oh fuck.* I can't find my tongue.

Adrenaline surges through me, and I jerk to a sitting position, somehow flinging my lead arm forward and up to smack myself in the chin. I proceed to bite the shit out of my no-longer-missing tongue, the metallic taste of blood melding with whatever the hell that other gross-ass taste is in my mouth. My fists land on either side of me on the mattress, and I slowly scan the room, because outside of knocking the hell out of myself, I'm too dazed to do anything fast. The good news, though, is that I'm in my Hamptons bedroom, and as a side observation, the throw that belongs on the chair in the corner is on top of me. The bad news is that I don't remember grabbing the throw, let alone how the hell I got into the bed. And unless I've suddenly added sleepwalking craziness to the list of crazy I already own, either someone put me here or I'm suffering from memory loss.

I try to move, but that leaden feeling in my limbs just won't go the fuck away, and the sensation of being trapped sends my mind to a dark, cavernous place: to the past. An image shoots through my mind of me on the beach, sand at my back, with the heavy weight of my attacker on top of me. No idea how I'd gotten there, but on some level, I knew

I'd been drugged. And then I'm replaying it. *Damn it*, I don't want to replay it. But it's there, in my mind, and it just comes to me.

I'm standing on the beach, the wind blowing in my hair, salt on my lips. And then there is a man grabbing me. I can't see his face. I can't see his face. *I start to fight, shoving and kicking. I need my gun. Where is my gun? I can't get my body to work. I can't get him off me. My shirt rips and sand is at my back. His body is on top of me.*

"I'll kill you!" I shout. "I'll kill you!"

His mouth presses to my ear. "You'll be too dead to kill anyone," he promises, his voice low, gravelly, accented. "But not until I'm done with you, which won't be soon."

"No! No!"

"No!" I shout, and still stuck in that memory, in that same heavily drugged sensation that I'd felt when trapped under that monster, I find the will to throw off the blanket. Fighting for control of my body, I lift my arms and start waving my hands in the air, forcing sensation to return. Once I succeed, I start moving my legs, and that's when my hand comes down on the heavy steel of Cujo, my trusty shotgun, resting next to me. Its presence infers that at some point I made an active decision to go to bed and have it by my side. And still I'm blank.

I press my fingers to my temples, and I force myself to focus. What is the last thing I remember? What? Nothing. I rotate and let my feet settle on the ground. Still nothing. I stand up slowly, testing my footing, and aside from the haze, I seem to be fine. I confirm this assumption with a few steps that gradually become me pacing. *Okay. Office.* I was in my office trying to find a way to clear Woods, the fall guy for the assassinations, which everyone else calls murders. Woods proceeded to confess on video and set himself on fire. Pizza arrived with a note from my stalker, Junior, attached.

I stop walking, memories now coming at me hard and fast: My decision to charge over to Kane's house and confront him about his secrets and the murders. Me cuffing him the instant he opened his door, and him telling me that I needed to see what was in the garage. The old man tied to the chair. The argument with Kane. I squeeze my eyes shut. "Holy hell," I murmur, remembering my pricked hand, my lashes lifting with a grit of my teeth. "That bastard drugged me."

My gaze jerks to my body, and I confirm that I'm still clothed, but my feet are bare, like I wouldn't notice that I was naked while pacing. Then again, maybe I wouldn't, because Kane fucking drugged me. And he drugged me knowing I was drugged that night on the beach.

"Bastard."

I glance down at my clothes again and flash back to being at Kane's door. The jacket I'd been wearing when I walked into Kane's house is also missing. My holster and weapon were still on my person, but now they are not. I scan the room and find them on the chair he'd grabbed the blanket from. The methodical way he handled this drives home the fact that Kane brought me here and he'd considered undressing me. And it *was* Kane, and not one of his men, because he's too damn possessive to allow anyone else to touch me, let alone enter my house. But the fact that he left me in my clothes, when that man's inclination is always to undress me, tells me that he knew damn well that he'd be absent at least one of his family jewels if he'd gotten me naked without my permission. He still might be when I'm done with him. And how did he know my security code? And why am I even asking that stupid question? Men like Kane can get anything they want.

Glancing at my nightstand, I find my phone plugged in and charging. "Such a gentleman," I murmur sarcastically.

I sit down on the bed again and grab my cell. Just thinking about Kane tucking me into bed like his precious property, while he sauntered his arrogant ass off to work—aka torturing and perhaps killing—agitates the hell out of me. Glancing at my display screen, I grimace at the late hour. Damn it. Aside from the other random, screwed-up pieces of my morning that thus far has not been bright and sunny, I don't have time to be sleeping until nine-oh-fuck o'clock.

In other cheery news, I've missed three calls from my boss and two from my brother, the police chief, who thinks he's my boss. And, of course, I have no calls from Kane, who probably thinks I'm still snoozing it off in hopes that I'll lose my job that obviously conflicts with his gangster lifestyle. I also have about ten calls and twenty text messages from my tech guy, Tic Tac:

Where are you?

Where are you?

Answer your damn phone.

Murphy asked for all the case data on Woods. I had to give it to him. I held back what I could.

Where the hell are you? You know, you want me to answer my phone whenever you call, but you don't answer yours. You better be dead or bleeding.

And on that note, I start to dial my boss but pause. I'm not dead or bleeding, but am I mentally equipped for this call? I test my mental faculties. "My name is Lilah-fucking-Love," I say out loud. "And Kane Mendez is not gangster enough for what he has coming his way."

Yep. I'm good.

I punch the Call Back button for my boss. "Agent Love," he bites out, answering on the first ring. "We have a communication problem."

Says every man I've ever known, I think, but what I say is, "I had a complication."

"I'm your complication."

Also said by a good majority of the men in my life, but before I can come up with a more acceptable reply, he adds, "I have dead bodies,

Agent Love. We also have a confession from a dead man, who set himself on fire on film after said confession, and the New York authorities are trying to close the cases. If they're connected to our two murders, that means I close our cases and you come home."

"Yes, but—"

"Unless you are dead," he continues, "which you are not, or bleeding profusely, or injured to the point of being incapable of communication, which you clearly are not, then use your damn phone the way you use your foul mouth. Liberally."

In other words, he expects an acceptable explanation for my silence, and sleeping late won't cut it. "Someone knocked me out," I admit. "Obviously I've rattled some cages."

"Who? When? Why? And most importantly, are you okay?"

"I'm just peachy," I say, and seizing every bit of honesty I can muster, I add, "but whoever did this won't be soon, I promise you. As to when it happened: sometime around ten last night. As to where: at my house, as I exited the patio door. I assume whoever it was searched my place."

"Any idea who it was or what they were after?"

"No idea who it was and I assume they wanted my investigation data."

"Do you have cameras?"

"No," I lie, even though I hate lies, but then I'm bad when I'm around Kane. That's just how it is. "But ironically," I add, "I called my service to have them installed before this even happened. They're backlogged."

"You need cameras now," he says, stating the obvious.

I move on. "It wasn't Woods."

"That's not what he said."

"Eleven percent of all confessions are fake."

"He *killed* himself, Agent Love," he bites out, sounding quite snippy at this point.

"Did he? Or was he killed? We need to analyze the footage of that suicide. And even if Woods killed himself, he did it under duress to save someone else. Woods is not our killer."

"That's an opinion. Make your case with facts."

"There is no evidence to convict Woods. That's a fact."

"And yet the locals are convinced it's him."

"Based on circumstantial evidence and pressure from the rich, famous, and powerful."

"Do I need to remind you that you're talking about your family?" he quips back.

"If you thought that would be a factor, I wouldn't be here."

"What circumstantial evidence?" he says, hitting me hard and fast.

"He had an affair with a famous actress, and her husband found out. He pointed a gun at the husband's head and then ran."

"Our victims died by bullets to their heads."

"Our victims died with bullets between the eyes, execution style," I say, "with the precision of a professional and no evidence left behind."

"How long ago was this?"

"Last year. Before the murders ever took place. Furthermore, that incident was fodder for the gossips in this town, of which there are many. Our killer is not a person who puts themselves in the spotlight, nor are they prone to outbursts. He, or she, wouldn't start killing people with a gun to the head after putting on a show like Woods did."

"*Come on*, Agent Love. Your mother was a famous actress. You've lived amongst the rich and famous. We both know that you understand double lives and good actors. Everyone isn't what they seem."

By the time he's finished those statements, I'm standing, and I don't remember standing, but something about his tone and the context is hitting me all kinds of wrong. Like he knows more about me than my proficiency with the word *fuck* and my history with Kane Mendez.

His phone beeps. "I have to take this," he says. "Hold tight."

And just like that the line is silent, and I'm flashing back to the night I arrived and my call to him.

"What do you have to report, Agent Love?"

14

"Same MO, different state." I don't give him time to ask for details. "How did you know I needed to be here tonight? How did you predict a murder?"

"That was a surprise."

"But you wanted me here tonight, earlier rather than later."

"Coincidental politics. Nothing more. Nothing I'm going to involve you in."

"But I am involved. I'm the one who's here."

"And well equipped to do a quick, thorough investigation."

"I have a history with Kane Mendez."

"Which makes you the perfect candidate to get into his head."

"Why do I need to be in Kane's head?"

"He's connected to this. Tonight makes that clear."

"I didn't tell you that. How do you know he's connected?"

"I looked up the crime scene address. I know he owns the property."

"But that doesn't make him responsible for the murder."

"That's true, but anyone else working this case would assume he is because of who he is, and I don't like the obvious as an answer to anything."

"Are you protecting Kane Mendez? Is he a part of the politics you keep mentioning?"

"There's always pressure to close cases and calm the public, and that doesn't always mean solving the case."

"You mean creating a fall guy."

"That's right. And I don't do fall guys."

"But Kane Mendez isn't anyone's easy fall guy."

"You're right," he says. "He's not, but when you appear invincible, you become a challenge."

My brow furrows. "I really don't understand what's going on here."

"Just go catch me a killer, Agent Love."

I return to the present, acutely aware of the fact that I wouldn't be in the Hamptons right now if he hadn't pushed me to come here. And he did so despite my many potential conflicts of interest. And that reference to politics and Kane leads me to one question: Is Murphy dirty?

CHAPTER THREE

I can't say that Murphy is dirty. Maybe he's just secretive, but I have to consider the possibility that he's a problem. And since I like dirty, two-faced people about as much as I like flip-flops, which is not at all, that's a problem for me. I don't like things between my toes or up my ass. It's just who I am. And two-faced assholes in law enforcement are no better than Bible bangers who praise God, sneer at my liberal use of the word *fuck*, and then turn around and fuck someone else's spouse.

And I'm really tired of finding out that everyone in my life wants to be a damn *gangsta*. Up until now, I've respected and trusted Murphy the way I *should*—after all, he's my boss at the fucking *FBI*. The idea that those things might be misplaced pisses me off. Which is probably why, when he returns to the line and says, "Back to Woods and his acting skills," I'm not exactly feeling as warm and fuzzy as usual.

"You can't seriously," I say, "with all your years of experience, believe that Woods planned the way things went down. That would mean that he had to orchestrate being caught with another man's wife and holding a gun to the furious husband's head. And he had to do so to hide the fact that he was a skilled assassin to complete a hit list. A list with no obvious connection to him, outside of the woman he slept with."

"It made you doubt him."

"Because it's absolutely stupid to put yourself on law enforcement's radar before completing a hit list," I argue.

"Serial killers taunt law enforcement all the damn time."

"Woods wasn't a serial killer."

"You know what I think?" he asks, but he doesn't give me time to reply. "His emotional outburst convinced you that he's not capable of calculated killing. Return to Profiling 101, Agent Love. Serial killers start small, often with animals, and then graduate to humans as they improve their technique."

I clamp down on about ten smart-ass remarks, of which at least one would likely get me fired, before I settle on, "Hit list. Skilled assassin."

"You're the only one who believes this."

I hold out the phone and silently yell at it before I calmly place it back at my ear and reply. "Why am I here if everyone is a better profiler than I am?" This time, I don't wait for *his* reply. "I know you asked Jeff Landers for our investigation material. Woods has no direct link to anyone but the woman he slept with. And if we're going to start convicting dead people just to close cases, I do hope there is going to be an agency announcement. I'm pretty sure we can clear at least some of the cold cases, since they can't defend themselves. Heck, why don't we look for homeless dead people? Then they probably won't even have family to defend them, which by the way makes Woods a perfect fall guy. He might as well be homeless. He had no one in his life."

"Cautious there now, *Special Agent* Love," he says, and I'm fairly certain the use of my formal title indicates his agitation. "I have to put my neck on the line when we end this call," he continues, "and I have to do so based on your investigative conclusions. I'm simply testing you to be sure you're certain you won't change your mind."

Whatever, I think, but I say, "If we call this done and another body lands on our doorstep, or even here in the Hamptons, or anywhere for that matter, you look incompetent."

He's silent for several beats. "You're right," he ultimately concludes. "We will indeed look incompetent, and yet I return to my original point: both the East Hampton and New York City officials are in agreement that all cases should be closed."

17

"And I'm back on repeat: Woods can't protect himself, and aside from that, we know the typical law enforcement motivation in these situations. A killer on the loose scares people. They want this to go away."

"But as you've voiced, another murder would come with public backlash and expose incompetence," he says. "Law enforcement is also smart enough to know that."

"The odds of another murder in the Hamptons is low, and thus closing out the case is an educated gamble. As for another murder in New York City, I've worked there. It's easier to bury another case there, especially when it's singular because the prior cases are closed and supposedly solved."

"And the murmurs of a serial killer are shut down," he says.

"Exactly."

"You're hanging your family out to dry here."

"I'm protecting them from their own stupidity. They need to slow down. Woods isn't going anywhere but into the ground."

"You have a bad attitude, Agent Love."

"That's what every criminal I ever took down said to me."

He laughs. "Indeed. You also make valid points."

"That you've made me repeat about ten times."

"And you stayed the course, which wins me over, but before I jump onto your ship and sail away, let's be clear. There is no middle ground any longer if you can't convince the locals to keep the cases open and allow us to assist. And if that's how this plays out, we have two options: We follow suit, close the cases. We claim jurisdiction. Which is it? And before you answer, be very sure about this decision. There will be heat from a hell of a lot of directions."

"No one is more aware of that heat than me."

"They have reason to fear a press leak and murmurs of a nationwide serial killer, and so do we."

"And if that happens, we have a rebuttal with a hit list, which calms the masses."

He pauses again, and this time it's so damn long I'm about to climb through the line and shake him. "Here's what's going to happen," he finally says. "I'm going to take some of that heat off you, at least momentarily."

"What exactly does that mean?"

"I'll contact the officials in both cities and request proof that connects all the dots to Woods. If they can't give me more than the confession, we'll reconvene one last time before we claim jurisdiction. In the meantime, continue your investigation."

"What's your timeline on this?"

"Today. I want to know where we're headed by tomorrow."

"I need a full two days to try to talk sense into everyone," I say, aware that this day is going to be about Kane and that man tied to a chair. "Make that three. I have to travel between East Hampton and New York City to do this right."

"You'll have it *after* I set the stage for you by asking for evidence that I trust they don't have, as I trust you. And that phone call I took was from Rich. He's staying with you."

"What? No. Rich is a tech guy."

"Rich is a damn good agent."

"Who I've fucked," I say, forgetting decorum and not mincing words.

"Well now, since we're pulling down the curtains and speaking frankly, I'm pretty damn sure you've fucked Kane Mendez as well."

"Which is why Rich can't handle this. He's too personally involved. That's dangerous."

"You're personally involved, which gives you advantages and disadvantages," he says. "And like it or not, you're human. If you claim jurisdiction, the wrath of your family will affect you, no matter how you try to pretend it won't. You need someone who knows you there. And aside from that, it's logical. He's there. You need extra eyes. He stays."

"Director Murphy—"

"End of conversation," he snaps. "We'll talk tonight."

He hangs up.

CHAPTER FOUR

My first thought in the seconds after Murphy hangs up is that I have to get to Kane before Rich does and Rich ends up tied to a chair. I dial Rich. His line rings. And rings. And then goes to voice mail. I dial Rich again. He still doesn't answer, when he *always* answers. I leave him a voice mail. "Call me, asshole," I say, and then I text him the same. I then immediately punch in the number to Kane's office that I unfortunately know by heart, refusing to analyze why I still remember it. I just fucking do, and since I don't want to talk to him just yet, I fact-gather. The line rings and I run a hand through my tangled hair, pacing a few steps before I hear, "Mendez Enterprises."

"Is Kane Mendez in the building?" I demand.

"May I ask who's calling?"

"Is he in the fucking building or not?" I snap.

"Lilah," the woman says, and I can almost hear her self-satisfied grin, as if she's just figured out a puzzle and she's anticipating the cookie she'll be awarded. "Mr. Mendez said you'd be calling," she adds as my stomach growls and I wish I had a damn cookie or ten.

"Is he in the building?" I ask.

"Yes, but—"

I hang up and grab my boots, pulling them on before walking to the bathroom, where I look in the mirror and cringe. "Holy mother of Jesus."

Raccoon circles have settled under my eyes, which is appropriate, since my mousy, tangled brown hair looks like something crawled around in it and created a nest. I desperately need a shower before I face off with Kane, and this damn taste in my mouth has to go.

No sooner than I set my phone on the sink, it rings with Rich's number on the display. I put my toothbrush down and answer the call, with one strategy in mind: controlling where he is at all times, especially this morning. "Asshole?" he demands.

He hates when I call him an asshole, since he prides himself on being a gentleman. "Yes. Asshole. We need to meet."

"Yes. We do. I'll come to you. Are you at your place?"

Me letting him come here, knowing Kane would find out, would be about as smart as the guy last year in Santa Monica who put a firecracker on his head and set it on fire. A bunch of the agency guys had then challenged me to profile his behavior. I had a one-word answer: *stupid*. And I'm not stupid. "Meet me for lunch," I say, because if I have to fight with him, my brother, and Kane in the same day, I deserve another strawberry pie. I give him the location of the diner that I've already frequented twice this trip before adding, "At noon."

"Noon," he confirms. "Look, Lilah. I know you called me an asshole because you're pissed, but—"

I hang up, and not because I'm trying to be the same asshole he's being by acting like a jealous shit with Kane. I simply can't risk getting into a conversation with him that sets him off and makes him do something stupid like the firecracker guy.

I set the phone down again and sway with a head rush, forced to grab the counter. *Damn it to hell.* I didn't eat last night but I was drugged, which translates to weak, and, with a glance back in the mirror, I add, just plain gross. I need that shower and some form of food in my stomach, or I am going to pass out or punch someone who isn't Kane. And Kane is the only one I know who can take the punch and not start crying, my damn brother included. Ironically, Kane is the only one of the three I want to make cry.

Thirty minutes later, I've showered, and with a robe around me, I walk into the kitchen, make a cup of coffee, and since I did go to the grocery store, I survey the cabinets and fridge for food. Apparently I suck at shopping, since within arm's reach I seem to have only strawberries and more strawberries. So strawberries it is. I grab a plastic container and my cup and trek back to the bedroom. Another fifteen minutes later, my coffee cup is empty, and my hair is not only dry but flat ironed. Makeup is next, as is my unskilled attempt to correct the vampirishly pale look I'm sporting today. I'm nearly done with the whole beautify-myself routine, and halfway done with my strawberries, when I feel human enough to answer one of three calls in ten minutes from Tic Tac.

"Dead or bleeding?" I say when I answer, referencing his voice mail.

"Holy hell, Lilah. I didn't really mean that."

"That really was coldhearted. Make it up to me. I need stuff."

"And here I thought a knock on your head would slow down the demands. I called you, remember?"

"And it was excellent timing. I need everything you can get me on Old Man Romano," I say. "Apparently he's the patriarch, not the other guy we've been chasing for years."

"How do you know that?"

I flash back to the old man tied to a chair in Kane's garage and decide Kane as a source doesn't work. I settle on, "Call it a theory I need you to prove." I switch gears then to my father's main campaign backer, Mr. Moneybags and the patriarch, aka CEO, of Pocher Enterprises. "Every instinct I own says Pocher has a Romano connection," I say.

"I've looked—"

"Look harder. He's one of the richest men on the planet. It's buried deep, but it's there."

"Aren't we trying to find a killer?"

"Yes," I say. "We are. And there are three powerful players in this territory: Kane Mendez. The Romano family. And Pocher. And since I'm convinced someone is trying to make Kane the fall guy, that leaves two." And because I don't want to answer questions, I throw him a bone he'll choke on. "Moving on." And because I know he's on his cell phone, not the agency phone, I say, "I need you to do something for me from home, away from the office. I'll owe you another big favor."

"I don't like how that sounds. No. The answer is no. So just don't—"

"I need everything you can find on Murphy."

"What?" he hisses, his voice lowering. "What are you doing, Lilah?"

"Just do it, Tic Tac. I wouldn't ask if it wasn't important."

"You didn't ask."

"I said I'll owe you," I say, my voice low, terse. "This is a big deal. I need you to do this and keep it between us."

"Holy hell, Lilah. You're going to be the death of me. You owe me big on this one."

"Let's hope that's all that comes out of this," I say before we disconnect.

I grab the sink and think of Murphy's words: *We both know that you understand double lives and good actors. Everyone isn't what they seem.*

He's right. They aren't. I'm not. But until today, I never read him as anything beyond appearance. And missing a snake in the grass at my feet is dangerous, not just to me but potentially to the other agents who work beneath him. Which, remarkably, brings me back to Kane and the one good thing I can say about the man at the moment: I know who and what he is. I'm not sure there's one other person in my life I can say that about right now.

That's not true.

Rich.

He's a nice guy who really *is* a nice guy, who is going to get eaten by the big bad wolf, which is Kane. And as pissed as I am at Rich right now, that's why I'm angry. He's not only going to get himself into trouble he's not equipped to handle, he's creating leverage for Kane against me. I have to get him out of here.

With that thought, I don't linger at the sink. I walk into the closet, and keeping with the New Yorker theme I've gravitated to since arriving here, I dress in black jeans and a black V-neck sweater, along with my Chanel boots. It's a generic look that my old boss in New York loved. It doesn't stand out because it's not me who needs to stand out, it's the criminals.

Once dressed, I realize that my shoulder holster is still on the chair in the bedroom where Kane apparently left it. I opt for my hip holster and attach it to my belt for easier reach. Once it's in place, I grab my wallet-sized purse—Chanel, because this town is all about brands—and slip it across my chest and settle it at my opposite hip. I then pull on a black Chanel jacket and call it done.

Exiting the closet, I hurry forward and enter the bedroom, pausing by the chair to remove my firearm resting there and holster it at my hip. That's when I rotate and take a step, only to stop dead in my tracks and stare at Cujo where it rests on the bed. Now that I'm clearheaded, that's not as insignificant as it was an hour ago. Cujo was in my office, along with the notes from Junior and all my case notes. Kane was in my office. I launch myself across the room, and I'm in the hallway and up the stairs in seconds. I stop in the doorway to find the pizza box I'd left on the top of the desk missing. My computer is open, my note cards stacked to the left of it.

Crossing the office, I round the desk and locate the pizza box where it now sits on the chest under the window. Where I know I didn't put it. *Kane was here.* That is the only explanation. Thinking back to last night, I recall pulling the note from the pizza box and setting it on my desk. Planning to sit down, I pull out my chair to find my briefcase on top—my briefcase, where I'd stuffed the rest of Junior's love notes. I grab it and sit down. Of course, the note that was on the desk is gone.

On the laughable chance that Kane didn't look in my briefcase, I unzip it, but as expected, those notes are gone, too.

Kane has every note Junior has left for me up to this point, unless he missed the one I balled up and threw on the floorboard of my rental, which I doubt. I glance up at my board on the wall. I've listed out names and pinned note cards there, all of which entail details about my thought process in this investigation that I would not willingly share with anyone. I punch my keyboard, and my computer comes to life with the open e-mail that included Woods's suicide video. "Stupid," I hiss. "Stupid, Lilah." I stand up, pressing my hand to my forehead. "I shouldn't have gone there last night, and yet I was about to go back there now. I can't. Not after last night, and not with my history with Kane. And now I'm talking to myself."

My hands flatten on the desk, a storm brewing inside me, and I let it. I embrace it. Being alone with Kane gets me fucked one way or the other, any way and every which way. The man drugged me. He then invaded my private space, stole those notes, inspected my evidence, and worst of all, left me with Cujo, as if I could really use him while sedated. If anyone should know what that means to me, it's Kane. Which is exactly why I never even considered him a risk last night. Because *that night* binds us together and forces trust. At least, that's my excuse for trusting him. But not again.

I consider looking at the security feed, but watching Kane carry me to bed and then search my house isn't good for him or me right now. Instead, I shut my MacBook, stick it inside my field bag, and zip it up. It's on my shoulder next, and when I would head for the door, I pause to look at the boards to my left, the words MURDER GIRL written in big, bold letters. Kane doesn't know about that nickname, but he'll know that's me. He knows Murder Girl. She existed long before the night I stabbed a man twelve times. She's the one who is too comfortable with dead bodies. She's the one who understands him. But what *he* doesn't understand is what the badge is to me or what I'll do for that badge. And how can he? He believes that night and the secret it created removed it from our equation. I have to find a way to add it back in.

I start walking and I don't stop until I'm at the door to the garage in the kitchen, standing at the security panel, and with a quick scan, I find Kane left it armed. "Aren't you a gentleman?" I murmur, considering he left me here, drugged.

Exiting the house, I'm inside the basic white rental that I'm quite certain will offend half the population of this town, but I like it simply because it reminds me of two things: I don't belong here anymore, and I'm not staying. It also stands out among the Mercedes and BMWs and tells people I'm coming, which isn't exactly a good thing. But then, today at least, Kane is expecting me, and I've decided I don't want to disappoint him. And his office is the exact right location for an official visit from Agent Lilah Love.

The moment I pull onto the road, I can feel the tug of another flashback: *The beach, salt on my lips. Sand at my back.* I turn on the radio, blasting the volume. A song I don't know comes on, but as soon as the lyrics "I hate you, I love you, Don't want to but I can't put nobody else above you" lift into the air, I turn the damn thing off again. I don't do music when I work cases. Lyrics tell stories that distract me from the story every dead body I study has to tell about how they died and who killed them. The one I stabbed over and over certainly told a story about me. I would call it an act of rage and passion. I'd suggest the person who planted that knife in a man's chest a dozen times would feel remorse, when I did not and do not. I'd suggest they wouldn't kill again, but I will.

And if all goes as planned, it will be called *my job* rather than murder, but nothing goes as planned in my world.

I pull into the parking lot of Kane's offices, and I don't bother to look for his fancy, sleek, sporty Mercedes because I know that it will be in the private garage underneath the castle that is the building. Lucky for once in this town, though, I snag a spot near the front of the building and open the door. I'm out of the car in an instant, and I grab my field bag with my MacBook inside and pop the trunk, sticking it inside before I lose it, too. My purse goes with it, but not before I attach my badge to my waistband.

Once I've shut the trunk, I face the building, and I start walking toward the main castle, ignoring the two side buildings, because Kane Mendez is always at the core of Mendez Enterprises. And per his near confession last night: the Mendez cartel. I cross the wooden bridge that is the path over a man-made moat. I enter the building and ignore the pretty brunette behind the triangle-shaped stone desk and head to the stairs.

"Excuse me," she calls out, but I ignore her. Kane knows I'm coming. He has people watching me and this building. He knows I'm in the building by now. I don't need "sweet thing" down there to announce me in yet another way. I'm at the top of the stairs before she finishes her fourth *excuse me*, which is now a bit louder, as if I just haven't heard her the other three times. I turn down the hallway and walk toward the desk outside Kane's office where Tabitha sits, minus any more originality today than the last time I was here. She's still bleached blonde, with her fake, giant-ass boobs hanging out of a silk blouse with numerous buttons undone that turn it into a slut show that could have been professional.

I pass her without a word, approaching Kane's double doors, when she says, "Drama follows you, Lilah Love."

"No," I say without looking at her. "Dead bodies follow me." I glance over my shoulder at her. "You should remember that."

And with that statement, which really had no purpose other than it felt really damn good, I open Kane's door.

CHAPTER FIVE

I step inside Kane's office and find him sitting behind his desk, just in time to hear him say, "She's here," into his intercom and then release the button.

With exaggerated drama that I reserve for moments when I want to be a smart-ass or simply announce my fucking presence, I use my body to shut the door, but I don't hang out and wait for it to grow roots. I rotate and charge toward Kane and that King Mendez desk of his that he doesn't get to use as shelter. By the time I round the wooden atrocity, he's standing, towering over me in a charcoal suit and a purple shirt with black stripes and some sort of black-and-gray tie. It's flashy, expensive, and works on him when it would not on nine out of ten other people. But then, while I keep a low profile—aside from the door drama, of course—and favor my black nondescript looks, his entire persona says "look at me" with the intended message of "I have nothing to hide." A lie he tells the world and, after he drugged me to keep me from knowing what happened last night, apparently me.

We stand there for a beat or ten without words before he says, "Lilah," and the very fact that he says it like sex is all it takes for me to snap.

I slap him in the face, because my bare fist is too small to hurt him the way his jaw would hurt me. It's also a disgrace to a man to be slapped, which is why one UFC fighter I've watched here and there does it to his opponents. And Kane *is* my opponent. He turns his head with the force of the blow, my palm stinging in the aftermath.

"Well now, beautiful," he says, fixing me with a brown-eyed stare. "I know you like it rough, but is now the time? We both have questions we want answered."

I slap him again, and this time he catches my wrist before I pull back. I try to slap him with my free hand, and he catches it as well, this time before contact. "You get two, not three."

My gaze flicks to the handprint on his right cheek that matches the one on the left before I meet his stare and say, "Two was pretty damn satisfying."

"Why didn't you tell me about your stalker?" he demands, his question low, lethal, his anger banked just beneath the surface, while mine is the cherry on top of every lie he's told me. "Because we both know that's what we're dealing with here," he adds.

"Let go of me, Kane," I bite out, my voice taut with impatience. No. Make that a desire to smack him again.

"After you tell me about your stalker and the notes."

"Let go of me, Kane," I repeat slowly, "or my next move will be a knee to your family jewels. And I promise you, it will be hard enough that neither of us will have to worry about our urge to fuck ever again." My jaw sets hard, but he doesn't release me. "You drugged me," I remind him, "and then searched my house before leaving me with a gun that I was too drugged to use. So if you think I won't do it—"

He releases me but doesn't step back. "I didn't leave you with a gun you couldn't use. I kept you at my house until sunrise, and I left a team guarding your place, front and back."

I don't analyze why that makes me angrier. That's for later. For now, there is this: "I'd pull my gun on you and back you off, Kane, but I swore the next time I did that, I'd shoot you. And I need information from you."

"I'm all yours, beautiful," he says, holding his hands out. "I always am." He motions to the sitting area to his left and behind him. "Let's sit and make this peaceful."

"Peaceful, my ass," I say. "You drugged me. Is the old man dead?"

"He is not."

"Is he in your garage?"

"He's been set free." And with that simple, unexpected answer, he sits down on the desk, hands on either side on him.

"Just like that?" I demand, claiming a new position in front of him with the window behind me, and not because that's what he wants: Me boxed in. Me closer to him. Because I don't want to shout across the room as I talk about his crimes that I haven't reported.

"We came to an agreement," he says without hesitation—not that Kane Mendez ever hesitates.

"What agreement?"

"Nothing that concerns you," he replies.

"But it does, doesn't it?"

"Nothing you need to know," he amends.

"Deniability, right?"

"That's right."

"Are you filming me now?"

"Yes."

"Ammunition, right?"

"That's not what last night was about, and you know it."

"It was a threat to expose me if I arrested you," I say.

"It was me giving you a reason to walk out of the door."

"And when I didn't, you drugged me."

A muscle in his jaw flexes. "It was necessary."

"Necessary? Really? That's your rebuttal? Even for you, that's lame, Kane."

"If you were ever questioned about Romano, you needed an out. You can now say that I drugged you. You woke up in bed. And I'll back that story."

"Taping me tells me that you'd bribe me."

"That isn't who I am with you, and you know it."

30

"But it's you with everyone else?"

"This is you demonizing me to avoid guilt and make yourself feel good about you. Everything I did, I did to protect you."

"That's how you justify searching my house and looking at all my research notes?"

"I saw someone hide their face and put a note on your car. I asked you about it. And like it or not, I know you. And I knew by your reaction that you were in trouble."

"I can handle my own trouble."

"In case you've forgotten, I'm ten feet under in this, right along with you."

"I'm crystal clear on how ten feet under you are in this, Kane."

"Are you? Because the tone of those notes says that your note writer is trying to turn you against me. And that's damn convenient, considering a woman was killed in one of my rentals and two of Romano's people had their heads chopped off. Obviously meant to turn attention on me."

"I never for a minute believed you killed that woman, and for the most part, I didn't believe you chopped off the heads."

He arches a brow. "For the most part?"

"Just being honest, the way you say you're honest with me."

"You know—"

"That you wouldn't leave a trail that leads to you?" I ask, and I don't wait for an answer. "Yes. I do, but I also know you're capable of killing. Because like it or not, I know you, too. More than either of us likes to admit."

"And yet at some point you convinced yourself that I'd act with stupidity and kill Romano's men." He doesn't give me time to reject that statement, continuing with, "And you didn't come to me about those notes. In other words, your note-writing stalker has succeeded in dividing us."

"For a Yale-educated attorney, you might not be stupid, but you're choosing to play dumb. Those notes didn't scare me and they didn't divide us. My badge did."

"You always had a badge."

"You didn't always run the cartel. Your father did."

"I don't run it now."

"You inferred otherwise last night," I say.

"Stop deflecting. Tell me about the notes, Lilah."

"Says the king of deflection. They started the night I arrived. I was on the beach, and when I got back to the house, someone had thrown a bloodlike substance on the sliding glass door and left a note. It spiraled from there."

"They read amateurish with an almost adolescent effort."

"Which could mean that this person wants me to underestimate them, or they're just plain crazy."

"Or they really are amateurish and adolescent."

"Maybe. I doubt it. Have you ever seen the notes Son of Sam left at his murder scenes? They were in childlike script, and one of them read along the lines of, 'I say goodbye and good night. Police: Let me haunt you with these words. I'll be back! I'll be back! To be interpreted as—bang, bang, bang, bang, bang—ugh!'" I pause to clarify. "He actually wrote *ugh*. And it was signed with, 'Yours in Murder, Mr. Monster.' His victims," I continue, "inclusive of those who lived and died, neared twenty."

"You're telling me you think this person is violent."

"I'm telling you that no two killers are alike. Just because he, or she, is not the kind of killer you understand does not make them not a killer. And furthermore, adolescentlike behaviors do not necessarily preclude or exclude a propensity for violence. Bottom line here, Kane: this person knows our secret. And if that person knows, so, most likely, does someone else."

"Which means we need to know two things: Who knows and what do they plan to do to use it against us? Because they wouldn't be taunting you unless that's what they intended."

"For two years there has been silence," I say. "And then I returned and the silence ended. This was never about you, was it?"

"No. In my world, people claim their sins. No one came forward. In fact, the more I dug for answers, the deeper they seemed to get buried."

"So whoever ordered my attack—because we both know it wasn't random—wanted me gone then. And they still want me gone."

"And yet someone was killed in your city with the exact same tattoo as the man who attacked you here."

"What are you saying?"

"Someone sent you a calling card to come home."

CHAPTER SIX

There's no such thing as a coincidence.

I live those words during my investigations, but somehow, I've missed the importance they play in these murders. "The murders in LA were to get my attention. The murder of your employee, at your rental, when I arrived, was to get *our* attention. Both assumptions worthy of a debate about where that might lead us."

"Agreed," Kane says. "Assuming those things are correct."

"Can we now also assume that Romano is behind all this?"

"He'd be dead if I believed that."

"But he approached me at the tattoo parlor," I counter.

"I'd refused his meeting and told him he had to meet with my uncle, who, contrary to your belief, runs the cartel."

"He approached *me* at the tattoo parlor. That's not a coincidence or just because he couldn't reach you."

"I said that to him, but he had a prepared answer. He'd been sitting on the anonymous tip for years. When you got back in town, he called me. That's proven true. His first attempt at contact was the day after you arrived. And when you showed up on his turf, and at the particular parlor that is known for that tattoo, he didn't want you to end up dead and have me look to him."

"But he knows about the tattoo. He told me that the tattoo was a blood tattoo."

"He shared that information with me as well."

"What does that mean? Blood tattoo?"

"There are whispers of a group called Blood Assassins who are supposedly inked in blood tattoos, but no one believes they really exist."

"The bleeding Virgin Mary? Is that the blood tattoo?"

"Yes."

"Did you know this from the beginning?"

"No. I knew they had ink but not what kind of ink. People clam up on this topic."

"Then they're afraid, which means they must have a reason. And I find that where there is fear there is fire."

"Perhaps not the fire you're assuming. These assassins could well be a story created to cover up a crime, and that snowballed into a bigger piece of fiction."

"Who do they work for?" I press.

"We can't even prove they exist."

"The man who attacked me had that tattoo. He tried to kill me. He had to be one of them."

"A dead man with a tattoo doesn't exactly scream well-trained assassin."

"You want to kill an assassin, you hire a better killer," I say. "Obviously I was the better killer in his case." I move on past that bad topic. "Romano. He said the words *She bleeds because you bleed.* It's a quote from a movie that has a hell of a lot of ties to me."

"In what way?"

"It stars Jensen Michaels, who went home with Alexandra the night I was attacked. He's why she left me alone at the bar. But it gets even weirder. The film also has a connection to the case I was working when I was attacked."

"Laney Suthers. The high-end call girl."

"How do you remember that?"

"I told you. I've been looking for answers. I considered a connection to the case you were working the night of the attack but couldn't find one."

"And without the clue Romano gave me, you wouldn't. That film with Jensen Michaels had the same Chinese financial backers as several B-list films Laney had starred in."

"Who was the investor?"

"Ying Entertainment. Do you know them?"

"I know everyone who has financial interests in my territories, and they do. I'll look into them further as well as the various connections to you they represent. Alexandra was with you that night. What's your read on her?"

"Do I think she's involved? We were close back then. It's hard for me to see it, but then again, I didn't see her with Eddie either." I set that aside. "I need to talk to Romano myself."

"I talked to him. He told me what he told you."

"I have to talk to him again now that I've decoded his message."

"He'll repeat what he told me, which is that he received an anonymous tip that amounted to nothing more than what he shared."

"Why would he even share a tip like that with me or you? I'm connected to you, and you two are enemies."

"And that makes him the person I'd look to if anything happened to you."

"But he came to me," I argue.

"I told you. I'd refused his meeting."

"Right," I say. "You told me. I'll get my own answers." I step away from the window, intending to place space between us. Kane moves with me, standing up and placing himself in front of me, his location and proximity all but caging me between his big body and the window.

"You will not approach him," he says, his voice hard, the set of his jaw harder.

"I'm a federal agent investigating a series of assassinations, not your little bitch, bedroom bitch, or stupid bitch. I *will* talk to him."

"You're a federal agent who was, and probably is, on an assassination list."

I grimace. "And your point?"

"Push too hard, in too obvious a way, and you could end up dead."

"I have more than my own life to think about, anyway."

"We had an agreement. You stay away from Romano."

"We did have an agreement," I agree. "You were supposed to find the assassin named Ghost. But not only is his name a little too literal for me right now, it doesn't sound like I'm looking for Ghost after all. At least not now. Not unless he has a blood tattoo."

"Who says he doesn't?"

"Are you saying he does?" I counter.

"Are you going to pass up the opportunity to talk to one of the most notorious killers in history, Agent Love?"

"That wasn't an answer," I bite out.

"You mean it wasn't the answer you wanted."

"I'm not negotiating. Ghost is still a suspect in these murders. You still owe him to me, but that doesn't change the fact that I'm talking to Romano. I'll let you set it up if it makes you feel better. And you're crowding me."

"Yes. I am. Get Romano killed and not only will his people look to me, there is zero chance of another message being passed to us."

"I need to talk to him, Kane."

"Okay. Done. Do you prefer Romano tied up in the garage or the living room?"

"Ha ha. Aren't you funny? Good to see that you grew a sense of humor since I left. You needed one. But jokes aside, I'll talk to Romano myself, but if you have tips, I welcome them. A favorite restaurant to meet. A favorite coffee shop. Lay it on me."

"You'll never get to him without me."

"I'm more resourceful than you think," I say. "Unless he's dead and you really don't tell me the whole truth and nothing but the truth."

His expression tightens, seconds ticking by before he reaches into his pocket and pulls out what looks like a disposable phone and punches a number before placing the call on speaker. *"Hola,"* a man greets in an aged voice.

"Old man," Kane says.

"Pinche, Kane Mendez. I have nothing more for you."

"Still feeling the rope burn, I see," Kane comments. "It'll get better soon and we can do it again."

"What do you want and why the hell am I on speakerphone?"

"Lilah is here. *Agent* Lilah Love."

"Agent," he says. "That's right. You get off on the forbidden. Obviously Agent Love does as well."

"Romano," I say.

"Whatever you want to know, Agent Love," Romano replies, "I can't help. I was given an anonymous tip to help me, not you."

"Why help at all?"

"Have you told her nothing, Kane?" he asks. "Or is she testing your answer?"

"Answer the question," Kane bites out.

"You die, Agent Love," the old man says, "and Kane looks to me first. And at that point, he's enraged, and others are, too."

"You lost two people last night," I say. "Did Kane do it?"

"What did he say?" he asks.

"What do you say?" I counter.

"No," the old man says. "He did not."

"Then who did?" I press.

"If I knew," he says, "I wouldn't tell you."

Of course he wouldn't, but I leave it alone, instead focused on a question that I should have asked Kane. "Why would that tip go to you and not Kane if it involved me?"

"Clearly whoever gave me the tip was helping me, not Kane. Other than that, I don't know what you want me to say. It was an anonymous fucking tip."

"The tattoos," I say. "The assassins—"

Sell your books at
sellbackyourBook.com!

Go to sellbackyourBook.com
and get an instant price
quote. We even pay the
shipping - see what your old
books are worth today!

00003423137

00003423137

"A legend," he says. "A myth. Fiction."

"And yet you seemed to indicate someone tried to kill me."

"If the Blood Assassins came for you and wanted you dead, you'd be dead." He laughs. "Or so the myth would have you believe. Maybe Pokémon is real, too?" He laughs louder and hangs up.

Kane holds down the Power button and then sticks the phone in his pocket again. "Satisfied?"

"No," I say. "I'm not. He knows more than he's saying, and you still haven't given me Ghost."

"You want a lot of things, Lilah Love," he says, his voice warm, his eyes hot as he adds, "but so do I."

"The difference is that I'll get what I want, and you won't." I try to step away, but his hand comes down on the window, his arm caging me.

"Tell me," he says. "What do I want?"

"Another palm, apparently."

"How about I give you my palm, but on a different kind of cheek?"

"Maybe I will give you that knee."

"And yet, I don't have it."

"And I don't have Ghost," I remind him.

"And if I give him to you? What do I get in return?"

Those questions make it clear that while he claims his recordings were not bribes, he knows they give me pause. They stop me from arresting him.

"What do I get in return, Lilah?" he presses.

"Satisfaction."

"I need more detail," he says.

"I won't fuck you," I say.

"But you like fucking me."

"A bad drug still feels good when you're doing it."

"And denial always feels bad and grows old." He pushes off the window, backing away and perching on the edge of the desk again. "I'll wait." He doesn't give me time for a rebuttal or to recover from his sudden withdrawal. Now he's the one quickly moving on. "Ghost got word to me that he'll be in touch. That's the best you do with Ghost, and even if you did shoot me, I couldn't change that. He watches you before he approaches you."

"Like you film me and watch me? How did you know I've been sleeping with Cujo?"

"It was an easy assumption. You're in the house where you were attacked, and it was on the desk."

He knows me too well. And I know him, which reminds me of one of the reasons I'm here. "Rich isn't leaving. My boss assigned him to my case."

His eyes harden, darken. "Isn't that interesting."

"He's going to come for you, push you."

"Will he be fucking you while pushing me?"

"I ended things with Rich before I even knew I was coming here."

"*Will he* be fucking you while pushing me?"

"No, Kane. He will not."

"And yet he thinks he will."

"He's a good guy who thinks that if he fights for my honor, he'll win me over."

"You mean he wants to ruin me to claim you."

"Yes," I say. "That pretty much sums it up."

"And I'm supposed to turn my cheek."

"Yes."

"All right," he says, a little too quickly. "I'll turn a cheek. For now, and that's the best you're getting, so take it."

I take what I can get but make damn sure he knows what to expect, so I know what to expect. "He'll be by my side while I investigate."

"Exactly why I'll tolerate him. He'll have your back as he tries to stab me in mine. But don't forget that your little investigation is about us and that night. No more secrets, Lilah, *Agent Love*. I know what you know. You know what I know. And don't tell me it's confidential on your end. These murders lead to you, a knife, a grave, and me. We need to end this before it ends us, and we need to do it together."

"You get what you give," I say. "Don't forget that, and leave out your myths and theories, or you won't like what I give back." And with that promise, I round the desk and start walking toward the door. I reach for the handle and then pause with a realization and turn to face Kane, finding him still on his feet and behind his desk but facing me now. "I know why the Son of Sam popped into my head."

"Tell me," he urges, his hands settling on the wooden surface of his desk, his body leaning in my direction.

"He was convicted in the seventies, and at that time, he claimed he killed alone. In the nineties, he amended his confession and said he was in a satanic cult. The tattoos and assassinations, my rape. The movie and the case I was working at the time. Maybe the Blood Assassins aren't assassins at all but cult members."

"Nothing about these murders read like satanic killings," Kane says. "They read like Ghost."

"Maybe," I say, offering nothing more. I exit his office, my mind focused on this cult idea, and I walk past Tabitha without so much as a glance. Kane's right in his assessment, but everything inside me says that he's wrong. My mind forms a theory. The Blood Assassins are a cult, and Laney, the call-girl case I was working during my attack, had to have been involved or a member. Which means my attack could have been a result of me getting too close to the cult or to someone involved in the cult.

CHAPTER SEVEN

I exit Kane's office building to find my brother leaning on the hood of my rental car, his long, jean-clad legs stretched in front of him, his wavy, thick blond hair lifting in a salt-kissed gust of wind. That ugly-ass tan uniform shirt he's always wearing, with a shiny police chief badge on the pocket, reminds me that brotherly love isn't the reason Andrew's here today. "Imagine seeing you here," he says as I stop in front of him.

"If you dent my hood, you're paying for it."

"Because you pissed away all your money in Tinseltown?"

"Because unless you have doughnuts in your car, like a good cop, I'm hungry, and your ass is in the way."

"Should I assume your visit with Kane was personal? Or professional?" he asks, obviously already past the sibling love.

"You have met Rich, right? The guy I dated after Kane."

"The one you dumped right about the time you came back here? Yes. I met him. He doesn't like Kane any more than I do."

"Rich and I broke up right about the time he insisted we move in together instead of just fuck and fuck and fuck." Andrew reddens and I smirk, loving the way I've made him uncomfortable, and not just because he was just an ass. Because it's my job as a sister.

"I could do without details, little sis."

"Really? Because I'm pretty sure you just demanded them when you inferred Kane and I were still a thing. And moving to business, Kane didn't behead Romano's people."

"Because you got naked with him, looked into his eyes, and saw the truth and honor?"

"Because I threatened to take Kane in for questioning last night," I say, not taking any chances he already knows I was at his place. "And in turn, he arranged a conversation between myself and the patriarch of the Romano family. Which I just had."

He blinks. "You talked to Angelo Romano?"

"No. I talked to Old Man Romano, who is, in fact, the patriarch of the family."

"The old man is not the patriarch."

"Kane and the old man disagree, but whatever. Talk to the cover guy yourself if you want. He's not going to turn on Kane. The real patriarch won't let him. Now get off my car. I need to get stuff done."

"If Kane didn't kill Romano's people, who did?"

"The old man said he wouldn't tell me if he knew."

"And what did Kane say?"

"That he's being targeted. The old man seems to agree with that as well. Actually, he didn't say that, but that was the vibe I got."

"Why would the old man protect Kane? The two families are enemies."

"Kane helped negotiate peace between the two families."

"Of course he did," he says dryly.

"You know, brother of mine, I get that Kane has slept with both your sister and your woman, and that you don't like him. I do. But you've known him a long-ass time. When has he ever been blatantly stupid?"

"If Kane didn't kill Romano's people, then another member of the Mendez cartel has to be responsible, and that means Kane, in my book."

"Since when is Kane a member of the cartel at all?" I ask, and for once it's not to be a smart-ass. "When I questioned Kane, he insisted that he's not that person. His uncle is, and operating far from our town."

"And the old man isn't the patriarch either," he says, "at least that's what law enforcement believed until you said otherwise. Kane's uncle lives in Mexico. Kane has to be running the US operation."

"If that's true, why have you allowed it to continue in your city?"

"You don't cross a man like Kane Mendez without proof." He doesn't give me the chance to beat that statement to death in about ten different ways, before asking, "Did you ask to speak to Kane's uncle or to Angelo Romano, the patriarch law enforcement knows?"

"If Romano thought Kane or anyone else in the Mendez cartel killed his people, we'd be dealing with war, like the good ol' days when Kane's father was in charge. In other words, it would bleed into the Hamptons and your life would be hell. You do remember what that was like, don't you? Because pushing them toward that again doesn't seem smart to me."

"The New York city officials want the crime solved, and they're looking to me because of Kane."

"Did they share the fingerprints lifted from the crime scene?"

"Not yet, but I talked to the lead detective. He's sending me the report. There were a dozen prints, two of which belonged to the victims at the scene."

"A dozen?" I ask, thinking of the crime scene. "Were they holding orgies in that tiny apartment or just selling drugs from the place?" I don't wait for a reply. "Email me the list of names when you get them."

"If this isn't a Mendez-Romano situation, who does Kane believe is targeting him?"

"Someone who hates him," I say, "and this is where this gets real big, brother. I didn't press for a name because I didn't want him to think of you. And you shouldn't either, or the town will end up with legal action. Chew on that one while I go find those doughnuts." I turn away and walk toward my door, and by the time I have it open, he's on the other side, staring down at me.

"Do you really want to continue this conversation?" I ask.

"Your boss called me," he announces.

"Then he's an asshole, too. He's not supposed to go around me. Did you take the opportunity to tell him I have a conflict of interest?"

"Yes. I did."

"And he told you that he knew that and that's exactly why he sent me," I say. "And thanks for trying to get me fired."

"I'm trying to get you away from Kane."

"Oh goody. I didn't know we were playing this game. I can think of all kinds of ways to get you away from Samantha."

"Leave Samantha alone."

"Leave Samantha alone. Live those words, Andrew." I motion with my hands. "Breathe them in. Record them and play them by your bedside."

His jaw flexes and sets. "Murphy wants proof that Woods is the killer we're after, and that proof has to hold up in court. That came from you, didn't it?"

"He asked me for proof that Woods is not the killer, too. It's just the way he is. All about dotting those damn *i*'s."

"What are you doing, Lilah? If you claim jurisdiction and news of a serial killer hits the press, this town becomes hell, and you hurt Father's chances of being elected."

"I can't even believe we're having a conversation about an election ranking higher than public safety, but since we are, let me put this in terms you might actually understand. This is a bad gamble you're taking. If someone else ends up dead, you look like you're incompetent, and the only way Dad saves himself is to fire you. So what am I doing? I'm saving you from yourself and him." I duck into the car, and Andrew stands at my door for several beats before shutting it. And damn it, I love that asshole, and right now, I really want to open it again and knock some sense into him before he ends up in trouble.

Unless it's changed, there's only one doughnut shop in East Hampton that I know of, and it's usually packed, which means people will see me, talk to me, and generally be nice, even if it's fake nice. I don't like fake. Not boobs, lashes, or even smiles. I don't even like nice. I just want a damn doughnut or three or four. Fortunately, with a quick google search, I discover that the shop still operates a truck, and I drive to a parking lot off the beach to peacefully have my sugar minus the conversation. I fail. The person inside the truck, while not familiar to me, is a talker. There are so many words between me and my doughnuts and coffee that by the time I have a bag with three plain and three cinnamon, I need more of the drugs Kane gave me.

I've also noticed a blue sedan sitting at the curb across the street between two houses that wasn't there when I arrived. Keeping a discreet eye on it, hoping I might have a lead on Junior, I climb into my rental. Once I'm sealed inside, I inhale a plain doughnut and down half my lukewarm coffee before it has time to become cold. Meanwhile, the blue sedan hasn't moved, but finally a thin, bald man in a dark suit, who may or may not be Mexican, exits. He walks to the doughnut stand, which seems innocent enough, but I am pretty sure that's the idea. The dude knows I made him.

I glance at his bunched-up shoulders before eyeing my car display, which tells me that it's ten thirty. Close enough to lunchtime to stop eating doughnuts, but I have no willpower. Solving that problem, I toss the bag into the back seat and start the car so that I won't twist around and grab them. I have time before my meet-up with Rich, and my mind goes to Kane's question about Alexandra and her involvement in my attack. Suddenly, I want to look her in the eyes and see how she reacts. I confirm the man at the doughnut stand is just as trapped by the chatterbox in the truck as I had been and pull up the number for the district attorney's office in South Hampton. It's an hour away, and I'm not driving there this afternoon if Alexandra isn't in.

I hit the Call button and speakerphone. I don't do Bluetooth. It can be hacked, and like sunglasses, I never can find the earpiece when I need it anyway. I have three rings to confirm that the doughnut man and the sedan man are still talking. "Is Alexandra Harris in today?" I ask when a woman answers.

"Do you mean Alexandra Rivera?"

"Yes," I say of her married name. "Her."

"Who's calling?" she asks.

"Agent Lilah Love," I say. "FBI."

"Agent Love, she's working at the East Hampton District Court at the town attorney's offices. Do you need that number?"

"I've got it," I say and then hang up, cranking my engine and placing the car in Drive.

I pull to the exit of the parking lot and pause, glancing back to find the bald dude in the suit fast-walking toward his car. And since Junior wouldn't be this obvious or stupid, I'm led one other place.

I dial Kane on speakerphone and then pull onto the highway, headed toward the courthouse. He answers on the first ring. "Already miss me?"

"Is the person you have following me in a blue sedan? Because if so, you need to hire better people. He sucks."

"I don't hire people who suck. He's not mine."

"I saw your man in New York, Kane. You need better people. Are you sure he's not yours?"

"He's not mine, Lilah."

"Huh. Okay. That's all I wanted."

I hang up and glance in my mirror. The sedan has yet to pull behind me, but then neither has anyone else, and yet it seems that I have eyes on me from all directions. I actually crave one of Junior's notes right now. At least that tells me where Junior's head is at, but I'm sure another one is coming. A lot is coming my way. I can almost feel the ball about to drop, and my mind settles on my mother, who loved her work but became scared of the rabid attention. I remember her saying: *It's unnerving. Every move I make, someone is watching, and you never know who might be crazy.*

But I don't get unnerved like my mother. I have a gun with bullets inside, and I know how to use it. And it doesn't hurt that I'm far more comfortable with dead bodies than a huge portion of the living. That thought thrusts me back to the past and to the dark beachfront on the night of my attack. The scene plays out in my head, almost as if I'm watching from above: My attacker is on top of me, and I can't seem to fight back. Kane pulls him off me, and the images shift. I watch myself grab the knife my attacker dropped in the sand, and then I'm shoving it in his chest. Over and over and over again. And I'd felt no guilt for the actual murder.

I still feel no guilt for killing that man. Even Kane, who seems to look straight to my soul and understand me, thinks that I do. Which lends credence to the suggestion that I'm good at my job for a reason: it takes a killer to outsmart a killer.

CHAPTER EIGHT

I arrive at the tiny East Hampton courthouse, and the parking lot is a clusterfuck of cars, Super Walmart–style. All I need is a shopping cart to ram into my rental, and the comparison would be real. But lucky me, for the second time today, third if you count my doughnuts, I manage to snag another front-door spot. In fact, despite waking up drugged and a mess, I'm so lucky today that I'm contemplating a trip to Vegas. Then again, two parking spots and doughnuts don't really constitute a change to my lifelong streak of bad luck, which is exactly why I'm here, prepared to drill Alexandra. I never count on luck leading me to answers. Doughnuts are another story. They lead me to tolerance, which I will need with Alexandra, and that's why I grab the bag from the back seat before I head for the front door.

Once I'm inside the courthouse, I give a quick scan of the dreary lobby, and I'm reminded that for a town dripping with money, none of it is in this building. The floor is basic white tile. The walls scuffed and white. The reception desk a simple light wood. The young chick with glasses behind the desk is so awkward with my entry that she's clearly a newbie and still in duty diapers. "May I help you?" she asks.

"No," I say, and because she might slow me down if I don't, I lift my jacket and flash my badge at my hip. "I know my way around." I start walking, and why wouldn't I? There isn't a cop around, which really isn't smart. It invites trouble from someone openly crazy, or even closet crazy like myself. Sadly, this fail falls under my father's and brother's responsibilities, but as I'm already turning down a hallway behind the reception area, I'm momentarily pleased with their current state of stupid.

Unavoidably, I travel a long path, passing random offices that I ignore in hopes that I won't hear my name. Luck still likes me. I make it all the way to the door marked **Town Attorney** with no one shouting my name at me, or any other name for that matter.

I step inside a workspace that appears to be a bullpen of sorts, the center without a receptionist, a half dozen doors forming a horseshoe. To my surprise, Alexandra's name is on the door to my immediate right, which tells me this is now her permanent residence—an odd setup for an assistant DA for Suffolk County. But so are a great many things, including the local victim's autopsy, which was done here rather than in the main location as would be standard procedure. It seems this town is interacting with other state officials in a great many ways that don't fit the established processes.

Embracing what appears to be a bit more luck on my side, I find Alexandra's door open and assume it to be an invitation I accept. I enter her office to find her sitting at a glass desk that is out of place in this shit-hole tiny office. A far cry from the corner office in Manhattan she'd always vied for.

On a gasp, she looks up from whatever papers she's examining, her heart-shaped face pulled tight beneath some sort of updo, her brows high, and despite this unappealing combination, she's still pretty—her brown eyes doelike, her skin ivory. Too damn pretty for the likes of Eddie, that's for sure, but then I've long ago learned that some of the pretty ones are the most fucked in the head.

"Lilah," she whispers, leaning forward, as if my name is a secret, my presence somehow scandalous.

"That's still my name," I say, claiming the seat in front of her and lifting the bag. "Doughnut?"

"What are you doing here?"

I grab a glazed delight and hold it up. "Eating doughnuts." I set the bag down. "You should take one now before I eat them all, and I have a lunch thing that might make that a problem." I take a bite. "God, these things are good." I reach behind me and shove the door shut. "Eat one," I urge.

"I have a meeting in a few minutes."

"I have murders to solve, and you had contact with the suspect. Is it more important than that?"

"What murders? The decapitations last night? That's not our jurisdiction, and I had no contact with anyone." She narrows her eyes on me. "I told Eddie and your brother that Kane Mendez was too smart to kill those people and lead law enforcement to his doorstep."

"I'm sure Kane appreciates your playing his guardian angel, but I'm talking about the cases everyone wants to pin on Woods." I finish off my doughnut and point to the unopened bottle of water on her desk. "Do you mind?"

"Woods confessed and then killed himself," she says.

"And your point?" I ask, and since she hasn't denied me the water, I claim it and open it.

"He confessed," she repeats, politely waiting until I guzzle her water and set the bottle down.

"How long have you and Eddie been married?" I ask, kicking my feet up on the desk, crossing them at the ankles.

"Two years."

"That means you jumped from Jensen Michaels's bed right into Eddie's. Talk about night and day. How was that for you?"

"Eddie's a good-looking man, Lilah."

"I don't remember commenting on his looks, but whatever the case, he's an asshole. When did he become your thing? Right after I left, or what?"

"Before."

"Really. As in before Jensen or after?"

"Before, but we weren't exclusive."

"But you didn't tell me," I point out.

"I wasn't going to upset you if nothing came of it."

I settle my feet on the floor and look her in the eyes. "Why did Woods call you to issue his first confession?"

"I told you why at dinner."

"Dinner at my father's house," I say. "That's right. I was distracted by the fact that you were actually at my father's house and married to Eddie. Tell me again."

"Am I being interrogated?"

"My boss is a pain in the ass. I have to write a report, Alexandra, and if there is one hole, we all have a problem. I'll have to claim jurisdiction, and your husband and my brother and father will lose their shit."

Her lips tighten. "Yes. They would. But Woods coming to me really isn't all that odd. The district attorney assigned me to East Hampton right after you left. But I also do some random guest spots on one of the mainstream news stations out of New York City."

It hits me now that she hasn't given up her corner Manhattan office. She's planning to go as part of my father's entourage. Better her than me, as long as that path doesn't include walking over Woods's grave and framing him for murders he didn't commit. "Has anyone but Woods ever randomly confessed to you?"

"No. He's the first."

"Do a lot of people come to you over my brother and his staff to confess?"

"No, but the TV segments have gotten more popular."

My gaze catches on a blue folder she has lying on her desk, my eyes narrowing on the label that reads "Pocher," before my eyes return to hers. "Why?" I demand. "Are you prosecuting a man funding my father's campaign?"

"Of course not. I'm helping with your father's campaign, and he's a major contributor."

Of course she is and he is. "Do you still talk to Jensen?"

She blanches. "What? No. I'm married." But she cuts her eyes to her hand, and that's her tell sign. That's what she does when she's lying. "And you're all over the board," she says when she looks at me again. "You're bouncing between unrelated topics and giving me whiplash."

"Really? Are they unrelated?"

"Of course they are. One has nothing to do with the other."

"But they do. Two things actually: me and you." And with that, I take my bag of doughnuts and her water, and I get up and leave.

Three minutes later, I'm inside my rental car, staring at the courthouse without really seeing it. She was nervous. Maybe she assumed I would disapprove of her role in my father's campaign, when it's not her I disapprove of. It's Pocher. I'm not sure that was it anyway. She didn't cut her gaze talking to me about Pocher. She cut her gaze talking to me about Jensen Michaels, who was with her the night I was attacked.

CHAPTER NINE

Realizing that your ex–best friend might have aided in an effort to kill you is like standing in the deep blue sea with colorful coral glistening beneath the clear waters: everything is beautiful until a shark shows itself and decides to take a bite. At which point you either fight, gouge its eyes out, and survive, or it's all blood and death—for you, not it. I might be comfortable with dead bodies, but not enough to join them six feet under.

Thus, by the time I pull into the packed parking lot of the diner, I've changed my perspective on where I stand in this investigation, which results in three conclusions. One: Murphy is an asshole, but he wasn't wrong. I need an investigator who I trust on my side, and Rich *is* the only shot I have of that happening. In other words, I have to shake some sense into him over Kane. Two: if he remains stupid over Kane, I'm getting him out of town, even if that means I grow some balls and do what I've resisted with him. I have to stop simply being resistant to his advances and start being a brutal-rejection bitch. It's for his own good. To keep him from ending up six feet under.

And three: good thing I didn't book that trip to Vegas, because my lucky streak has ended. There is no front-door spot for me at the diner. After fifteen minutes of trying, I accept this as fact and pull around to the side parking lot. "Damn it," I curse, squeezing into a spot between a truck and another car, which offers shelter for Junior to leave me another literary masterpiece of love/hate in the form of a note. And hey, I'm down with the love/hate thing we have going on. The sooner we get to full-blown hate, the sooner we have a confrontation and end this matchup. Bring it, and all that grand shit. Except for now, when Rich will want to walk me to my car.

Though, I think, killing my engine, it *will* be interesting to see if Junior wants to remain secret, as in for my eyes only, or if he flaunts the notes in front of Rich. I open my door at the same moment my phone rings. Grabbing it from inside my jacket pocket, I glance down to find Rich's number. "Are you here?" he asks the instant I connect.

"Parking lot. You?"

"I'm here, but there are no seats."

"How long is the wait?" I ask.

"I'm trying to find out."

With my strawberry pie in jeopardy and a to-go order in mind, I say, "I'll be right there," and end the call. Shutting my door, I lock up before weaving my way through the parked vehicles, but I never round the corner to the front of the building. Rich steps in front of me in a long-sleeve light-blue T-shirt and jeans; with his blond hair lying in waves, he looks every bit the hot surfer dude who makes women swoon. Just not me. Not that I swoon at all. Ever. For anyone. "An hour wait," he says. "And I doubt you want to hang out here that long."

"They do have good pie."

"You want to wait an hour for pie?"

"No?" I ask.

His brow furrows. "Yes?"

I wonder in that moment if our communication has always been this stilted and I chose to ignore it, before I offer him a firm "No," though I'm going to have to come back later for that pie.

"Where else can we go and talk?" he asks.

"Right here and now works just fine," I reply. "Are you here to help me with this case or stalk Kane?"

His eyes glint with anger. "Kane is part of this case. He's probably behind every damn last one of these murders. And the sick fuck was probably just trying to get you here. How does that feel? To know people died to get you here?"

Considering my earlier conversation with Kane, Rich has hit about ten nerves. "What kind of prick lays that kind of guilt on someone? Oh right. The kind thinking with the head in his pants, not the one on his shoulders."

"I don't know how else to make you see him for what he is."

"This isn't going to work." I turn and start walking away.

"I'm here because you can't see him clearly," he says from behind me. "That's why Murphy sent me."

I whirl around to find him on my heels. "Is that what Murphy told you?"

"It's pretty obvious."

"So that's not what Murphy told you," I say.

"No, but—"

"What did he say?"

"That you needed backup you can trust."

"I do, and do you know why?"

"He said you'd update me."

"And you actually thought my update would include my plea that you save me from Kane Mendez?" I don't give him time to reply. "You're here," I say, lowering my voice, "because Woods didn't kill those people. A professional assassin did. He's just the fall guy."

"Then Kane ordered the assassinations."

"Oh fuck, Rich. Get over Kane. He didn't do this. He's not that stupid."

"Then why does his name keep coming up?"

"Perhaps he's a distraction. It's damn sure working on you. Set Kane aside and ask the right questions."

His expression tightens. "Eddie says—"

"Eddie is part of the cover-up."

"Does your brother know this?"

"Yes, Rich. And so does my father, who's going to run for governor of New York."

He blanches. "Your father's running for governor?"

"Yes. He is. And a killer on the loose doesn't exactly work in his favor. I'm either going to have to talk sense into my brother and my father or claim jurisdiction."

He shakes his head. "I can't believe Murphy has you on this case."

My mind goes back to that talk with Murphy yet again:

"I have a history with Kane Mendez."

"Which makes you the perfect candidate to get into his head."

"Why do I need to be in Kane's head?"

"He's connected to this. Tonight makes that clear."

Is Murphy protecting Kane or working against him? Rich is against him, and Murphy pushed Rich on me and this case. "I need to go," I say, rotating with the full intent of leaving and confronting Murphy.

"Lilah, damn it," Rich grinds out, putting himself between me and the car. "We aren't done."

"I'm done with this argument, Rich," I snap. "I'm going to go make a phone call and then catch a killer. You go chase Kane Mendez and end up dead."

"Why the hell would you date a man who requires that warning?"

"Food for thought, Rich," I say, trying to jolt him into pleading off this case as I add, "Fucking someone isn't the same as dating him." He blanches again, and I step around him, leaving him to wonder if I'm talking about him or Kane or both of them.

I click my locks open, climb inside my car, and lock up. Almost instantly, Rich is pounding on the passenger door. I have a short, pleasant fantasy in which I leave him outside and drive away. But that won't do anything but restart the battle we're presently fighting, and I need him on board with me or gone. There is no in-between. I hit the lock and let him join me, then he turns to face me. "I'm here to help."

I study him for a few beats, searching his chiseled face, which still manages to be etched with fifty shades of hate for Kane. "This isn't going to work."

"You need someone you trust at your back. You trust me."

He's right, at least partially. At my back, in a professional capacity, I trust him. But I don't trust Murphy, who insisted Rich stay here. Maybe that means I need to trust Murphy, or maybe it means I shouldn't trust Rich. My cell phone rings with Tic Tac's number displayed. I study Rich for another beat and then answer the call on speaker. "Agent Moore is with me, Tic Tac," I say, warning my tech partner in crime that we are not alone.

"Agent Love."

At the sound of Director Murphy's voice, I stiffen, a bad feeling sliding down my spine. "Director," I say, glancing at Rich for some sort of guidance. He shakes his head, telling me he knows nothing. "What happened to Tic Tac?" I ask.

"If you mean Agent Landers," Murphy says, "he's right here."

Tic Tac clears his throat. "I'm here."

"Tell me, *Special Agent* Love," Murphy says, his tone and the formal use of "Special Agent" telling me that he's pissed, "why exactly did you have Agent Landers looking into my history?"

Oh fuck. How did he find out?

Rich gives me an incredulous look and mouths, "What the fuck, Lilah?"

"How did I find out?" Murphy asks, apparently reading my mind. "I found out because Landers here used the company system for research."

"You searched on the FBI system, Landers?" I snap.

"Yes," Murphy says. "He did. And what kind of example would I set if I didn't have alerts set up, particularly as they relate to myself?" He doesn't wait for a reply. "Agent Landers," he adds, clearly talking to Tic Tac. "Share the details you've learned about me."

Tic Tac clears his throat. "Director Murphy came up the ranks with his New York City equal, Assistant Director James Carter. Carter has a variety of political scandals surrounding him. He was involved in an investigation with at least three high-powered political figures funded by you can guess who."

"Pocher," I say, and glancing at Rich, I explain, "*the* Pocher of the Pocher family, who's my father's main financial backer for his run for office." Refocusing on the call, I say, "Carter made those political cases go away in Pocher's favor."

"Unproven," Murphy says. "But that's how it reads to me, especially knowing Carter as I do. He's ambitious in all the wrong ways. Which brings me, Special Agent Love, to your poor communication. Why the hell do I not know about the double beheading last night linked to Kane Mendez?"

I bristle with the reprimand, opening my mouth to remind him that he ended our call this morning by hanging up on me, but Rich reaches over and grabs my arm, giving me a warning look. My lips thin, and I nod before reframing my planned smart-ass remark as something a bit more professional. "I had just returned from consulting on the case when I ended up knocked out. But I followed up this morning. I spoke with Kane Mendez and Old Man Romano. Kane didn't do it. It's some sort of setup."

"I didn't ask if Mendez did it. I asked why the hell I didn't know. Agent Moore," he says, addressing Rich. "Based on what you've learned in this conversation and the fact that Lilah strongly believes that Woods is a fall guy, tell me why we now have jurisdiction issues?"

Realization hits me, as does dread. "I have a bad feeling that I have the answer."

"I said Agent Moore," Murphy replies.

Rich looks over at me, my realization now in his eyes. "Kane's linked to the murders we're investigating through the one murder on his property of his employee," he says. "He's linked to the beheadings simply because that's a signature Mendez kill. He's a local with a long family history of crime, which means the local FBI could easily fight to claim jurisdiction."

He's nailed my thoughts exactly, and I am not pleased when Murphy validates his statement and my thoughts with, "You're exactly right, Agent Moore. Which is why you are not there to fuck Kane Mendez and us right along with him. You're there because between you and him, Lilah stays alive and catches us the real killer. Protect her. Protect the case. And make sure she communicates." He turns the attention back to me. "Agent Love. Spend your energy hunting a killer, not me. And I need that killer now, not later."

"Or what? We lose jurisdiction?"

"I don't lose, Agent Love. Make sure you don't either. You get me my killer. I'll get you jurisdiction. Just keep your mouth shut about it until I say 'go.'"

He hangs up.

Rich and I sit there for a good thirty seconds without speaking before Rich says, "Kane Mendez is a problem I don't plan to forget, but I will put him on hold for now." He looks over at me. "I'm in this. I'm with you. What's the plan?"

I turn to face him. "We need to avoid the battle of jurisdiction, which means we can't let the locals close the case."

"That's a touchy order."

"But you can buy me some time."

"How?"

"Keep playing the bad guy," I say. "Convince Eddie and my brother that you can influence me to back out of this. Get them to keep the case open for a little while longer."

"All right. I can do that."

"Can you?"

"You might not know this, Lilah, but I'm more than the surfer dude you called me. I'm a damn good agent."

"I know you're a good agent."

"A *damn good* agent."

"Okay. A damn good agent."

"What are you going to do if your family crosses the line?"

"The right thing."

"Translated to mean any number of things," he says, "but I won't push. We'll take it one step at a time. Let's go inside and get lunch."

I reach to the floorboard and shove the doughnut bag at him. "There's your lunch."

He doesn't look inside the bag. "I get it. You want me to go. And I will, but Lilah, this is my last word on this for now. I'm the good guy. Kane Mendez is not. And I'm not going to let you forget that." He opens the car door and gets out, shutting me inside.

I start the car, ready to get out of here, and I'm not even sure where I'm going. I just need to be moving. And *damn it*, I didn't get my pie and I gave up my doughnuts. I kill the engine. I need to eat and think, but I don't get out of the car. My fingers thrum on the steering wheel, my mind going back to Laney's case. I know that case is connected to my attack. And my attack is connected to the current murders by way of the tattoo. And the old man's clue led me to Jensen Michaels and to Laney, who connect by way of the film company. Pocher, or someone just as powerful, has to be connected to that film company.

I grab my phone and start to dial Tic Tac, then think better of it. Murphy is watching over him, and this all connects to me and to the night that I stabbed a man twelve times. I should never have asked Tic Tac to look into the film company, and yet I did. I practically invited him and Murphy to discover I'm a killer hunting a killer. That means I'm dependent on myself and Kane to figure out the connection between that film company, my attack, Laney's case, and the murders. Actually, there is one more person who might just know something. The person who was working the Laney case with me but didn't end up raped and nearly killed: my ex-partner, Greg Harrison.

CHAPTER TEN

I dial Greg and, *of course*, I get his voice mail. "Greg," I say. "It's me. You know. *Me.* The one whose calls you never fucking take. And I don't know. Maybe you have a good excuse for ignoring me. Like you're drunk and feeling sorry for yourself. Or maybe you're naked with that party-planner chick I saw you cuddling up to at the party the other night. I wouldn't want to interrupt you while you're getting a good piece of ass because Lord knows, based on the way you looked and smelled last week, you aren't getting much. Maybe—" The voice mail buzzes. "Damn," I murmur. "I wasn't done." Especially since that party planner is a Romano.

I disconnect the line only to have my cell ring again, and assuming that it's Greg, I answer without looking at the number. "Screening your calls?"

"What the hell, Lilah?"

Not Greg. "I don't know, brother of mine," I answer at the sound of Andrew's voice. "What the hell?"

"Why are you harassing Alexandra over Woods?"

"Friendly questions over doughnuts does not constitute harassing. And if she needs you to fight her teeny-tiny battles, I know why she didn't end up with a corner office in Manhattan."

"Unlike you, she's invested in this community and our father's future."

I'm officially bordering on angry. "You know, Andrew, even for a brother, that was low. Especially since I'm the only one who seems to have the common sense to see beyond shortsighted decisions."

"Whatever the hell that means, Lilah, I don't care. We need to end this Woods situation here and now."

"And there it is. The shortsighted decision."

"I should have dragged you to the station this morning. Where are you now?"

"Have you gotten Murphy the paperwork on Woods that he requested?"

"We both know he's pushing for proof Woods is guilty at your encouragement. You can end this."

"That's a no. You have not gotten Murphy the paperwork that he wants. I can't do anything to help you until he finishes his evaluation. Believe me. I tried to get him to make a decision now, not later." My phone beeps. "I need to take this call."

"We need to finish this conversation," my brother argues.

"I'll come to the station."

"When?"

"Soon," I say.

"Today," he insists.

"I'll try." I end the call and answer the next line, this time a little more cautiously. "Agent Love," I say.

"Aren't we formal, Agent Love?" Greg says. "Where's Ms. Fuck-fuck-fuck?"

"Where are you?"

"Still in East Hampton," he says. "Are you?"

"Why are you here?"

"You know the ex-supermodel Misty Morgan?"

"Yes. I know her. She and my mother were friends. Why?"

"I'm doing security for her book tour that launches tomorrow. And holy hell. Did you just say that she was your mother's friend?"

"Frenemy. Misty's attacks on my mother were so frequent that Misty might as well have been a Vegas hooker in a five-and-dime."

"Great. This just got weird."

"You're fucking her and the Romano chick? Jesus, Greg. She is old enough to be your mother. And to think we used to say you were the normal one."

"She's hot. She's famous. Life is short."

"And that mentality gets a lot of people in trouble. You know it. I know it. We need to talk in person."

"Whatever you think you know, you don't."

"Meet me and look me in the eyes and answer every question I have," I say. "Make me believe you."

"Bring it," he says, accepting my challenge. "When and where?"

"Now. A diner ten minutes from Misty's."

I give him the address and we disconnect, my fingers thrumming the steering wheel. He was with the Romano woman. Now he's with Misty. I'm not sure what to make of Greg's recent behavior, but I'm not ready to write him off as bad. I exit the car and walk to the trunk, grabbing my briefcase from inside before locking up. Rounding the front of the building, I see there are now open parking spots, which I hope equate to open tables. I need that second cup of coffee, right before I have a third.

Entering the diner, I find that my luck has returned. There are several open tables, and one of them is my favorite corner booth. The hostess, a forty-something woman with her hair clipped at the back of her head so tightly I think she might pop a seam, greets me. I point to my table. "That's my reserved seating."

She frowns. "Reserved?"

"Yes. They didn't tell you?"

She doesn't laugh. She looks confused. Either she really is about to pop a seam, or I'm clearly really bad at fitting in and making small talk. Either is highly possible, which leads me to believe that I need coffee. Or booze. Maybe both. "I'll grab my seat," I say, heading in that direction, and the good news is that she doesn't stop me. I'm also pleased to note that of all the people in the place, I recognize absolutely no one.

That's hard to do in this town, and yet this place has continually over-performed in that aspect. And it has good pie.

Win.

Win.

I settle into the booth, my back to the wall and my eyes on the front door. Rose, my waitress from my prior visit, is quickly beside me, filling my coffee cup—proof that good tips to good people pay off. Which is a nice change of pace, since in my business, good tips often come from bad people, and good tips sometimes go to bad people. I've just opened my computer to start digging into some research on the Chinese production company on my own, but I find myself staring blankly at the monitor, my mind going back to the past: six days after my attack and the night Laney died in her Manhattan apartment while out on bail.

Greg and I step into the elevator, and I hit the button for the thirtieth floor of the Central Park apartment building, then head to the $20 million apartment Laney owns. A luxury her nickname, "the Princess of Call Girls," has allotted her.

"What's wrong with you, Lilah?" Greg asks the minute the doors seal us inside the car.

That's a loaded question he doesn't really want answered. I don't look at him. "I'm two candy bars shy of my chocolate quota for the week. That kind of shit fucks with a girl."

"At least I got a smart-ass reply out of you. That's the first time in days."

"Fuck you," I say, glancing over at him. "How's that?"

He punches the button on the elevator to halt us at floor five. "Talk to me," he demands.

I whirl around to fire back. "What the hell are you doing, Greg? We don't have time for this."

"Why? Because Laney is going to run off to Brazil before we talk to her? She's under house arrest. What the hell is going on with you? What is wrong?"

"You, right now. My job is to work the case, not entertain you with my attitude."

"Your attitude is who you are, and if that part of you isn't present, you aren't present, and that's dangerous to us both. Are you and Kane having problems?"

"What the hell is it with you men? You think that if a woman's upset, a set of balls is to blame?" And because he's still staring at me, I give him a nibble, and it's not a lie. At least not fully. "It's the anniversary of my mother's death. And I'm like this every year around this time, so I really don't know why you chose to be less self-absorbed than usual and actually notice. But don't. Go back to being your regular insensitive self. I like you better like that." I punch the button to start the elevator moving, facing forward again.

He faces forward, too. "When is the anniversary?"

"Just drop it," I say, and thankfully he does. Right now, we both need to focus on our case and our boss's directive to reveal Laney's entire client list.

Floors tick by, and as I have many times in the past few days, a flashback of me driving a knife into my attacker's chest is shoving its way into my mind. And damn it. I don't think it's supposed to be a memory that calms the storm inside me, but it does. It's a good memory.

We arrive on Laney's floor and the elevator opens. I shove aside everything but this case and step into the corridor beyond the car. I've met Laney several times while she was in custody. I fought to get her home, where I could actually break down her walls, and I'm hoping today is that day.

Wordlessly Greg and I walk the hallway until we are outside of Laney's place, ringing the bell. Laney opens the door almost instantly. Her blonde hair is tied back, her skin free of makeup. She looks younger than her twenty-six years, and her eyes are puffy as if she's been crying. She glances at me and then at Greg. "Who is he?"

"My partner. You can trust him."

"No. Not him. He can't come in. Just you."

I glance at Greg and he nods, leaning on the wall. I enter the apartment foyer, a modern chandelier dangling above me that looks more like a wood sculpture than a light.

Laney points to a doorway directly to the right, and I follow her into a small library where we settle into the two leather seats framed by bookshelves. "You got me out, didn't you?" she asks.

"Yes," I say honestly. "I did."

"I'd say I appreciate that, but we both know you did it to get me to talk. And I can't talk to you."

"I can get you a deal. A good one. We don't want you. You're not the objective."

"How many names get me my freedom?"

"I want them all."

"I won't give them all to you."

"Then you won't give me the most damning ones. And that doesn't work for me."

"Then we're at a stalemate."

I consider my options for all of two beats. "Give me more than names, then."

She laughs without humor and looks away. "I could. Oh God. I could tell you things you'd never believe."

"Try me."

"No."

"What kind of things? Let's narrow the list and find you an opening. An escape from all this."

She looks at me. "Why would you help me? I know who you are. Your mother was a movie star. You understand these high-profile people. You know how much they need privacy and someone to trust."

"My mother's fame controlled our lives when I was growing up. Which makes me understand what it's like to be powerless in your own world. My mother felt trapped. She created her identity, but it held her prisoner. Like yours has you. I see you in her, not them in her."

"Did your mother find an escape?"

"Only in death," I say. "Don't let that be you. I'll protect you. I'll make sure the information you give me doesn't come from you."

"You can't do that and get me a deal."

"I will. You have my word. But I need the information you share with me to be provable. It can't be just words."

"How about murder by a very powerful man? Would that do it?"

There is a chill in her voice that sends ice down my spine. "Do you have that proof I just mentioned?"

"Yes. The problem is that this person will know it came from me."

"I won't let that happen."

"He'll know." She stands up. "They'll know. No. I can't do this. I don't want to die."

"Think about it. Trust me to protect you, because right now you're going to jail, and you're going to be old and gray when you get out. Do you really want that?"

"Please go."

"If you have these secrets and they're about someone powerful, you won't be safe in jail. You won't be safe anywhere unless you're hidden."

I leave her there, but as I reach the front door, I feel her behind me. I don't turn. "I'll be back in the morning."

I exit to the hallway and shut the door behind me. Greg pushes off the wall, and we head toward the elevator. We don't speak until we are on the street. "Well?" he asks.

I turn to face him. "I'm close to a breakthrough. I'm coming back in the morning."

"Define 'breakthrough'?"

"She says she can give us proof that one of her high-profile clients committed murder. And that's just for starters."

I blink back to the present, my gaze on my now-empty coffee cup, remembering the most brutal part of my Laney experience: arriving at her apartment that next morning to her apparent refusal to open the door, only to later discover her hanging from a bedsheet in her closet. Murdered, I knew, but I couldn't prove that based on the crime scene. I think back to Laney's fear when she'd made me leave the night before. *I don't want to die,* she'd said, with real terror in her voice. She was murdered.

And in that moment, I have a revelation. If the murders I'm investigating tie back to Laney, and they seem to do just that, then could she be the common denominator we've been missing? Are the victims all names from or related to her client list, which she never got the chance to reveal before she died?

My gaze lifts and lands at the front of the diner, where I find Greg standing in the doorway. With broad shoulders and standing six feet four inches, he consumes the entire archway. His jeans, boots, and burnt-orange Texas Longhorns shirt are all throwbacks from his college days in Austin. He scans the diner, but he misses me, which allows me to watch him, study him for telltale signs of his mood, his state of mind. He runs fingers through his full, curly dark-brown hair, which he does often, before walking to the hostess stand and, proving he's in his comfort zone, grants the woman a charming grin.

It's all a part of his teddy-bear quality that earns him immediate favor, even trust, from strangers. He earned my trust, and I'd planned to knock sense into him, not second-guess his character. Until this moment and two profoundly fucked-up realizations: I still believe Laney was murdered to shut her up, and the only person I told that she was about to talk was Greg.

CHAPTER ELEVEN

I wave at Greg, and the moment his eyes land on me, he grins a familiar grin and heads in my direction, his stride long, his presence somehow big yet unintimidating. He winks at a woman giving him the eye, his demeanor friendly, not arrogant, and it's not long before he slides into the booth in front of me. "Lilah-fucking-Love." And damn. He feels like friendship and warmth, like hot chocolate on a cold night with your favorite blanket wrapped around you. Safe. Comfortable.

So comfortable that I give him a middle finger and use it to point to his face. "Still clean as a baby's butt. Does that mean you showered for me, too?"

"I smell like fresh-baked cookies, and I know how much you like fresh-baked cookies. Want to come over here and find out?" Of course, I'd never smell his cookies, and he knows it, and the invitation is quickly withdrawn anyway. He reaches for my cup, contempt in his blue eyes when he finds it empty. "None of my cookies for you."

Rose is beside us instantly, filling our cups, and Greg has her smiling in about thirty seconds flat. He's just one of those huggable people, while I'm one of those punch-you-in-the-face kind of people, a contrast that worked for us as partners. However, we are not wholly opposites. His sweet tooth is the size of mine, and clearly leaning on this knowledge, he takes it upon himself to assume lunch is a sugar high. "We'll take two of those mammoth cinnamon rolls I saw at one of the front tables," he says to Rose, and she's barely left the table by the time he's dumping sugar in his cup. "You really are a bitch," he says nonchalantly. "You know that, right?"

"Practice makes perfect."

"God, I miss your smart-ass remarks, woman." He sips his coffee. "Damn, I needed this."

"Up late last night with Misty? Or that Romano woman at the party the other night who you were cuddling up to?"

"Olivia Mason is not a Romano, thus the name Mason."

"She's niece to the Romano brother general believed to be their pack leader."

"Stepniece, and I've been around the block, Lilah. I know dirty. She's not dirty."

"Are *you*?"

He gives a humorless laugh. "You think I'm dirty now? Is that how this plays out now? You're the good guy and I'm the bad guy?"

"Nelson Moser's a dirty cop. You worked with him before you got suspended."

"Exactly. He got me suspended."

"He got you the job at Blink Security."

"We talked about this. I know it could be a setup of some sort, but I have to pay the bills. And so far, all I've gotten out of this is a good job and fucking fantastic pay."

"Maybe he wants you out of the picture. Maybe he hopes you'll quit the force."

"Then he got what he wanted. I quit this morning."

I blanch, a rare reaction for me. "What?"

"You heard me. I quit. I called in this morning and gave my notice. I'm working full-time for Blink now and making four times the money."

"It's not about the money to you. You loved your job."

"Loving it wasn't enough apparently, and being broke and unappreciated really loses its appeal fast."

I narrow my eyes on him. "There's more to this. What aren't you telling me?"

"Like there was more to you leaving for LA?"

"I was suffocating."

His eyes meet mine, a cutting understanding in their depths that sends a razor blade of unease slicing down my spine. And for the first time ever, I consider Greg might know more than I think he knows about me and the reasons I left. "So," he adds, "there's more. You tell me your more and I'll tell you mine. Or"—he pauses for obvious effect—"we can just settle on that we both needed to move on."

Our cinnamon rolls appear on the table in front of us, and after a brief conversation with Rose, we're alone again, an awkward pause between us that isn't us. We aren't awkward. Greg picks up a fork. "Sugar makes it all better." He eats a forkful and gives a moan. "Holy fuck. Set aside your pissy mood a minute and just take a bite."

I grimace but pick up my fork and dig in and do as ordered, mimicking him with a moan. "Sugar does make it better."

He laughs, and we both tear into another bite and another, that awkwardness fading into the comfort of silence we've always shared. "So. Did you call me over here this morning to lecture me on good vs. evil or just to see my pretty, clean-shaven face?"

I want to talk about Laney. I want to trust him just like old times. But I am reminded of something my father says often: *You can't keep doing the same thing and expect different results.* I trusted Greg. Laney died. "I was worried about you," I say, and that's the truth. I was. I am.

He narrows his eyes on me. "And what else?"

"Nothing else."

"Bullshit. Talk to me. Is it your family? Your case? Kane?" He holds up a hand. "Not that I'm assuming a set of balls is your problem."

"Well actually, on that, I was wrong and you were right. Someone with a set of balls usually is my problem. Which is why me and Moser don't get along."

"Right. You kneed him to his knees."

I laugh. "It was fucking beautiful, too."

"Damn, I wish I could have seen that." He scoops up icing with his finger and licks it off before adding, "You know how to bust some balls. Like mine, the first time we met. Oh fuck. You called me a 'wimp-ass baby.'"

I give him a disbelieving look. "You threw up at the crime scene and contaminated evidence."

"I didn't contaminate evidence. And the damn eyes were missing. I still have nightmares about that scene. Sick fuck. I was wishing the death penalty still existed when we arrested that bastard." He gives me a keen eye. "And you didn't even act affected."

"I have a place I put things. You know that."

"Yeah, I know, and it's kind of scary sometimes. But you catch bad guys. We did good things together."

"Yes," I say, and seeing an opening, I take it. "And you want to know part of the reason I left? Part of my more?" I don't wait for him to reply. "Two of three of our last cases went unsolved. I felt stale. Like I'd lost my touch."

"Are you fucking with me, Lilah? We had a bad streak that had nothing to do with us. We had a cold case that should never have been reopened, and our call-girl case ended in suicide." He starts lightly running his pinkie finger over the table. It's his nervous twitch, his tell. Wherever that pinkie is, if he's nervous, it will move.

"Laney was the call girl," I say. "And you know I never believed she killed herself."

"The evidence said she did."

"She didn't want to die, and what's pathetic is that when she did, a whole lot of people breathed a little easier."

"On that you won't get an argument from me. That case was the window to enough dirt to funk up a hell of a lot of people. We would have needed a task force to manage the funk, it would have reeked so badly."

His cell phone buzzes and he digs it from his pocket. "And that would be Misty," he says, reading the text message without replying. "She has some tour staff she wants me to meet." He sets his phone down on the table, his attention on me. "Apparently, at least one woman misses me when I'm gone."

"I missed you," I say, and it's not untrue, which is why the sledgehammer of doubt about him is pounding on me so damn hard.

"We've talked, what? Two times since you left?"

"Three. And that's only because I really like you."

"Fuck, Lilah. I'd hate to be hated by you. And that's for real." He tosses money on the table. "It's on me. I got a big payday this week. And damn it feels good not to be the broke one of the two of us."

"How big a payday? Because I have plans to buy a pie I need to pay for, too."

"Big enough for pie," he says, tossing a fifty on the table and picking up the twenty. "When are you leaving?"

"I haven't decided."

"Does that mean your case hasn't closed or home is calling you back?"

"The only thing calling me is that pie I ordered. It's the only thing in this town I can't live without. And maybe these cinnamon rolls, too."

"I hear that New York City case you were asking me about is ready to close, right along with the East Hampton case. That Woods character is your guy, right?"

My eyes narrow on him. "You hear a lot for a guy who resigned."

"I'm still connected. So yeah. I hear things."

"From Moser?"

"Yeah, but I called my ex-partner, the one who got shot before I landed Moser as a partner, and asked about the NYPD case for you."

"And?"

"He heard the same about Woods being guilty, but he didn't have anything else to add." I grimace. He narrows his eyes on me. "You aren't sold on Woods as the killer, are you?"

"Why do you say that?"

"You aren't calling it done and over. And you haven't packed up and left town again."

"My boss is making the call," I say. "That's the joy of the FBI. I don't say when I come. I don't say when I go."

"Interesting."

"Not really," I say, downplaying it. "There're more power plays in the FBI than with that Colin dude we arrested a few years back."

"Colin? Which one was he?"

"That pimp we took down three times before he finally got fucked in jail instead of getting everyone else fucked."

He laughs. "Right. Fucking Colin."

Sensing his guard is down, I dive on past it. "Resigning won't stop IA from looking into your case."

His glower is instant. "I didn't do anything wrong, Lilah, if that's what you're getting at." His phone buzzes again. He grabs it, and this time he types a reply before looking at me. "I need to go."

He starts to get up when a realization hits me. "Wait," I belt out.

He gives me a narrow-eyed look. "What?"

I lean close to him. "The Romano chick. You were working on a Romano case when you were suspended. You're using her to prove your innocence, aren't you?"

"I quit, Lilah. I'm not doing anything but getting off on living. And if that comes in the form of a hot Romano chick, so be it."

He looks me in the eyes when he says those words. He makes me believe him, but I don't want to believe him. I don't want Greg to be dirty. "I need to go, Lilah." He stands up.

"I'll walk out with you," I say, grabbing my briefcase and pushing to my feet.

He walks on ahead of me, almost like he can't get away fast enough, but I stay the course, on his heels with each immediate step of my own. He's stalled at the bakery counter, which bottlenecks the door, a cluster of people blocking our exit. And that line ruins all interest I have in my to-go pie. We literally can't get to the door, and Greg turns to face me. "You said a diner. Not a Black Friday fucking extravaganza."

It's in that moment that a woman shoves through the bodies and steps between us. "Samantha?" I say of my brother's prissy, rich bitch of a girlfriend, who just happens to be Kane's fuck buddy.

"Lilah," she greets stiffly, and then, glancing at Greg, she asks, "Who are you?"

"Lilah's other brother," Greg says.

She frowns and glances at me. "You have two brothers?"

"He's a brother from another mother," I say, and before she can ask what the hell that means, I look at Greg. "Samantha's dating Andrew but fucking Kane."

Greg's eyes go wide. "Really?"

"Not really," Samantha snaps, bristling, her arms folding in front of her and hoisting up the deep V of her black T-shirt. "I'm with Andrew now."

"Except for the other night," I say to Greg. And then to her, "What are you doing here?"

"Your brother likes the strawberry pie. It's famous here, you know."

Greg chooses that moment to touch my shoulder and motion toward the door. "I'll call you," he says and turns away.

"Wait," I call after him, not even close to done with the bombshell or ten I'm thinking he has going on right now, but he's already disappeared behind several big bodies.

I take a step, but Samantha maneuvers in front of me. "I know you don't believe this, Lilah," she says, "but this thing with Andrew and me is real."

"This thing," I repeat. "Well yes, Samantha. Everyone you fuck is a real fuck. I guess it's extraspecial, though, when you buy pie instead of cigarettes afterward. Enjoy the pie. We both know it won't last." I step around her and find a clear path to the door, quickly exiting the diner. Pausing just outside, I scan for Greg but realize now that he was a subway rider in NYC. I don't even know what kind of car he's driving.

Cutting left and then around the corner, I find most of the cars now gone, no sign of Greg, and my car in view. I hurry in that direction, and as I approach, I spy the white piece of paper flapping in a gentle breeze. Samantha, I think. Someone must have spotted her, and she needed an excuse for being here, one I myself would validate, thus the strawberry pie.

I stop at the car and pull the note that actually seems to be on a napkin, which is new for Junior, from the windshield. Flipping it open, I read:

Strawberry pie, my ass. WTF was that all about?
Dinner. Soon. —Greg

He's right. Strawberry pie, my ass, especially since my brother hates all things strawberry. That encounter felt very stalkerlike, very *Juniorlike*, and yet it was Greg who left me a note on the car. Which leaves me with only one clear-cut conclusion: I can't ever eat strawberry pie again without thinking about Samantha, which means she's ruined it for me forever. And with a killer and Junior on the loose, if that's all I've got right now, I'm in trouble.

CHAPTER TWELVE

I don't know why Samantha showed up and disrupted my personal space. Though unlikely, maybe she really *is* Junior. Maybe she hired someone to be Junior. Maybe she's just a crazy, whacked-out bitch who is obsessed with everything *me* for God knows why. I'm sure as hell not. Or maybe she is part of a bigger picture, a minion of Pocher who spies on Kane and tries to control my family from the inside out. That means keeping an eye on me. Or I'm back to that maybe she *really is* just a whacked-out bitch. Whatever the case, I start my car with no intention of lingering to watch Samantha exit with a pie my brother won't eat. I'm not even going to ask him about it because come *on*. She'll take it to him to cover her story. She'll flash her boobs and pretend she thought he wanted it. And he's so balls to the wall for that woman, he might even eat it. What the fuck has happened to my brother?

I back out of my parking spot, driving toward the exit, where I glance at the short handwritten sign on the curb that reads **Our Strawberry Pie Is Famous**. Those were Samantha's inspired words, an advertisement she latched on to when she had nothing better to say. I'd dismiss that if I wasn't concerned she was going to cut my brother's heart into pieces after dragging him into corruption. For now, though, I set that problem aside and scan for the familiar and unfamiliar, for those who are following, of which there are at least two: Kane's person and the doughnut-chasing fool. Hell, maybe the assassin is watching me, too, and this is one big fucking Lilah Love porn show, only with clothes. I've never liked being the show. I like ending it, and that's what I have to do now. I need to find answers before another dead body shows up and I end up being pulled back to LA, powerless to end this once and for all.

I pull onto the main road, and while I see no one in my rearview mirror, I still believe that Laney saw too much and that got her killed. And since dead bodies are the only clue I have right now, and they aren't exactly talking to me, I decide to go to the one man who might actually have something to say: Laney's brother. He'd had influence over her. He'd known things, and at one point I'd thought he'd help me. Then he clammed up, and that didn't change when Laney ended up dead. I need to have another talk with him, and this time, I'm not leaving without answers.

That said, the last I knew, Laney's brother was in Westbury, Long Island, which is two hours away, and not a drive I want to take without a plan. I pull up to a stoplight and dial a guy I know from high school who is now at the DMV here in New York. We dated one time, way back then, and somehow, we don't hate each other. "Nicolas," I say when he answers, scanning my rearview for followers that still haven't appeared.

"Lilah-fucking-Love."

"I need stuff," I say.

He lets out a bark of laughter. "Believe it or not, I miss hearing that. Are you here?"

"I am."

"Then you owe me dinner, remember? You said if I helped you again—"

"That I'd buy you a slice of pizza. That's not dinner."

"Steak. It was a steak, but what do you need?"

"An address for a Rick Suthers. Should be in Westbury."

The keyboard clicks and my light turns green. "345 Plainview Drive," he says as I accelerate and pull away from the light.

"Got it," I say. "That's what I remembered."

"When do I get that steak?"

"Pizza," I say, "and it's coming." I hang up and note the black sedan that pulls in behind me several blocks back. My very special doughnut-loving stalker. In response, I turn right and into town when I'd planned to turn left toward the highway. And since it's obvious that this investigation ties to my attack, I'm done fighting Kane's role in this investigation, which is why I dial him now.

"Yes, beautiful?" he answers.

"My tail is back. I need the license plate number. Have your guy text it to me."

"I'll text it to you," he says, not even bothering to deny he has someone following me. Neither of us is big on games.

"Whatever," I say. "I just need it. And I need the tail to go away without ending up dead or hurt. I'm following up on a lead, and I don't need it to get back to the wrong people."

"Where and what lead?"

"If your Lilah stalker is good, he or she will find me. Just make sure they're the only one that does." I hang up. He calls back. I don't answer.

I turn my car down a country road that I know will lead me back to the main highway. Whoever is tailing me will expect me to exit at a certain location a few miles away. Instead, I do a U-turn, pull to the side of the road, and wait, planning to exit the way I came from. My phone beeps with a text. I glance at the screen and, to no surprise, discover Kane is my messenger.

What the fuck happened to 'being in this together'?

I think he might need some clarification on what "being in this together" means to me, and feeling generous, I give him some: If you can keep up, I type, you're in this with me.

You doubt me? is his instant reply.

I snort and type: What do you think?

No, he replies. You don't doubt me. But you think it would be easier if you did.

I grimace. He's right. It would be easier to doubt him because as an FBI agent, that's what I'm supposed to do. Doubt people like Kane. And I do. Everyone *but* Kane. Which is why I don't reply. And it's also why I know that my doughnut-loving stalker will be handled. This is Kane. He's good at being bad. I glance at the clock and count down five minutes. On the fifth, another text message beeps, and I glance at the screen to read Kane's newest message: Your rogue stalker is detoured. And don't fret, beautiful. He's alive, unharmed, but most likely irritated. License plate number AXL-285 New York.

I don't reply. I don't ask details. I dial Nicolas again on speaker. "I need stuff," I say, even as I pull back onto the road.

"When you're back, you're back. Hit me with it."

I give him the plate number. Listen to his keys clacking before he says, "Martin Walker. Albany, New York. Eighty-nine years old. Sounds stolen to me."

"Got it. Expect something from me tomorrow."

"Do I even want to know what that means?"

"It's from me. You know it's wonderful."

"You mean I know it's fucked up."

"Maybe," I say, laughing and hanging up with a mental note to order the man a stripper and a steak lunch.

I pull to a stop sign and glance right and left, looking for trouble and finding none, though I know Kane's person is nearby but obviously damn good at hiding. Cutting right, I reenter the main road and take it slow and easy through town until I hit the highway. While watching my mirrors, I formulate a plan that ensures no one, not even my invisible stalkers, knows my next move. I need cover, a place to disappear.

I dial my pal Beth at the medical examiner's office in Suffolk County, which just happens to be a short drive to Suthers's work and home. "Lilah Love," she greets.

"I'm headed in your direction," I say. "Can we meet?"

"Why? What's happening?"

"We're friends."

"Why? What's happening?" she says again as if I haven't spoken.

"Seriously, Beth. I just want to catch up."

"Okay. I give up. Of course, we both know this is about the murders you're investigating and the body I autopsied, but you'll admit that when you get here. When do you want to meet and where?"

I glance at the clock to read one o'clock. "Three thirty and I'll come to the medical examiner's office."

"I'll see you then," she says before ending the call.

And yes. She will see me and so will everyone else, which is my plan.

~

I arrive at the eighty-five-thousand-square-foot Suffolk County medical examiner's office fifteen minutes early and park at the front of the building. I'm just about to open the car door and exit when my cell phone rings. "Yes, brother of mine," I answer.

"We have a problem."

"We? As in you and me? Because it can't be just one. For starters—"

"Lilah," he bites out.

"Yes, Andrew?" I ask sweetly.

"A Detective Moser from the NYPD was just here with an NYC FBI agent named Smart."

"Really?" I ask, aware that this is the power play Murphy expected. "How'd that go for you?"

"I told you to get your ass here and close this case. They're on their way to Kane's office to talk to him."

That earns my laughter. "Really? They think that's going to work for them, do they?"

"What part of this are you not getting? They're going to claim jurisdiction based on him, and we're all fucked. There's no telling where this will lead and what kind of press will follow."

He's pissed and obviously distressed, which means that either the FBI in NYC isn't in bed with Pocher and helping my father, or my brother just doesn't know, and therefore isn't as dirty as I'd feared. "There's no evidence against Kane," I assure him. "None. And showing up at his office is going to make them an enemy they can't beat."

"You really think they can't beat him?" he demands, his tone incredulous.

"You really think they haven't tried before now? *Relax.* The only one you have to battle for jurisdiction is me. Just stay away from the flame. Let them burn themselves. Did you get that information over to Murphy?"

"I got it to him, and we both know how that looks. We need to have a sit-down. Where the hell are you?"

"The medical examiner's office in Long Island."

"Why the hell are you there?"

"Murphy wants me to make my case, just like you have to make yours."

"I could say about ten things about your case and what you're doing right now, but I won't. Just get your ass back here."

"Okay," I say before ending the call, and my agreement stems from one place: I do plan to get my ass back there. When I'm ready.

Right now, though, I'm working on my communication skills. I dial Murphy. "Agent Love," he greets, because he's really the only person who doesn't greet me as *Agent-fucking-Love.*

"The NYC FBI is headed to Kane's office to question him."

"And?"

"And . . . I'm just doing that communication thing you seem to love."

"And you want to do what in response?"

"Depends. What's your position on Woods's guilt?"

"There is no proof that Woods is guilty, and before you ask, I've stated our intent to claim jurisdiction to my counterpart in NYC. He requested that we hold, and I moved my request to a higher level that's waiting on approval. That said, how likely is it Kane goes down tonight or connects himself to the murders?"

"Zero."

"All right. You're confident. I'll run with that. How will Kane respond to an FBI probe?"

"A probe done professionally is one thing. He won't be humiliated at his office and do nothing."

"That's what they're counting on. That he lashes out or makes a move they can use to burn him."

"The man has a degree from Yale and graduated top of his class. He's not stupid. He'll defend his reputation, but he won't give them leverage against him, which means he won't be their excuse for pushing us out."

"You're certain?"

"I'd bet your firstborn," I say.

"My firstborn?"

"People like me don't have kids. When can I expect an answer on jurisdiction?"

"Tomorrow, if you're right on Kane."

"I am."

"You better be."

He hangs up, and I don't even consider calling Kane. He can handle himself, and besides: a surprised Kane is a pissed Kane. I have a crazy kind of kinky attraction to the pissed-off Kane that always does me right when it does everyone else wrong. Sometimes I think that's a problem. This isn't one of those times. This isn't going to work out badly for me. It will for them. And that means we get to catch a real killer, not blame an innocent dead man.

With that certainty and my field bag on my shoulder, I exit the car and head toward the medical examiner's building. Once I'm inside the lobby, I announce myself to the receptionist. She buzzes Beth, and it's two minutes at the most before Beth appears in the lobby, her black pantsuit accented with a hot-pink silk blouse. Her blonde hair tied at her nape.

"There's a coffee shop on the second level," she greets as we move to the rear of the lobby.

"Actually," I say, "I need a place to join a conference call that's private." I don't try to be apologetic. It's just not my thing. And it's not necessary anyway. Shit happens in this job.

"Oh," she says, giving me a curious look. "Yes. Sure. You can use my office." She motions me forward and we enter a hallway. "Anything you can talk about?"

"To summarize: a demanding boss, a crazy ex who isn't Kane, a killer I haven't caught, and this call is a prelude to me having to skip our coffee."

"God, no wonder I like you. You just replayed my life. No. I need a life."

"Would you settle for old times? Weekend yoga with pizza as a reward for surviving."

"In other words, I do yoga and you watch and eat pizza?"

"Right. Like old times."

She laughs and stops at an office door. "Call me for the yoga-pizza party," she says. "I have an autopsy I was waiting to start until you left." She unlocks the door and gives me a knowing look, like she knows this is all a setup. "You can let yourself out."

"Thank you, Beth."

"Catch that killer," she says. "Because we both know Woods isn't the one." She turns and starts walking away.

I enter her office for show and shut the door, leaning against its wooden surface, to take in the mahogany desk and the corner table. There is a picture on the wall of the building I'm in. It's a sterile environment that infers she's emotionally detached. The office of a woman who spends more time with the dead than the living. I wonder if that detachment is innate or learned. One certainly could reason that it's a necessary skill for people like her and me. A skill Beth and I share with the assassin. A skill *Kane* shares with us and the assassin.

But Kane aside because, well, Kane is fucking Kane, and I've already considered him and marked him off the list. I'm back to Beth, and I don't like where I'm leading myself right now, which is to add a suspect to my list, one I don't want to add. But I have no choice. She lives and works near here, yet she was in the Hamptons the night of the murder. She was one of the first people at the crime scene.

Okay. This is insanity. It's not Beth. She is not an assassin. She is not Junior. She did not hire an assassin. This is one of those times when my mind takes me one place to go another. It has to be.

This craziness has to wait, at least momentarily, while I focus on the real reason I'm here: Laney's brother. I pull out my phone and arrange not one but three strategically placed Uber pickups. Only then do I return to Laney and where my thought process about her guides me. I call Tic Tac.

"Lilah," he greets me, his voice a tight ball of awkwardness and anger.

"Okay," I say. "Clearly you have your panties in a wad. Un-wad them now. We got bitch-slapped by Murphy. It's done, and I have a killer to catch before I lose jurisdiction. Look for anyone inside the system who had contact with the victims' cases. Obviously, there is you, me, and Murphy. Look deeper. Medical staff. Technicians. Clerks."

"You think there's an insider?" he asks, that tightness in his voice easing.

"Just look. If you find anything, text me, don't call me. I'll call you." I hang up and look around the office again. *Damn it.* This place is as sterile as her procedure room. However, it's reasonable to believe that she quite possibly can't deal with those she loves in a place where she deals with those who've died. But did she have any connections to

Laney Suthers? We were close then. She knew I was on the case. "Damn it. Damn it. *Damn it.*" I need to know.

With few options, I dial Tic Tac again. "It's too soon, Lilah," he says. "I haven't even typed ten words. I'm good, but not that good."

"Ha ha," I say, but I suddenly have second thoughts about where I was about to lead him. If I connect this case to Laney, I need a reason that isn't me killing a man with the same tattoo as a victim.

"What do you want, Lilah?"

"Just making sure you un-wadded those panties."

"I'm fine," he says. "I don't have wadded panties."

"Okay. Good. Because they aren't fun, I promise."

He hangs up.

I push out air. *Damn it.*

I refuse to believe Beth is involved, but I have to do my due diligence. That's all. This is due diligence, and since I'm considering the idea that someone in law enforcement might be involved in this mess, I have resources I can use to help me. They aren't legal, but we do what we have to do. And if that's what I have to do in the name of justice, that works for me. Just like stabbing a man twelve times also seemed to have worked for me.

If there is one thing this return home has proven, it's that I didn't kill my enemy. I killed my enemy's messenger. My enemy is still out there, with me and Kane in their sights, which means we had better get him, or her, or them, in view now, before someone else ends up dead.

We.

Me and Kane.

One of us experienced with a knife and the other with a shovel. And therein lies the problem. We have a body that is our secret and can be used against us. It's us or our enemy, and it is going to be us. Apparently, those who kill and dig graves together stay together. Because Kane is right. We *are* in this *together.* And anyone who thinks that's good for them and not us is going to find out they're wrong.

CHAPTER THIRTEEN

I leave Beth's office, walking a long hallway, with two goals playing out in my mind: catch a killer and defeat what appears to be a long-standing enemy. More and more, those things appear to be related, and I'm hoping like hell Laney's brother will help me look deeper and in the right places. For now, though, I shove aside anything except my surroundings, and with good reason. I knew a cop who was followed. He didn't cover his ass, and now he's dead and so is the informant he was meeting.

And that's exactly why my path to Rick Suthers is going to be turned into one of those algebraic equations you figured you'd never need again in your lifetime because they're stupidly complicated.

Reaching the glass door that is my destination, I push the bar down and exit the medical examiner's building. I immediately step out of the view of prying eyes and into the shadows of the dumpster I've identified to Uber as my pickup spot, the one with the big yellow *X* on it. I scan for trouble and any remnants of my collection of stalkers, which I don't find. I check the time on my phone. Four thirty. It's then, and right on time, that my Uber pulls into a spot beside me, having actually followed the directions I'd given.

I climb inside and shut the door. A wrinkled, overly tanned grandma with a baseball hat covering her long gray hair twists around to greet me. And I know she's a grandma because it says so on her hat. "Where to, honey?" she asks.

"The park, sweetie," I say, which earns me a laugh and a wink along with a look that's a little bit too intimate to be innocent.

I'm being flirted with by a grandma. I think that means that I'm in the Grandmas' Club now, and I can't say it's nearly as appealing as the Mile High Club, of which I am also a proud member. Thank you, Kane Mendez. And Rich. Once. Sort of.

Grandma pulls us onto the main road, and a tour bus for some musical group called Big and Rich pulls past us. *Fuck*. Rich. Kane. The FBI. I dial Rich's phone, and he doesn't answer. I dial my brother next. "Where is Rich?"

"He went with Tweedledee and Tweedledum to Kane's place. I thought you knew."

"No. I didn't know, and how are we born of the same womb and you could think that was a good idea? I have to call Kane."

"No, Lilah," he orders firmly. "That could potentially be bad for you. It'll look like you're guiding him through an investigation."

"Damn it, I hate when you make sense, but Rich—"

"Could be in danger because Kane really is a criminal?"

"Two exes together is a volatile mix, and you, as a long-standing member of law enforcement, know that. And the idea here is that Kane is pissed enough to act out against everyone but us." My line beeps. "That could be Rich. I'll call you back."

"Don't call Kane," he warns.

"I get it," I growl, before I click over.

"Rich?" I demand.

"Yes. *Relax.* I got this."

"Got this? What the fuck does 'got this' mean?"

My old driver glares over her shoulder because apparently my language is an issue for her.

"I'm playing the role," he assures me. "I'm on their side just enough to hear their side."

"By giving them a conflict of interest they can use against us?"

The car jolts to a stop at the park, and I don't have to look at the driver to know she's glaring at me again. I get out on a curb beside a grassy median, and she screeches away like a mad teenager. "Hold on," I say, my gaze scanning the huge mass of grass where dogs and people play.

"I don't have much time," Rich snaps.

"You don't need time," I say, walking toward a giant, old oak tree on the opposite side of the sidewalk, where I stand in the shade. "You need to pull back."

"I'm not stupid, Lilah," Rich says. "And neither is Kane or he wouldn't have you convinced he's one of the good guys." He doesn't give me time to counter. "This gives us insider information."

"Kane *is* our insider information."

"Because Kane will tell you everything, right?"

"*Yes*. He will. Kane and I communicate. That doesn't mean we're fucking. Do not face him with that in your head because you won't like where that leads us. Understand?"

"*Yes*, Lilah. I do."

"How are you calling me? Where is—"

"I have to go."

He hangs up.

Damn it to hell, why is everyone always hanging up on me?

I glance around me, slowly scanning the area again, taking in faces, making sure that I'm familiar with who is around me right now. Once I get my bearings, I start walking, and it takes me a full ten minutes to travel to the other side of the park, where my second Uber is waiting. I'm on my third Uber in thirty minutes when finally, my driver drops me at the Long Island train station, which happens to be only a few miles from the accounting office Rick Suthers owns and operates. Not that I plan to ride the train, but crowds and transportation equal visibility.

I start the short walk on what has become a chilly day toward Suthers's downtown Westbury office, which is more like a subdivision than a town and not an exciting one. It's most definitely no New York

City. There are no street vendors. No dogs pooping by street poles while owners happily scoop it up in little baggies like it's the best gift ever. There aren't even homeless people hanging out while fancy stuffed suits walk by and try to pretend they don't exist. There is just a sidewalk that leads me past run-down offices and stores, all of which contrast with the fancy houses only blocks to the east and west of the road.

I stop at Rick's office to find a **CLOSED** sign on the door, which works just fine by me. I'd rather talk to him in his home, which is to most people their safe zone. Cutting down a side street, still not a person or moving car in sight, I walk toward the east neighborhood, traveling several blocks straight and then to the right. The houses are big, their look old but elegant, the yards neatly manicured. An old lady waves to me from a porch. A middle-aged man rakes leaves one house over. Another block and I'm at Rick's white wooden house, hurrying up the porch steps to ring the bell. After a respectable thirty seconds, I knock. And knock again. Still nothing.

My mind goes back to the last time I'd been here. He'd called me. He'd wanted to meet. I'd been in the city, hours away, but I'd hurried here. He'd taken forever to come to the door. He'd opened it quickly and stared at me. He'd looked like her, despite being in his late thirties when she'd been only twenty-seven. Good-looking. Blond. Blue eyes. Easygoing, but not that night.

"Go away, Agent Love."

"You called me."

"To tell you to go away. My sister is dead. It's over."

"Someone killed her."

"She killed herself. She was weak. I am done. Respect that or I will report you for harassment."

He'd shut the door.

He'd been scared. He'd been afraid to talk to me. And he'd called my boss the next day. I'd conveniently been sent to LA to consult on a double homicide shortly after, and that had led to my introduction to the FBI. I'd walked away then, but I can't do that now.

I head down the steps again and around the side of the house to find his gray Ford Focus in the driveway. A bad feeling slides through me, and I head to the fenceless backyard. The only door I can find is at the bottom of a set of steps that seem to lead to the basement. I hurry down them and again find a locked door. I really don't contemplate my next move. I go with my gut, and my gut says I need inside that house. Now. I grab a brick and knock the side window out just enough to slip my hand through the glass, unlock the door, and open it.

I enter through a laundry area and shut the door behind me. My hand settles on my gun, and I hurry through the unfinished concrete room and up a set of wooden stairs. I pause at the open doorway, where I find the lights on, but there are no active sounds. No voices. No television. No footsteps. Just a clock ticking somewhere. A chunk of ice falling from the ice maker into the freezer a few feet from where I stand just off the kitchen. A foreboding knot forms in my belly and I call out, "Mr. Suthers? Rick? It's Lilah Love. Agent Lilah Love. We met about your sister, Laney."

I wait for a reply and get nothing.

No words.

No steps.

No sound.

I check my phone and ensure it's on vibrate, despite checking it in the last Uber, and then pull my weapon, easing into the kitchen. The hardwood floor creaks beneath my feet, and I pause, waiting for some replying action that doesn't come. I'm still sheltered by the stairwell, but at this point, a sink and a window above it sits directly in front of me. A small hallway is to my left and right. I take the final step and ease into the doorway, now able to see a full U-shaped kitchen before me. I look right to a hallway that leads to a front door and a stairway to the second level. I look left to another hallway that leads to an archway, which I assume is the living area. I head that direction with the intent of circling back to the stairs. I check a small bathroom and then ease into a sitting area that leads directly into a living area. I pass through it, and I'm at the front door. There's an office directly in front of me that I check as well and find it clear.

That brings me to the bottom of the stairs, where I call out again. "Rick? Are you up there?"

I listen again, and there's a creaking sound that is followed by a swish. This repeats. And repeats. That knot in my gut tightens and grows. I start up the steps, and the sound continues, becoming a little louder as I approach. I take a few more steps and pause, but I don't call out again. I ease forward and repeat the process of pausing, listening, pausing, listening, until I reach the top level. The sound is coming from the room to my left. There are two more rooms to my right and one directly across from me that appears to be a library with no obvious occupant, but I can't see every nook and cranny.

I turn toward the sound and enter the room, quickly placing my back to the wall, gun in the air. And that's when I find Rick Suthers hanging from the closet that sits immediately to the left of the door I've just entered, with a bedsheet around his neck in the exact way I'd found his sister, the tug and sway of the body creating the swooshing sound. And I'm back with Laney for just one minute:

"Did your mother find an escape?"

"Only in death," I'd said. "Don't let that be you. I'll protect you. I'll make sure the information you give me doesn't come from you."

Only I didn't protect her. I didn't save her. She's dead. I found her, and the fact that I'm standing here looking at her brother's dead body—that I found him, too—is no coincidence. It's my enemy's plan.

I know dead bodies, and Rick Suthers is dead, and I don't plan on joining him. I exit the bedroom and search the remainder of the upstairs before I harness my weapon, open the field bag that's at my hip, and pull out a pair of gloves. I slip them on but I don't touch anything. I step closer to the body and study it first, noting the jeans and white T-shirt that appear neatly pressed. The face is blue, lips and cheeks swollen, eyes bulging. His skin is still pink and that, along with the limited rigor mortis, tells me that he hasn't been hanging there long. I skip by the implications of that realization, considering my visit, and focus on what I believe to be a crime scene. There's a double stack of books at his feet, as there had been with his sister. And just like then, I question a person's ability to stand on those at all without them tumbling. I simply don't believe it's possible.

I close the space between me and the body, kneeling down and doing just what I did at Laney's feet. I look through the titles of the books. Looking for a message, like the one left for me with the beheaded bodies. With Laney, I'd found nothing significant. That's how this begins. I search titles, reading each, considering the content. The bottom book freezes me in place: the unauthorized autobiography of Laura Love, a Hollywood legend. *My mother.*

CHAPTER FOURTEEN

I have a moment of shock at the presence of that book, and then it's over. I set it aside and mentally step into my Otherworld, my name for my emotionless zone where I focus on facts and the necessary tasks at hand. I grab the book and thumb through the pages, finding no message or note, but then again, the book itself is a message. I hunt down another book to replace it and then stick my mother's biography in my bag. I'll analyze the implications and content of the message it's meant to deliver, along with who could be behind it, later and alone. Right now, I need to search the house and deal with the crime scene, which is going to be called a suicide. The chance anything is found to prove otherwise is next to zero. This killer is that good. I learned that when I tried to prove murder with Laney. As good as that assassin, and it wouldn't surprise me at this point if they are one and the same.

I start a methodical search of the house, starting with the body, checking his pockets and his wallet, and the closest thing to interesting is the odd way he's folded a dozen or so Starbucks receipts with his cash. That tells me he's a man of habit and he doesn't let go of things easily, and yet, he pushed me away. He let go of Laney.

Moving on, I check drawers, mattresses, pillowcases, underneath the bed. Next, I hit the library, searching books, chair cushions, a small desk. Every room is checked, but there is nothing to be found. Peculiarly, not even a photo of Laney. *Note to self: make it clear to Andrew that if I die, I don't want a shrine, but a good "Fuck you" coffee mug in his cabinet would feel like love.*

I'm finally done with my search, and I walk back to the bedroom and stare at the body, waiting for one of those random deep ideas to come into my head, but there is just one word: *murder*. And that leads me to contemplate my next move. I could leave. No one would know I was here. No one would know that I broke the window. Unless, of course, a neighbor reported seeing me, and that could get complicated. So could explaining my presence here, but I decide it's better than explaining my absence. And at this point, all my role-play as 007, along with three Ubers and a walk, is for nothing. I'm exposed. I'm here. It's known by my enemies, and it didn't protect Rick, a part of this equation that I can't let myself linger on right now or it will fuck with my head.

I dial the locals and the reply is quick. "Nine-one-one, what is your emergency?"

"This is Federal Agent Lilah Love from the LA bureau in town on official business. I have a probable suicide. A man hanging by a sheet with no pulse. The address is 345 Plainview Drive, Westbury. To clarify: I'm on scene and will remain on scene and meet them at the front door."

"Backup is on the way."

I end the call and walk down the stairs to the front door, opening it and stepping onto the porch as the sun sinks rapidly on the horizon. With no time to spare, I dial Murphy. "Agent Love. Do you have news?"

"I have a situation outside my brother's territory."

"Where?"

"Westbury, Long Island. A suicide that I've called the locals on. I'm on scene now."

"And this relates to our investigation how?"

I stick to a shortened version of the truth. "I stopped by to check on the brother of a woman who died on my watch. She killed herself. When I got here, the brother had killed himself in the exact same manner as his sister."

"And you just happened to show up when that happened?"

"Apparently I did," I say.

"And how exactly did you end up in the house?"

"His sister killed herself. He wasn't at his office. He's not overly social, and I had a gut feeling. I have no other answer."

"What aren't you telling me?"

"You're highly suspicious by nature, aren't you?"

"I have one hell of a bullshit detector, Agent. Need I remind you of our earlier conversations on this very day?"

"You just did," I say, one dead body and a book too far gone to bite my tongue, "but I get it. Bosses get to be assholes."

"Glad we're on the same page. Now. What aren't you telling me?"

"I could make a smart-ass remark, but I don't want to get fired," I say as sirens sound in the not-so-far distance.

"You just made about three smart-ass remarks," he snaps.

I open my mouth to argue the definition of smart-ass, but he's already moved on. "We both know you're wading knee-deep in bullshit," he says, his tone thunder that borders on a roar. "But," he continues, "that bullshit story is the one you need to stick with for everyone but me. Understand?"

"Yes," I say, deciding that if I want to stay on assignment, and employed for that matter, right now might not be the time to add any additional dialogue.

"You better," he says, "because I'm about to repeat it to the local officials. You call your brother and give him the heads-up. And make damn sure your exit is fast and simple. Get the hell out of there."

He hangs up, and a fire truck pulls up in front of the house, followed by a cop car. I greet the officials and answer questions, but I don't get the hell out of Dodge. I want to see them pull the body down. I want to look for answers in the sea of questions. I back off, though, standing outside, giving the locals space to work while I dial my brother. "I've got nothing for you," he says. "They left Kane's offices and Rich hasn't returned here, nor will he answer his phone."

"I'll find out what happened," I say, "but right now, this is an official call in case you get an official call." I relay the situation exactly as I'd explained it to Murphy as well as to the locals on scene. It doesn't go over any better with big brother than it did with my boss.

"Lilah, damn it," he says. "What the hell are you thinking? You got hit with all kinds of trouble over that case."

"I just explained what I'm doing here," I say. "I need to deal with this here. I'll deal with our situation and Kane when I'm done, but call me if there is a development. If I don't answer, I'll call you back as soon as I can."

We disconnect as a car pulls to the curb, and I cringe as Beth climbs out. I also find it interesting that with so many medical examiners in this county, she just happens to be the one on the scene. I walk toward her, and we pause together midway up the sidewalk. "Do I even want to know how we both ended up here?" she asks.

"You tell me," I say.

"I got the directive from above on a possible homicide."

"Huh. Interesting. I called it in as suicide."

"You're FBI. They're covering their asses. But how did you end up in the middle of a suicide scene?"

For about the sixth time now, I run through the story, which at this point is already about as palatable as old bubblegum. "Strange you say suicide," Beth observes when I finish. "I remember the Laney case. You were obsessed. You thought she was murdered."

"You have a good memory."

"You asked me to consult. I read her file. But I didn't get to see Laney's body. Let's take a look at Rick. Maybe I can find something that helps with both cases."

"You won't," I say. "I had the best of the best try with Laney, and this is an identical situation."

"And yet you called this one suicide and that one murder?"

"I said it looks like suicide. I didn't give my opinion otherwise."

She narrows her intelligent eyes on me. "Right," she says. "Let's go see the body." She steps around me and heads for the house.

I rotate and follow her, and *damn it*, it's irritating to distrust everyone but two men who hate each other and who I used to prefer naked. They're both less complicated that way. I enter the house and follow Beth through the process of meeting everyone before we head upstairs into the bedroom to find that Rick is still hanging from the closet. I stand back and watch Beth pull on gloves and then do a detailed inspection of the body. At the end of which, she glances at the books and then me. "He stood on books?"

"Same as Laney," I tell her.

"I'd have thought they'd tumble over. That's odd to me."

Agreed, I think, though I'm not comforted by the observation. For all I know, she's in on the big picture here and taunting me with the absence of one. Though admittedly, Beth isn't likely to believe I'd be taunted easily.

She motions to the EMS team, and two minutes later, Rick is on the ground. Beth and I kneel beside him, doing a complete inspection of the body. "He's got ink," she says, pulling up the sleeve of his white T-shirt.

I stand with the announcement and move to her side of the body to squat next to her, studying the etched heart on Rick's shoulder that reads RIP Laney. He didn't let her go. He just made the rest of the world think he had. And now, more than ever, I believe that he was killed to shut him up. My distance kept him alive. My nearness did to him what it did to Laney: *killed him.* And that's a poison pill that's going to be a bitch to swallow.

Otherworld, I remind myself.

Focus, Lilah.

I push to my feet and leave Beth to her work, stepping around the body to inspect the closet I couldn't get to earlier for the dead man hanging in front of it. I start searching pants, shirts, and finally jackets, hitting all the pockets. A bagged black jacket in the very back catches my attention. Bagged means "special." Black means "funeral." His funeral jacket is my best bet, and I reach inside the pocket to remove a necklace of the Virgin Mary. And while that might not be significant to anyone else, I now have two dead bodies with a bleeding Virgin Mary tattoo on them, one of which I killed. I pocket the necklace and continue my search.

By the time I'm done, Beth is standing. "I'll need to look closer at the facility, but as it stands—"

"You see no signs of struggle or foul play," I supply.

"Correct," she confirms, "but those books just don't make sense to me. Did you do models and reenactments with his sister's case?"

"I did, and the books scattered every time, but I still couldn't get anyone to buy into murder. There just wasn't anything else that pointed in that direction."

"You didn't have me working the case," she says. "As for the here and now, I'm ready to go if you are."

Considering Murphy wanted me out of here about thirty minutes ago, I'm quick to agree, and we weave our way through the gaggle of uniforms and out the front door. "I need a ride back to your office," I say, joining her on the sidewalk beside her car.

"You don't have your car with you?"

"Nope," I say, walking around the rear of hers to the passenger door.

She clicks the locks and I climb inside. Once she joins me, she glances in my direction. "Don't ask about the car or Rick and Laney Suthers because you aren't answering, right?"

"That works for me."

She accepts that reply and starts the car. I like a person who knows when to just leave things the fuck alone. I also like a person who knows how to be silent, and during our short ride back to the medical examiner's office, Beth proves she's still really good at saying nothing.

For my part, my mind is already on the people who knew I was headed toward Long Island and might surmise I was headed toward Rick Suthers's house. The list is surprisingly long: My brother. Rich. Kane via his hired stalker. The man at the doughnut stand. Greg, perhaps, since I brought up Laney, though that was a cautious, barely there mention. And Beth. Then, of course, there is the assassin and Junior, who could be connected to any of the other names, or not.

Beth pulls into the parking lot. "I'm at the front door," I say.

With a little direction from me, she pulls in beside my rental. "You want to stay for the autopsy?" she asks.

I do, but that would bring attention to a case I can't afford to have attention on. "I don't need to be here for you to find nothing." I pop the door open. "And that's what you're going to find. When are you back in the Hamptons?"

"This weekend. Want to eat pizza and watch me do yoga?"

"No yoga," I say, barely in this conversation while my mind is racing other places. "But I vote yes to pizza and—" A sudden realization hits me. The assassin is done killing. That's why Woods was killed. That's why they want the cases closed. I really need the assassin, and whoever contracted the assassin, to believe that I've given up.

"And?" Beth prods.

"Tequila," I supply. "If I'm still here."

"You're already going back to LA?"

"It's looking that way," I say. "I'll let you know if I leave before the weekend."

"What about the case you came for? Are you closing it?"

"It's not my case to open or close." And because I don't want to seem suspiciously uninterested, I add, "Call me if you find anything in the autopsy, will you?"

"Of course."

I nod and exit the car, walking toward mine, a new strategy burning through my mind. Pull down everyone's guard but mine. I have to convince Murphy to let the locals close the case but allow me to stay on some pretense of personal matters—my father's campaign could work.

I unlock my door and glance at the windshield. There's no note from my stalker. I climb inside and consider Junior's silence. Perhaps I've parked strategically within a camera's view, but Junior has been highly creative and resourceful up until now. This feels like a choice. The question is why, and I tick through the options:

A: Junior's strategy has been deemed unsuccessful;

B: Junior feels that he has succeeded and moved on—though I'm not sure what success has been found; or

C: Junior wants to make me squirm with, or without, a plan to kill me, since Junior may or may not be the assassin.

I vote *C*. And since I don't let anyone have that kind of power over me, Kane included, I'm damn sure not giving it to Junior. I start the car and decide that Junior and Kane have more things in common than not. Both are stalking me, and both have me chomping at the bit for payback.

And Kane might just get his tonight.

CHAPTER FIFTEEN

A starless night has fallen by the time I'm on the road, thunder rumbling in the far distance. My mind has shifted from the storm I've left behind me in Westbury to the one in front of me in East Hampton. And that brings me to two conclusions:

I need Kane.

I'm worried about Rich.

Those things are not mutually exclusive, considering Rich has placed himself in Kane's path, while in turn, Kane and I are in the line of fire from our unknown enemies, who seem to be stepping up their game. Once I'm burning up the highway miles at a steady pace, the traffic light and my rearview clear, I dial Rich, only to be sent directly to voice mail. I try again with the same outcome. "Damn it."

My fingers itch to dial Kane, but the circumstances haven't changed. Tonight is not a good night for us to have documented communication. My phone buzzes with my brother's number, and I quickly answer. "What's happening?" I ask.

"Rich isn't answering his calls or text messages. I drove by Kane's offices. I don't see that FBI agent's car or Rich's there. Have you talked to either?"

"No," I say. "And I tried Rich and was sent to voice mail, but I can tell you that Kane wouldn't have allowed them to stay in his building for any period of time. Certainly not this long."

"Then they must have taken him in for questioning."

"They would have taken him to your location," I argue.

"Not if they were planning to arrest him," he counters.

"Unless they have something on Kane that we don't know about, there is no evidence against him. You know that. Taking him in, removing him from his office building, would be harassment."

"And you've never seen the FBI harass anyone? They're squeezing him."

"They didn't arrest him, Andrew, but call NYC and ask if it makes you feel better."

"I tried. I failed. The ball's in your court."

"I'm not calling my boss," I say.

"He's pissed that you walked into trouble tonight, right?"

"Yes. So I repeat, I'm not—"

"I need you to call Murphy, Lilah."

"Andrew—"

"For me, sister."

"Fuck, Andrew. I hate when you pull that brother shit."

"Yeah, well, back at ya, sister. Because I've heard the sister card about a hundred times in this lifetime."

My lips tighten, right along with my fingers around the steering wheel. "I'll call." I hang up and dial Murphy.

"Agent Love," he greets, my name quite precise on his tongue. "Do we have yet another problem I don't expect that you've created?"

Bastard, I think. And I hope the fuck not. "Has Kane been arrested or taken in for questioning?" I ask, sounding calm and almost sweet. Okay, probably not sweet.

"What do the locals say?" he asks.

"Rich went with the NYC assholes to talk to Kane, and we can't reach him now. And I don't think I have to tell you the issues of Rich and Kane together, let alone Rich, Kane, *and* two assholes from New York who want the jurisdiction we're about to take."

"How the hell did Rich end up in the middle of that situation?"

"With two feet and a smile," I say. "He doesn't belong in the field."

Murphy makes sort of a grunting sound that brings to mind things I don't want to think about. "I'll call you back," he says, and disconnects.

As if I'm single-handedly trying to prove that saying, "Don't keep trying the same things and expecting different results," I dial Rich again, and I get no better results than before. My phone buzzes with a call almost instantly, but any hope that it's Rich is dashed by my brother's name. I answer to hear, "Did you—?"

"Seriously?" I demand, cutting him off. "You gave me five minutes?"

"Ten. Did you call your—?"

"Yes. He's trying to find out what's going on. I'll call you back when I know something. Don't call me in five minutes that you will call ten. Don't call me in ten minutes that you will call fifteen. I won't answer if I don't have news. And you had better call me if you hear something, too, or I swear—"

"You just told me you won't answer."

"Okay, smart-ass. Don't call me without news and we're in good shape."

"You really are a bitch, Lilah."

"I know," I say. "But you love it."

"Are you sure about that?"

"Of course. I'm your sister." My phone beeps. "That will be him. Hold on." I confirm the caller ID and click over. "Director."

"Why do you keep putting me on speaker?"

"Right this very moment, I'm driving in a cheap car with no other option."

"It's called Bluetooth or a headset. I don't like speakerphones. Get a headset." He moves on. "Kane wasn't arrested or taken in for questioning. That's all my insider can tell me right now. But I've been instructed to be on a conference call with my boss and my counterpart from NYC tomorrow in the morning to discuss jurisdiction."

"So tonight was a setup for that call," I assume.

"That's how it seems. Any word from Rich or Kane?"

"No," I say, "but I won't hear from Kane. Like I said, he's no fool. He won't pull me in and lose me as a potential ally later, and anything that would be considered inappropriately timed contact could do that." Did I really just say that? I think before I continue. "And Rich," I add, "must still be with the enemy, playing his game. He's in over his head, Director."

"You've said that," he comments dryly. "Kane isn't a fool and I'm not stupid. I don't need things repeated over and over, and I don't do things without a reason."

My line beeps. "Is that him?" Murphy asks.

I glance at the screen. "It's my brother, who I've apparently just hung up on."

"Update him. Keep up this new communication thing you're doing. It works for me."

He ends the call, and I answer the line. "Kane wasn't arrested or taken in for questioning."

"Then where is Rich and why isn't he answering?"

"I have no clue," I say. "I'll be back there at about nine. If he's not there by then, I'll go hunting for him."

"I'll be here when you get here. I'm not leaving the station until I hear from him."

"I'll come to you."

We disconnect, and my phone rings immediately, but it's still not Rich. It's Greg, and this call can be about only one thing. "News travels fast, and you're not even on the inside anymore," I say.

"Yeah," Greg agrees. "It does, and I'm still connected. You know how that works. But that aside, Holy Mother of Jesus. Rick Suthers is dead?"

"Hung himself just like his sister."

"Damn. Did he know you were coming? Was that the trigger?"

Fuck me. And fuck *him.* I want to reach through the phone and punch him in the mouth. "You're an asshole, Greg," I say. "And I really can't deal with one more asshole today. Go away." I hang up.

He doesn't call back. He knows me. I won't answer. Bastard hit the same raw nerve Murphy did a few minutes ago, their joint effort dragging that nerve from outside my Otherworld before I was ready to chew on it, rather than it chew on me. But now I'm in a car alone, on the road, and suddenly my crazy ringing phone isn't ringing anymore. The silence is inescapable, the implications of Greg's words with it. My mind goes to the book left with the body. The message behind it that makes a few points brutally clear: Laney died because I got too close to someone. Rick died because I'm close again. And my decision to go there tonight isn't one I can change.

Someone wanted me back here. Kane and I have established that fact. And now they're taunting me, punishing me, like they did the night I was raped. Maybe I'm next on the assassin's list, but that's just fine by me. I'll be waiting, and I'm going to be really fucking pissed off when we finally meet.

～

I'm almost to the police station when my brother calls. "Rich just called me. He's about to pull into the parking lot now."

"I'm three minutes away. What did he say?"

"Nothing yet. I'm going to meet him outside and find out."

He ends the call, and I turn right, driving a few blocks until I pull into the station parking lot. Rich and my brother are standing beside Rich's rental car, Rich leaning on the door and my brother standing tall and stiff in front of him, obviously as irritated as I am. I pull up right beside them, place my car in Park, but don't kill the engine. I get out, leave the door open, and walk to stand in front of Rich and beside my brother, my wrath aimed at Rich. "Glad to know that you aren't dead or bleeding out somewhere."

"My cell phone battery went dead," he says. "I left my charger in the hotel room."

"You're an FBI agent and you don't have a fucking backup phone battery?" I demand. "*Jesus*, Rich. You don't belong in the field."

"And the woman who wants to fuck Kane Mendez, when Kane Mendez could be involved in all of this, should be?" he snaps.

"Holy fuck. Did you fight with Kane?"

My brother's hand comes down on my arm. "Easy there, little sis. He's not the enemy."

I ignore him and keep that wrath aimed at Rich. "What happened?" I bite out.

"Kane and I hate each other's fucking guts," he says. "But we were civil, Lilah."

"Then you both get a damn cookie."

"I sure as hell deserve more than that," he says, giving me a direct look. "And I know you know what I mean."

"Hey," Andrew says. "Not in front of me. She's my sister, fucktard."

Rich snaps a look at him. "And I'm not Kane."

"Good point," Andrew says. "Continue."

"About the case," I say sharply, while considering something else sharp, as in an elbow to my brother's ribs. "Tell us about the meeting with Kane," I add.

"Those New York assholes made a completely unprofessional scene in Kane's office."

"What kind of scene?" Andrew asks.

"Nothing like throwing things around or shoving Kane against the wall," he says. "But they loudly announced themselves, flashing badges in the lobby. It drew attention."

"And Kane did what?" Andrew presses.

"Kane was surprisingly gracious. He invited us to his office, but as hard as they pushed him, he owned the office and the meeting."

"What did you do?" I ask.

"Observed everyone involved," he says. "Everyone in that room, Kane included, was new to me. But it was fast. We were out of there in thirty minutes."

"And then what?" Andrew and I say at the same time.

"I followed them to a restaurant in the Seaside Hotel in South Hampton," Rich says. "I thought they were staying at the hotel they were there so long, but they left an hour ago. I followed them until I was certain they were headed back to the city."

"Did you figure out what they're after?" I ask.

"It seemed like they were laying groundwork," he says. "They asked him about Woods. They seemed to be connecting people he knows to people Woods knew. It was a weak angle, but they hit him hard about it."

"But they're going to use it to claim jurisdiction," Andrew says. "How did Kane handle the questions?"

"Like I said," Rich replies. "He owned the meeting."

"That's it?" I press.

"No," Andrew says. "That's not it. We all know where this is headed. Close the case. Let them deal with Kane on their own."

"And then an assassin goes free," I say, "because Woods and Kane are innocent."

"Are you sure about that?" Rich asks, and he's not asking about Woods or playing a role.

"I'm going to leave now," I say, looking at Rich. "Call Murphy." I look at my brother. "Don't call me."

I walk to my car, get in, and drive away, pretty fucking done with men for the day. My brother is willing to let Woods take a fall for my father's campaign. Rich wants Kane to go down. And if Kane decides he wants to, he can take them all down. And I'm the one who has to keep peace and sanity in place. No wonder I'm so damn comfortable with dead bodies. They're a hell of a lot less complicated than the men in my life.

CHAPTER SIXTEEN

It's a short drive to my cottage. I resist calling it home, but for reasons I can't quite name, or maybe I just don't want to name, my apartment in LA doesn't feel like home either. The truth is, it never felt like home. Nothing has since my mother's plane crash except Kane, and that worked for me for a while until I started to resemble him far more than felt acceptable. Maybe I already resembled him. Maybe that's why we get each other, why we connect. And we did and do. We always will, I think, but I don't think it's healthy for either of us to feed those things in each other. *Those things.* What the hell are *those things*? I think I'll avoid naming them on a night I was responsible for a man's faked suicide. I'll find a vice and drench myself in it instead. Chocolate, or perhaps . . . chocolate.

I pull into my driveway, the yard etched in darkness too thick for shadows, the stars covered by clouds. Obviously, I need to set a motion detector on the outdoor lights and perhaps even install more. Though I hope like hell I catch a killer and get the hell out of here before I have time to make that change. The garage door lifts, the light inside flickering to life, and I am more than aware that I'm being stalked, and that this is where someone can follow me inside. But leaving my car outside allows someone to tamper with my vehicle. I pull into the garage and allow the door to close before I even unlock my doors. I slip my field bag back across my shoulder and unlatch the door, my hand on my weapon as I kick it open and stand up.

From there, I stand with my back to the wall as I search my surroundings and clear my path. I reach inside the interior door and flip on the kitchen light and then scan the room before stepping inside and shutting the door. I arm the system and start a search of the house. Ten minutes later, I've cleared the entire place and returned to the kitchen with my shotgun, Cujo, in hand. I set him down on the counter next to my cell phone and my field bag.

Hands pressed to the counter, my mind flickers with an image of Rick Suthers's body hanging from that doorframe. "Shit," I murmur, dragging my hand through my hair and shoving aside the claws of guilt ripping through me. That thinking serves no purpose but to weaken me and give the enemy what they want.

Right now, I need food and then to dig into my work. I open the fridge, where I'm reminded that any real grocery shopping has not occurred in a number of years as it relates to this particular house. Or to me, actually. I'll need to order pizza again. *Again.* Fuck. The pizza box and the note. I was drugged and in chaos today, or I would have thought about it sooner. I walk back to the counter and grab my phone, dialing the same pizza place I called last night. "Pizza Jacks," a man answers.

"I want a large pineapple and Canadian bacon with medium crust," I say. Then, considering breakfast, I amend, "Make it two larges and what do you have for dessert?"

"Chocolate chip—"

"I'll take one of those. And is there any chance you could send the same driver as last night? I forgot to tip him, and I want to make it right."

"Hold on one moment." He punches computer keys and then, "Odd. I don't seem to have a driver's name."

"He was short, with brown curly hair."

"Mick," he says. "Yeah. He's here tonight. He's your guy anyway."

"Oh good. Great. Thanks." I end the call and set my phone down, a memory surfacing of Rich accusing me of not saying *please* and *thank you. Asshole,* I think. *I say* please *and* thank you. I walk to the living room and the cut-out bar and bring a barstool to the island, removing my computer from my bag and cranking it to life. I set the book I'd retrieved from the crime scene on the counter as well, a reminder to me of how personal this case has become. Another flash in my mind of Rick hanging in his closet door and I turn to the coffee machine and get a good chocolate-flavored pod of caffeine brewing. Because who doesn't need caffeine when they're wired and on edge?

Once it's doctored up just right, I sit down at the island and drink my first boost of chocolate for the night, which will not be the last. It's also the closest thing to food I've had since the pure sugar of the cinnamon roll earlier today, which explains why I'm feeling light-headed again. I set the cup down, intending to turn my attention to my computer, when my gaze lands on the cover of the book—on my mother—and my heart squeezes. I love this picture of her. A pink gown and her hair brown, not blonde. She looks beautiful and natural, more like the person I knew than the one Hollywood knew. My throat thickens, and my mind throws me into the memory of the night of her death. I'd been in the law school library, studying for a debate the next morning, when an official-looking man in a suit had suddenly appeared, standing over me.

"Come with me please, Ms. Love," he says.

"Why? What's happened?"

He's tall and stone-faced. "You need to come with me."

I shut my books and shove them in my backpack, and I can almost feel part of my heart bleeding. Something is wrong. Very wrong. My knees are wobbling and I think someone calls my name as I follow the man through the hallway, but I don't hear them. I barely remember how I end up in an office of some sort. "Call your father," the man directs and shuts me inside.

I dial the number, my hand trembling. "Dad?" I say.

"Your mother's helicopter has gone down."

"What? When?"

"An hour ago. There are search-and-rescue teams."

I blink back to the present, shake off the memory. "Fuck. What are you doing to yourself, Lilah?" I reach for the book to move it out of sight, when my gaze catches on the Barnes & Noble sticker on the top right edge. There's a Barnes & Noble a few miles from Rick's house. There will be cameras and sales records, but without going to Tic Tac, it's going to have to be part of that illegal activity I've anticipated in the form of a favor. A favor from someone who owes me one. I plan to call it due tomorrow morning.

I open the drawer next to me and pull out a pad of paper to begin a list of things I need hacked.

Barnes & Noble sales records

List of books that were at the scene of Laney's murder

List of personnel at Laney's murder versus Rick's

An in-depth search on the production company

The doorbell rings and I stand up, hurrying toward the front of the house, unzipping my purse at my hip as I walk. Once I'm there, I remove a $100 bill meant to be a tip, zip it back up, and glance out the side window and confirm my visitor is my pizza delivery boy. I disarm the alarm and unlock the door before opening it to find the same short, curly-haired, older teenager in front of me as last night.

I hold up the hundred. "How did the note that was in my pizza last night end up in my pizza?"

He blanches. "What?"

"The note. How did it get in my pizza box?"

"They put coupons in the boxes. Do you mean the coupons?"

The sound of music touches my ears, and I wave him backward. He eases out of my way and I step outside to find his passenger door open. "Why is your car open?"

"It's faster. I can't get the bag over the steering wheel without tipping the pizza sideways. I run. Grab the bag, deliver the order, and return it back to the seat."

"Right," I say. "Of course you do. I hope you don't have anything in there that might get stolen." I don't wait for a reply. "How about those pizzas and my dessert?"

He pulls out my order and hands it to me, and I offer him the cash I've teased him with. His eyes light up. "Thank you. Thank you so much."

He all but skips back to his car, and I can think of any number of people, starting with Kane and Rich, who wish I was that easily satisfied. Then again, I doubt Kane would even want me if I was easy anything. I enter the house, kick the door shut, and juggle the three boxes in my arms to lock up and re-arm the security panel.

The walk back to the kitchen includes the spicy, cheesy smell of real food that has me ready to open one of the boxes and inhale a slice of pizza. Maybe I'll even stuff a bite of whatever that chocolate chip thing I got is, in between slices. I set my order by the coffee machine and inspect the giant chocolate chip cookie before I load a slice of it and a slice of pizza onto a paper towel. I grab a bottle of water from the fridge, and the action begins: Pizza bite. Pizza bite. Cookie. Water. Repeat. I've only managed this process two times before the doorbell rings again.

I decide that if this is my brother, I might punch him with no regrets. He has to back the fuck off and let me do my job. Ready to blast him with that exact statement, I hurry to the door again and peer outside, only to press my back against the wall and groan at the sight of Rich. "Lilah! I know you're there."

He knows no such thing, and I'd just pretend that I'm not here, except that he'd start calling and possibly sleep on my doorstep. I straighten and disarm the system, opening the door and stepping into the opening. "You shouldn't be here."

"Because it will piss off Kane, or because you don't want me here?"

"Don't do this."

He presses his arm to the doorframe above me, his big body close to mine. He smells good. I'll give him that. Fresh and masculine. I always liked that about him. I like a lot of things about Rich, which is why my inability to fall in love with him confuses him and frustrates me. "Don't do what?" he asks.

"Why are you here?"

"There were things I didn't want to say on the phone or with your brother present."

"Rich—"

"About the case, Lilah. Invite me inside."

"You aren't staying. Say it."

"Lilah—"

"Say it."

"I'm not staying."

I back up and give him space to enter. "Do I smell pizza?" he asks.

"You aren't staying," I repeat, holding firm, and not because I'm the bitch he thinks I am. Because I'm protecting him from Kane. And me. I'm protecting him from me.

"I haven't eaten," he says. "Lunch didn't exactly become lunch, remember?"

"The case, Rich."

"We're doing this right here, in the foyer?"

"Yes. We are."

His jaw sets hard. "I know who those New York City assholes had the long dinner with, and I want to tell you, not your brother."

"Fuck. My father?"

"Close. Pocher, who I know supports your father."

"Pocher," I repeat. "Of course."

"Don't make this a huge blow," he warns. "We knew he was connected to the director of the New York bureau."

"Yes," I agree. "But now we have confirmation that he's involved in what's going on right here in this city. And in what looks like an attack on Kane."

"Kane's a criminal, Lilah. He's an easy target."

"Such a criminal that Pocher wanted in on his oil business. Kane refused, and Pocher hates him now. And Kane isn't a fucking criminal, Rich. His father was a criminal. His uncle is a criminal. This is about hurting Kane while they take control and clear the case. It's about my father's reputation, which sucks, considering Kane has done things to protect him."

"What things has he done to protect your father?"

Buried a body, I think. "Irrelevant," I say. "The point is that Pocher is pulling strings to help my father, and my father is going down the toilet in a hunt for fame and power. He was always jealous of the attention my mother got."

He studies me for several beats. "This doesn't mean your father is party to Pocher's activities."

"My father is not a naive man, and I'm not a wilting flower who needs to have the truth softened. And right now, I need to be alone and to think."

He steps toward me. I back up. "Rich, not now."

"Let's go eat that pizza I smell and talk about this."

"I want to stay friends. I do. We *are* friends, Rich. I would take a bullet for you and not blink, but we aren't a thing anymore. And later, you will thank me when you find the person you deserve."

"Friends can share a pizza, Lilah."

Except that he vowed to ruin Kane and prove he's the right man for me. "The breakup is too raw right now. It's too soon."

He stares at me for several beats that stretch eternally, that I'm about to end when he beats me to the punch. "I'm going to be here, though, when you wake up to the truth about him. I'm going to catch you when you fall." He turns and walks to the door and leaves.

I rush forward and lock the door, re-arming the security system before I lean against the wall. *Holy fuck*, this day has been a bitch trying to bend me over and paddle the fuck out of me. And *holy fuck number two*: that reminds me of Kane and his hand-on-my-cheek comment this morning. I need more chocolate. I shove off the door and walk toward the kitchen, but as I leave the hallway I stop dead in my tracks as I bring the living room into view. Kane is leaning on the archway of the open sliding glass doors, his jacket and tie gone, his sleeves rolled up to the elbow.

Clearly, he and his people knew when I opened the door for Rich, and he used that opportunity to get in. As for how he managed to get past the locked door, clearly he took some sort of liberties while I was passed out to ensure he could. That infuriates me, and I want to cock block him again. But that's what he's waiting on. For me to go to him. Which is why I leave him standing there and walk to the kitchen. The bastard can come to me.

CHAPTER SEVENTEEN

I round the island, grab my half-eaten slice of pizza and piece of cookie, and toss them in the trash, then set my coffee cup in the sink. By the time I'm back at the island, Kane is entering the kitchen. He saunters toward me, all dark good looks with a touch of the criminal I just denied him to be radiating from him. *Fuck.* He must have heard me defending him. He steps to the counter directly in front of me. I press my hands to the counter. "Of all the people I have stalking me right now, you are the worst."

He mimics my position, pressing his hands to the counter as well. "Am I?"

"*Yes.* You are."

His lips curve, eyes alight with amusement, not regret. *Bastard.* "Your pretty boy, Rich, was a perfect gentleman today," he says. "Seems he's been disciplined by Agent Love."

"This spoken by a man who still has the imprint of my fingers on his right cheek."

"If that was your attempt to discipline me, I was playing the wrong game. But I'm here now. Give it a go again."

"Don't tempt me, Kane. I'm still furious with you for drugging me. And how did you get in here?"

"It wasn't locked and the bar wasn't in place."

"Bullshit."

"It wasn't locked, Lilah, and I checked it before I left this morning. You haven't used it?"

"Fuck. No. I haven't, which means someone's been in here again."

His brow lifts. "*Again?* What the hell does that mean?"

"I have it handled."

"We do this together, Lilah. We agreed."

"Together means together, Kane. Not you charging forward and dragging me along."

"Just dragging you to my side, beautiful, instead of letting you run ahead of me. What the hell does 'again' mean?"

"I'm not running from you, Kane, which we both know was your inference. And to answer your question, one of the first notes was left on my desk upstairs."

"Which means Junior saw your investigation notes."

"And you know this because *you* looked at my investigation notes."

"*Yes.* I did. Don't expect guilt. I prefer my dirty emotions to include you naked. Otherwise, I don't waste the energy. I assume since you're you, you've checked the house and it's clear?"

"I did, but obviously I need a new security system."

"I'm your new security system. Have you received any more notes?"

"You are not my security system, and no, I have not, which brings us back to you and your protection. Obviously, Junior knows I'm being watched. We can't catch whoever this is if your person is breathing down my throat."

"There are too many dead bodies for me to back off, Lilah. And whoever this is won't stay hidden long. They have an objective."

"Maybe it was to scare me off." My brow furrows. "Unless . . ."

"Unless?" he prods.

"If the murders in LA were meant to bring me here, and Junior seems to be driving me away, then Junior isn't the same person."

"Possibly, though Junior could simply be taunting you with a bigger endgame."

"Taunt me and then kill me?"

"Or taunt me and then kill you."

"Whoever hired the assassin clearly wanted them disrobed and humiliated before they were killed. That speaks of anger and hatred. What if, in my case, that anger and hatred runs deeper, thus my humiliation is to be drawn out?"

"You need out of this house. You need to stay with me."

"I don't need a babysitter, Kane. I'm an FBI agent and you're—"

"My father's son? Like you're your father's daughter?"

"That line is getting old. Come up with a new one."

"You want new? How about this? Quit the FBI. Consult instead."

"And then I can be with you?"

"Yes. Then you can be with me."

"Then you lose your insider in law enforcement."

"I have insiders in law enforcement," he says. "What I don't have is you."

"You want what you can't have."

"And yet," he says, "I've had you and I still want you."

"Had," I say. "Not anymore."

"Are you sure about that?"

"Yes. Tell me about your meeting with those New York City assholes."

"They tried to connect me to Woods. And you're right to assume that they're posturing to take over and push you out. Your turn. Tell me about Rick Suthers."

"You know." I don't give him time to respond. I hold up a hand. "Of course you know."

"Was it suicide?" he presses.

"No. It was not. It was just like with Laney: a copycat murder of hers made to look like suicide. He was standing on books that should have scattered, but they didn't: just like Laney." I grab the book and set it between us, a fist forming in my chest. "And this was one of the books."

He looks at it and then me. "How long had he been dead when you got there?"

"Fresh."

"Who knew you were going there?"

"No one knew I was going to see him, but obviously the right someone knew I was in that region of the island. I assume that was the trigger. Whoever this was may not have planned for me to find the body."

"The book says you were expected."

"I would have asked to see the case-file notes no matter what." My mind tracks back to the crime scene, and I reach into my pocket for the necklace. "I found this in what I believe was the bag holding the suit I'm fairly certain he wore to Laney's funeral," I say, setting it on the counter.

He picks it up and holds it in his hand before looking at me. "Virgin Mary." He sets it beside the book. "And there's no such thing as a coincidence, right?"

"You know way too much about how I solve crimes. And I don't believe for a minute that the necklace isn't connected to those tattoos. Shared symbols mean an organization." I lift the book. "And this. This was someone telling me to back the fuck off, which makes me believe that I wasn't lured back here at all. I'm being told to get the hell out of town."

"A tattooed victim in your region can't be a coincidence."

"Maybe not," I concede. "And on that note, was the lead the old man gave me a setup?"

"Could be, or the person who gave us the clue got busted and confessed what they told us."

"Right. Talk about a cat-and-mouse game. I'm feeling like we're the mice."

"We're not the mice. Not even close."

"Our enemy knows who we are, but we don't know who they are. What do you know about the production company?"

"On the surface, there are no connections that look interesting, but I have their banking transactions being traced. That's where we will find the answers we're looking for."

"When?"

"By tomorrow." He circles back. "Are you sure no one knew you were going to Suthers?"

"I called Beth hours before I got to Long Island. She knew I was headed that way. We sidetracked the tail I had, and then there was my brother and you." A thought hits me. "Actually, I did mention Suthers to Greg at lunch today, but it was a flippant, barely spoken mention."

"He knows you. You don't do flippant and meaningless."

"I don't believe it was Greg. And you like Greg."

"I don't *like* Greg. I simply don't dislike him. And everyone has a price."

"What's yours?"

He pushes off the island and walks around it. By the time he's on this side with me, I'm facing him, the barstool at my back. "You are, Lilah." He steps closer, and I don't back away.

"I don't want to be a weapon that can be used against you."

"Anyone who believes they can get away with turning you into that will suffer, and painfully." He doesn't give me time to object. "You didn't cause that man's death."

"I know that," I say, and I feel the pull between us, a warning to back away, and I do, hitting the stool. Kane moves with me, and I end up with my back to the island, his hands on either side of me.

"You didn't cause his death," he repeats.

"I told you. I know."

"Do you?" he demands.

"Yes, damn it, I do."

"Because if you let it fuck with your head," he says as if I haven't spoken, "you'll get careless and end up dead, and you don't get to die, Lilah. Understand?"

"I'm not going to die."

"No. You are not. And as for me wanting what I can't have, we both know you have me confused with Pretty Boy." He pushes off the counter. "You know where to find me," he says before he walks away.

My jaw sets and I follow him, bringing the living room, and him, into view as he reaches the sliding glass doors, at least ten things on my tongue ready to be shouted. All of which I know will piss him off and bring him right back to me. But I'm saved from that stupidity, which would have created a fight, followed by fucking, when he steps outside and shuts the door. *Gone.* He wants me to follow, but he's smart enough not to expect me to. And I'm not going to either. But I do charge forward, locking the door and sliding the bar back into place.

I lock him out and then turn to face the house. Someone was here again. The question is, what did they do when they were here?

I search my house and check my camera feed, which is illogically clear. Every window. Every door. Every drawer. And I come up with nothing. There are no signs that anyone has been here. Once I'm 100 percent certain that the house is clear, I grab everything I've set up in the kitchen and move to a big cushy chair in the corner of the living room that gives me a view of every door in the house. The giant ottoman becomes my table, and I settle on the floor in front of it with my back to the chair. Everything I need is nearby. Note cards and Cujo to my left. Pizza and cookie boxes, field bag, the book, and necklace to my right. My computer and a plate of pizza and cookie in front of me. I also have a towel over the cream-colored cushion, guarding it from my ravenous, hunger-induced messiness. Not because I care about the cushion but because my mother would care, and this house still feels like hers.

I log on to a private e-mail server and find Tic Tac online. I direct-message: What do you have for me? A tactic that spares him the necessity of hearing me talk with my mouth full, which my current state of starvation would otherwise require.

> The murders are spread out: two in LA, one in New York City, one in East Hampton. You are the only common denominator to tie the cases together. You were on three out of four of the cases. I'm e-mailing you the list anyway.

Four out of six, I think, if we include Laney and her brother, but, of course, Tic Tac and Murphy have no idea there's a probable connection. I finish a slice of pizza and drop another on my plate before typing: What else?

> I'm also e-mailing you a list of anyone I can find who is easily connected to that production company you asked about. I don't see anything that stands out, but you might. I don't know what you're looking for to dig deeper.

This is dangerous territory I should never have ventured into with him and that I now attempt to sidestep by typing: It's a far-fetched lead anyway. I'll look and let you know if you need to continue.

I disconnect with him and go invisible online before pulling the e-mail list he's sent me. By the time I'm done, I've shoved aside my pizza and come up with nothing. The murders are spread out, with different case personnel. I really am the only common denominator. I pick up the book and the necklace and set them on the ottoman. Correction: me and the Virgin Mary are the only common denominators. Correction again: me, the Virgin Mary, and the killer. And Kane. He's connected to my attack, the Virgin Mary, and the local murder.

I grab a stack of note cards and write out all the names Tic Tac e-mailed me, but after that I have nothing. "Damn it." I toss the cards in the air and across the room, watching them flutter everywhere. Why can't I figure this out? My gaze lands on the cover of my mother's book, the message left for me. There's a bigger picture in all this, and I have to figure out what it is. What I'm missing.

I lie down on the floor with it on my chest, staring at the ceiling. "Think, Lilah," I murmur. "Think."

I force my mind back to the bar the night of my attack. I tell myself to relive it, but instead I'm remembering the first night I met Kane. I'd been at the Cove, on top of the boulders where Kane and I met several days ago. The place that became our secret escape. The place where no one could hear what we said. The place my mother had also used as an escape from everyone who wanted a piece of her, including my father.

I don't know why this is the memory I've chosen right now, but my mind takes me in circles, leads me places to find other places. I know this, and so I shut my eyes and let myself sink into that moment, the wind lifting my hair, the salt on my lips. I can even see what I was wearing: black. All black because death was consuming me, eating away at me. I sink deeper into the memory, reliving it as if it were happening right now.

Wind lifts around me, blowing off the ocean, waves crashing on the rocks, salt on my lips, and for the first time in the month since my mother was declared dead, it's not from my tears. It's changed tonight, more of a cutting, biting pain, not an emotional storm. Exhaustion is starting to take hold, weeks of barely sleeping finally catching up with me, but I don't want to go to the cottage, to my mother's home. I remove my jacket and lie back on the rocks, stuffing it under my head, the moon casting me in a beam of light. I shut my eyes, just needing to rest a few minutes, but a sound jolts me, and I sit up. That's when a man I didn't even hear approach squats down in front of me, his jacket and tie gone, sleeves rolled to the elbows.

"Lilah Love," he says, and though we've never formally met, it's a small town. We know of each other. And considering who he is, and who my father is, I know on some level I should feel fear, but I don't. But then, I've already decided I'm not going to die boxed in by other people's limits, as my mother did.

"Kane Mendez," I say. "I've heard stories about you. Are you here to fuck me or kill me?"

"Are you saying you want me to fuck you?"

"You look pretty good in a suit from what I remember, so maybe I might fuck you."

He laughs. "Is that right?"

"Yes. That's right. Why are you really here?"

"I come here when I want to think and be alone," he says, sitting down next to me and looking over at me. "Why are you here?"

"My mother used to come here for the same reason as you. Did you ever see her?"

"No," he says. "I did not, but I met her a few times. She was not only stunning but gracious to everyone around her."

"Yes. She was."

"I've met your father, the police chief, as well. He's a prick."

"Yes. He is." I glance over at him. "Did I read that you have a Yale law degree?"

"I do."

"Does your father?"

"No. The law doesn't appeal to my father."

"Are you dirty like your father?"

He glances over at me. "You're direct."

"Yes. I am."

"Why?"

"I don't like junk conversations. They waste time."

"And I don't do anything like my father, dirty or otherwise. What about you? Are you going to be a law enforcement officer like your father?"

"The FBI recruited me back when I started college. I was supposed to finish law school this year and head to Virginia."

"Was?"

"I took a job at the NYPD. I start next week."

"Why?"

"I need to be here. That's my gut. I don't have another answer."

"Death either draws you to the familiar or pushes you to the unfamiliar." He looks over at me. "Sometimes a combination of both."

"Spoken like a man who's lived that experience."

"Yes. I have." He offers nothing more.

"Your mother is gone, too, right?"

"Yes. Killed by one of my father's enemies when I was eight."

He says those words matter-of-factly, but there is a grit beneath his tone that hints at much more. "You hate him."

"He's my father. And this time, I don't have another answer."

Being my father's daughter, I accept that answer. I even understand it. "Tell me about your mother."

He looks at me, surprise in his eyes. "You want to hear about my mother?"

"Yes. I do."

"Why?"

"Because. Just because."

"There's no such thing as just because, Lilah Love. There is always a deeper meaning, intended or unintended."

I open my eyes and replay those words in my mind: *There is always a deeper meaning, intended or unintended.* I sit up, and my mother's biography tumbles to the floor. I pick the book up and stare at it, something clawing at my mind. Something I need to discover, something that the book tells me. "Intended or unintended," I whisper. A crazy thought hits me, and I set the book down on the stool and key my computer to life. I go to my mother's IMDb profile and start researching. An hour later I have the answer I'm seeking. I dial Kane.

He answers on the first ring; no playing hard to get for Kane. "Miss me already?" he asks, his voice rippling with arrogance.

"Kane," I breathe out.

"What is it?" he asks, his voice somber now, matching my urgency.

"There is always a deeper meaning, intentional or unintentional."

"Yes. There is. Where are you going with this?"

"The book made me start thinking about my mother's death."

"Your mother died two years before any of this started, and before your attack."

"Two years before we know it started. The Chinese investment firm that financed Laney's movie financed two of my mother's." My jaw clamps down. "I might need you to bury another body before this is over."

"I'm coming back over."

"No. I'm not going to be fucking you tonight, Kane. I'm going to be too busy figuring out how to fuck someone else." I hang up.

CHAPTER EIGHTEEN

My mother was *murdered*.

The very thought has me pacing and tangling fingers in my hair, anger burning a hole in my gut and chest. It consumes me. It hurts. *God*, it hurts, and I find myself standing at the foot of my bed, staring at my mother's photo in her most iconic role: Marilyn Monroe. My mother was an amazing talent, but most of all, she was good. She was kind. She was gentle. In my youth I wanted to be like her, but not for years. And not right now. Right now, I want blood. I want answers. I inhale sharply, lowering my chin to my chest and deep-breathing, images of my mother's casket in my mind, followed by another of Rick Suthers hanging by a sheet. I huff out a breath and look at my mother again.

"Otherworld, Lilah," I whisper, forcing myself into the place I normally reserve for crime scenes but aware that I need to step back and away from the personal side of my investigation. I need to be Agent Love: cold, thoughtful, calculating, and driven. I inhale again, slowly letting the air flow back out of my lungs and over my lips. "Otherworld," I repeat as I turn away from the photo and exit the bedroom.

Fifteen minutes later, after fighting an urge to confine myself to my office, my self-declared Purgatory, the place I confine myself until I find the answers I need, I settle in the living room. It's the only way I can keep the doors in view. I turn the living room into my new workspace, my temporary Purgatory. Once I have note cards, pens, coffee, and cookie slices within reach, I get to work. And as my trips to Purgatory always begin, I alternate between pacing and cursing, with random time at my computer and scribbling on note cards. At three in the morning, I summarize the points in my mind and discussed with Kane up to this point:

JR. AND ASSASSIN—THE SAME PERSON? UNCERTAIN

MY RETURN TO NEW YORK COULD BE A BY-PRODUCT OF THE MURDERS, NOT NECESSARILY PLANNED

OR THE ASSASSIN WAS TOLD TO HUMILIATE THE VICTIMS BY UNDRESSING THEM BEFORE KILLING THEM, BUT I'M EXTRASPECIAL: I GET TAUNTED FIRST

At four in the morning, I wake up in the center of the floor with a cramp in my leg, note cards scattered everywhere. I have a cookie. It helps. At five, I repeat this process, but this time I wake up with my arm so asleep that I have a panicked moment when I think it might not ever wake up. Because, you know, bad guys and bodies don't scare me, but not being able to control my arm scares the fuck out of me.

At six, when the same arm is asleep, I'm done with this hellish cycle. I give up on sleep and do so despite the fact that I have a minimum four-hour sleep bar. Without it I'm a bitch, which really wouldn't worry me, considering all the enemies I have biting at my heels, except for one thing: it also means that my brain gets stupid. I can't be stupid today. I head to the shower, and with hot water running over me, I devise a plan to stay on my game today, which includes extra coffee and real food that is not laced with sugar. Once I'm out of the shower, I dress in brand-name everything, because that's what this fucking town likes: Black slacks. A pink blouse, because as bitchy as I am I need something to soften me the fuck up, if that is even possible. High-heeled boots that I can use as weapons to complete my outfit. My gun goes to my hip, and with a blazer in my hand, I'm ready for the bed everyone is going to wish I was in.

By eight, I am sitting at the island in the kitchen with the news on subtitles, coffee in my cup, and a slice of cold pizza, my version of wholesome, being shoveled down my throat. By eight fifteen I've finished up a spreadsheet of the crew for every movie the Chinese production company has ever done. Finally, after hours of work last night and early this morning, I sort it by like names. A few more key punches, and I have several hits:

ROBERT NEIMAN, EXECUTIVE PRODUCER OF FIVE OF THE TEN FILMS. TWO WITH MY MOTHER AND ONE WITH LANEY.

GUY SANDS, PRODUCER OF THREE OF THE TEN FILMS. HE WAS ON LANEY'S FILM.

KELLI PEARCE, ACTRESS ON FOUR OF THE TEN FILMS. SHE WAS ON FIVE OF GUY SANDS'S FILMS.

I dial Kane.

"Did you sleep?" he asks.

"Two hours. I'm a bitch. I can't help myself."

"I know how to fix that."

"Chocolate," I say.

"Me," he says.

"A knee," I offer.

"For Pretty Boy?" he counters. "I approve."

"Stop while you're ahead. I'm texting you three names. They all have strong ties to the Chinese investors connected to Laney's movie, and now two of my mother's. Two producers and an actress. I know nothing more at this point."

"I'll find out the rest. What else?"

My gaze catches on the television above the bar, which is showing an image of my father. "I'll let you know. Something just came up." I hang up and push the Volume button on the remote to hear: "Mayor Love will host what is expected to be a celebrity-riddled crowd at the Children's Museum today, and all in the name of a good cause: the battle against children's cancer."

"A good cause, my ass," I say, turning off the television, wishing I could believe this was about the charity, not politics, but I can't. Not with everything that's come to light about my family this past week. Whatever the case, my father needs a visit from me, but first things first.

I dial Rich. "I need to see you."

"When?"

"Now."

"Where?"

"I'll come to you. Where are you staying?"

"Apple Cove Inn," he says.

"I know it." And because the location might send the wrong idea, I add, "This isn't a naked meeting in a hotel room. Meet me in the lounge." I hang up and then write the three names down on a piece of paper, along with the details on the Chinese investor, before pulling on the black blazer I've draped over a chair. And because nothing about my research stays in this house for prying eyes, I walk to my newly minted version of Purgatory, the room others call the "living room," and load my field bag with every note card and scribble I've made. For good measure, I check the sliding glass door. It's locked. It better stay that way.

It's nine fifteen when I arrive at the Apple Cove Inn, where Rich is staying, and park near the door, locking my field bag in the trunk. I walk across the short, graveled parking lot and up the wooden steps to find Rich sitting on the wide wraparound porch in one of about a half dozen wooden chairs. He stands to greet me, his hands settling under the thin tan leather jacket, exposing his badge and gun at the waistband of his jeans. "What's going on?"

"I need a favor," I say, moving to join him.

"Not 'I need stuff' but 'I need a favor,'" he says as I sit next to the seat that he reclaims. "That sounds serious," he adds, his elbows on his knees. "I'm all ears."

"I need you to go back to LA."

He makes a frustrated sound and straightens, running his hand through his longish blond hair. "No. I'm not leaving." He grimaces and then gives me a dead-on look. "Murphy wants me here. I want me here. You're going to have to deal with it."

I hand him the piece of paper. "This is why I need you to go back."

His lips thin, but he reluctantly accepts it, glancing down and then up at me. "What is this?"

"Three people who live in LA who might have answers I need. Off the record, Rich. This is potentially tied to my family and corruption. I can't trust anyone else to do it."

His spine softens and he leans closer. "Explain."

"The Chinese financier I've written on the paper is my focus. I need to know who is behind them, off the books. The people who hide behind other people. All these names I've given you are individuals who have been on multiple projects for them and who might know something. Unfortunately, the two producers are both out of the country, filming separate projects. But that doesn't mean digging around their backyard won't produce answers. And the actress is working on an independent film in LA. You can talk to her."

He studies me for several beats. "This is important to you."

"Very."

"All right. I'll do it."

"It can't be on the books, and Murphy is too smart not to know you're back in LA. It's a lie I don't want you to get caught telling. You have to request removal from this case. And you have to do it urgently."

"What corruption, Lilah?" he says softly.

"I don't want you to be able to answer that question. You need to be able to say 'I don't know' if you're asked."

"Damn it, I want to push. You know that, right?"

"Yes. But don't."

He seems to struggle with that but thankfully moves on. "If I leave," he says, "and you claim jurisdiction, your family is going to lash out at you."

"The answers you're trying to get will help me deal with them."

He runs his hand over his perpetually clean-shaven face, as if the man carries around a razor blade. "I'll call Murphy," he says.

"Now. Call him now."

"He has that conference call."

"Try," I press.

"You never get less pushy, do you?" he asks, but he does it. He dials Murphy, only to shake his head. "Voice mail," he says before he leaves a message. "I'll book a flight," he says after he sets his phone aside. "Where are you going now?"

"Research stop," I say. "Call me when you talk to Murphy." I stand up and start walking.

"He's dangerous, Lilah."

I stop in my tracks with that warning, which is obviously about Kane, my lashes lowering with the realization that despite how much Rich wants to stay here with me, he's in fact leaving for me, to help me. And I do trust him, which means he deserves honesty from me. I turn to face him. "You see what I wish I was, Rich. He sees who I am. I will never live up to your expectations, but I wanted to. I tried. But I will *always* live up to his expectations, when I wish I wouldn't. But I'm me. I can't be something I'm not."

"I see more than you think I see, Lilah."

"Part of me wishes that were true. The other is really fucking happy it's not." I turn, and this time I hurry down the steps and don't look back. Once I'm at my car, I'm aware of the absence of a note. Junior has disappeared. I settle into the driver's seat of my rental, and I decide it's good that Rich is leaving. I can't be around him right now, not when this investigation has turned to my mother, who may very well have been murdered. I don't want the pressure of being good. In fact, I want to let myself be really damn bad.

CHAPTER NINETEEN

Fifteen minutes later, I've just pulled into the driveway of my father's sprawling white mansion and parked under the willow tree, with no other vehicles in sight, when Murphy calls. "What happened with Rich, Agent Love?" he asks.

"I don't speak for Rich."

"I asked you, not Rich."

"It's not safe for him here."

"Are you suggesting Kane Mendez would kill him?"

"I don't remember bringing up Kane's name at all, and frankly, I'm the one who wanted to put a knee in his groin and grind it a few times before repeating."

He's silent. "*Agent* Love."

I'm pretty sure that's a reprimand, but I'm not feeling all that willing to accept it right now. "I didn't sleep last night. That comment was my version of nice today."

"Pretend you're undercover and the person you're pretending to be has slept and get a better attitude."

I bite back a smart reply about preferring my role-play to end in the pleasure this conversation is not giving me. "Did you have the conference call?"

"Yes. I did. And Kane gave us an asset by filing a lawsuit against the NYPD along with our New York City bureau, while leaving us, you, out of the picture. Therefore, you have two options: claim jurisdiction today or come home today and let the New York City bureau claim jurisdiction. There is no in-between. There is no extra time."

"I have balls in the air I can't let fall. I need until tomorrow to do this right."

"You have until midnight to either tell me, or I expect you on a plane back here tomorrow. Don't argue. You won't win. Understand? Say 'yes, Director' or say 'yes, asshole.' Say no. It still changes nothing."

"Yes, Director," I bite out.

"Ah, submission. Oh how sweet it is." He disconnects.

I grimace and slide my phone into my jacket pocket, exiting the car and crossing the yard, my fingers brushing my mother's ivy on the exterior of the stucco as I pass. "Otherworld, Lilah," I whisper, trying again to force myself to live in that mental zone beyond a short, intense crime scene.

I climb a dozen stone steps to reach the wide porch, where two heavy wooden rocking chairs frame the entrance left and right. Once I'm there, I reach for the door handle and hope it's unlocked, but I hit a roadblock when it doesn't budge. I ring the bell. A twentysomething pretty blonde in a lilac-colored velvet sweat suit and a cleavage-dipped T-shirt answers the door. "Lilah," she greets.

"You know me?"

"I've seen tons of pictures. I'm Katie, the new house manager."

"House manager," I say, nearly choking on the laughter I hold back. "I won't ask what that job description entails. Step aside."

"Your father isn't here."

"And?"

"And I can't—"

I step forward and come toe to toe with her, crowding her to the point that she instinctively backs up. I enter the half-moon-shaped foyer and turn to her. "Where is Jennifer, by the way?" I ask of the *house manager* who preceded her and practically raised me and my brother.

"I have no idea. She was gone when I started."

"Right. I'll just wait for my father in the other room." I ignore the stairwell directly in front of me, which is made of the same gray wood that is beneath my feet, and cut right, walking into my father's office. I turn and Katie is rushing toward me. "Sorry. I need to make some calls and need privacy. FBI business." I shut the double doors and lock them.

Certain I only have a few minutes before my brother storms over here at my father's demand that I be removed, of course, I hurry forward, round my father's heavy mahogany desk, and sit down. My gaze lifts to the bookshelves framing a sitting area full of big, comfy furniture, and I have a mental flash of my mother curled up on one of the chairs reading while my father worked. I shake it off and reach for a drawer, only to find it locked. Knowing my father more than most might think, I stand up and walk to the bar in the corner, open the leather case that holds an expensive-ass bottle top, and remove it to grab the key. Returning to the desk, I open the drawers and start going through files, using my phone to take photos of various financial transactions, contracts with vendors, and pretty much anything I'll want to analyze in more detail. I even take photos of all the business cards he has stuffed in a top drawer, as well as a few numbers scribbled on a pad of paper.

At twenty minutes, I know that I've pushed my luck, and I lock the desk and return the key to the leather box at the bar. I'm about to leave, but the forty-year-old bottle of scotch sitting on the bar works for my plan for the rest of the morning. I grab it and head for the door. Katie is sitting on the stairs and jumps up when I exit. She places herself directly under my mother's teardrop chandelier, which bothers me for personal reasons that are likely misplaced and ridiculous. I have many things to worry about other than who my father is bending over his desk.

I walk past her and exit the door, pulling it shut behind me. I hurry down the steps and turn to the sidewalk only to find the billionaire asshole himself, Pocher, walking toward me, his Jaguar Roadster parked next to my piece-of-shit rental. "Lilah," he greets with a smug look on his face that makes me want to punch him.

"Pocher," I say, his navy-blue suit fitted perfectly to his slender frame, his salt-and-pepper hair sprayed to an unmovable freeze. "Do you know what they say about suits as perfect as yours?"

"They wish they could afford one?"

"Money mobsters," I say. "At least that's what we call you people at the agency."

"*You people?* Like Kane Mendez."

"Kane isn't as gentle as your kind. You know that. Why are you here?"

"Your father left a file he needs for today's charity auction here, and he's tied up preparing for his speech. Are you joining us?"

"Since I wasn't invited, and since I have dead bodies and money mobsters to contend with, no." I start to step around him.

He steps in front of me. "What brings you here, Lilah?"

"I wanted to roll around on my old bed and see if I could smell my mother's perfume. You remember her, right?"

His eyes narrow. "Yes. I do. You are more like her than I realized."

"You need to step aside," I say.

"Of course." He rotates to allow me to pass, and I walk to my car, feeling him watch me every step of the way. I open the door and turn to find him standing in the center of the sidewalk, just staring at me. "I forgot," I say. "I came for this, too." I lift the bottle. "My father owed me this."

"That's an expensive bottle of scotch. Why'd he owe you that?"

"For putting up with you, but it's only going to take the edge off. The pain will be right back in the morning." I climb into the car, seal myself inside, and drive the fuck away.

Asking for favors when I feel like a bitch who wouldn't mind having a baseball bat in hand—because my gun would be a little too extreme—isn't easy, which is why I show up at Lucas's door bearing gifts. I ring the bell and wait for about thirty seconds for him to answer before I start knocking. He yanks the door open, his preppy Tarzan good looks in full force today, complete with a sunburn across his nose, a snug white T-shirt, and ripped jeans.

"Must be nice to work from home and investment-bank or whatever you do," I say.

"Or whatever I do?" he snaps. "I make a shit-ton of money for most of this town and beyond."

"Right. Money. Lots of it." I hold up the scotch but don't fully allow him to see the bottle, and I step toward him. "I bring gifts, well, *a gift*." He backs up and allows me to enter, and I pause in the foyer in front of him. "It's a really good gift," I say, presenting the front of the bottle.

He glances down at it. "Holy fuck. Forty-year single malt. You brought me a fifteen-thousand-dollar bottle of scotch?"

"Yep," I say, heading down the hallway. "I brought *us* a fifteen-thousand-dollar bottle of scotch."

The door shuts behind me. "Is there a body you want me to bury?" he calls out as I enter the living room framed by windows, the curtains drawn to display his massive egg-shaped pool. I head to the white stucco bar in the corner, grab two crystal glasses, and turn to look at him.

"Kane buries my bodies," I dare to say, joining him on the smoky-gray couch and setting my field bag down on the floor.

"Right," he says as I set the glasses down and he opens the bottle. "How could I forget Kane? The bastard who won't let you go on a date with me." He fills our glasses.

"You're my cousin."

"Are we doing this again?" he asks, screwing the lid back on the bottle. "By marriage."

"Yes, well, people date, fuck, and hate each other. We get to love each other forever." I hand him his glass and pick up mine, offering him a toast. "To love and cousins."

"To fucking, hating, and making up," he says, clinking my glass. "Unfortunately, with other people. I officially give up, cousin."

"Finally," I say, and we both drink and savor the warmth of the woodsy flavor. I down mine.

"Tell me you didn't just down forty-year scotch," he says. "You're supposed to savor it."

"I savored a swallow." I sink back on the couch and grab a pillow. "And I slept about two hours. I needed to de-bitch myself." I laugh, the heat of the drink warming my limbs. "Un-bitch? Stop the bitch? Whatever you want to call it."

"You're always a bitch," he says, sinking back and lounging next to me, his glass in his hand. "But it's oddly endearing."

"Ahhhh, cousin. You're so sweet."

He takes a drink. "This is a damn good scotch. How'd you get your hands on it?"

"I took it from my father."

He laughs. "Like I said. Oddly endearing." He hands me his glass, and I sip before giving it back to him.

"I've been thinking about my mother a lot the last two days," I admit.

"What about her? Aside from the obvious that you miss the fuck out of her."

"I've always thought it was odd that your father and my mother were in that plane when it crashed. *Alone*." I flash back to my brother's claim of an affair. "Do you think—?"

"Yes. It's true."

"What's true? Be clear."

"They were having an affair."

I sit up and rotate to face him. "You're sure?"

"You aren't?" He sips his whiskey but doesn't sit up.

"No. I don't want to believe it."

"I hear ya. Parents banging other parents blows the whole fairy-tale, happy-family shit to hell and back. But it's true. I heard them talking, and it was one of those kinky, hot, burn-my-ears-because-it's-my-father-and-your-mother kind of talks."

"*Fuck.* How long was this going on and *my cousin* didn't tell me?"

"A year that I knew of, but I'm pretty certain longer."

"Did my father know?"

"I have no idea," he says.

"Why *the fuck* didn't you tell me?" I demand.

"You were in law school miles away. And what were you going to do? They're adults. They *were* adults. Fuck. I still speak like they're alive."

But they're not alive, I think. And I'm a law enforcement officer who now suspects murder. And I know all too well that you look close to home, to the spouse first, especially when an affair is identified. In this case, that means *my father.*

CHAPTER TWENTY

I stand up and walk to the windows overlooking the pool but without really seeing it. My father *did not* kill my mother. I refuse to believe that is possible. I *won't* believe that, but the comment Pocher made about me being more like my mother than he knew comes back to me. It didn't hit me wrong then, but now, it hits me ten ways of wrong. Did he kill my mother and Lucas's father? Was she in the way? Was the affair the scandal that kept my father from the limelight?

Lucas steps beside me. "You okay?"

I glance over at him. "Most of the time. Not all the time. You?"

"The same. You know how close I was to my father."

"Yeah. We were both lucky to have those relationships." I glance back out the window. "I knew she wasn't happy with my father. I should have convinced her to leave."

"Don't do that. 'Should have, could have' does no good for anyone. It solves nothing."

I fold my arms in front of me, and we turn to face each other. "For me, that's not true. It often does solve cases."

"This isn't a case," he says, having no idea that, indeed, this may very well tie into the murders I'm trying to solve. "And people, family included, get angry when you get in the middle of their personal shit. It's just how it is."

"My father is running for governor."

"No shit? So the rumors are true."

"Yes. *And* I think my father's banging his young housekeeper."

"He better watch that shit if he's running for governor." He glances over at me. "And just so we can get past why you're really here. Love forever and all that stuff, cuz, but I'm not hacking for you."

"You have to. It's life or death, literally."

He holds up a hand. "No. I'm not doing it." He walks back to the couch and refills his glass. "You're the one who shut me down and saved my ass. I could have gone to jail."

I walk to the opposite side of the table and stand above him. "And I could go to jail for what I did to keep you out of jail."

"It's a drug to me, Lilah, an adrenaline rush. I took the hacking jobs for that high. Even then, before I inherited my father's money, I didn't need the money. But I needed that rush, and I can't do it again or I will keep needing it."

I squat down in front of the table and him. "No, you won't," I assure him. "I'm not going to let that happen. I'll grab you and hold on. I promise. There are dirty cops involved. There's a body count that might be closer to a dozen after I finish connecting the dots."

"And you think your people are dirty so you want to make me dirty again, too?"

"I think my father's dirty. I think he's involved."

His eyes go wide. "Are you serious?" He sets his glass down. "Your father? In a dozen murders?"

"In a cover-up of at least half of them. Maybe it goes deeper. I don't know. I need you to help me find out."

"Damn. Yeah. I'm in." He stands up and I follow. "Follow me."

I grab my field bag from the couch, follow him up the stucco-encased stairwell to our right, and pause at the top as he unlocks a door. He turns to look at me. "Welcome to the addiction." He shoves open the door and steps back, allowing me to walk inside. I walk through the doorway and find myself in a giant room that is walled off by floor-to-ceiling windows, the beach crashing against the shore beyond the glass. The only solid wall is lined with blacked-out monitors, the center of the room filled with random tables and tech equipment.

I face him. "This is insanity."

"I had money that became even more money with my addiction."

He backs up and punches a button, and the room churns and flickers to life. Monitors power up, buttons and machines lighting. He points to a horseshoe-shaped workspace with, of course, a white tiled top. "Let's sit there."

I follow him, and we claim spots in rolling chairs behind the countertop. A few minutes later, my computer is fired up, phone by my side, along with my note cards and a notepad. Lucas has a heavy-duty gaming-style notebook computer in front of him. He rubs his hands together. "What am I after?"

I decide to start with the part I want to supervise. The rest he can do on his own. Not to mention he might lose his mind right now if I say "assassin" and infer any connection between Ying Entertainment and my mother, which means his father. I slide a piece of paper toward him with a list of all the murder victims, including Laney and her brother. "I need complete case notes, inclusive of all personnel who came anywhere near the cases or crime scenes, down to the janitors. I wrote the location and investigating agency next to each name."

He shoves back from the counter and rolls around to face me. I do the same with him. "You want me to hack law enforcement? Are you fucking nuts?"

"That's one way of putting it, but that's to the point. It's the only way to do this. And if you get busted, I'll say I bribed you with some family secret."

"I'm not going to let you do that." He shoves fingers through his hair. "Damn it, Lilah."

"If you're not good enough—"

He points at me. "Don't do that. Don't play me. You know I'm good enough. I hacked some of the most secure systems in the world before you reeled me in. If I do this, I do it for you, but you better really need this."

"I really need this."

He presses fingers to his temple. "Okay. Fine. I'll do it." He turns to his computer.

I start to do the same and change my mind. "Actually. One thing I really need right away."

"If you want me to write a personnel review for you while I'm in the system, I'll do it, but you won't like it."

"My attitude doesn't suit you, Lucas," I snap, getting back to business. "There's a Barnes & Noble in Westbury, Long Island. Can you find out if they have cameras in the stores? If they do, can you download the feed for the cash registers for the past twenty-four hours for me?"

"That's a piece of cake if they have cameras online. What are you looking for? Does the killer turn books into a deadly weapon?"

"Ha ha," I say, ready to shake his attitude and him with it. "Not really funny." I turn away.

"It was funny," he says, giving his attention to his keyboard. "I'm ordering us lunch online from my favorite spot up the road. Then I'll start with Barnes & Noble."

I pull a cord from my case and connect it to my phone, downloading the photos that I took at my father's office. I start tabbing through them when my phone rings. I note my brother's number and hit Decline. I return my attention to the photos that look to be city business receipts and nothing out of the ordinary. My phone buzzes with a text. I glance down to find my brother again.

Did you hear that Kane filed a lawsuit against the NYPD and the NYC bureau? he asks.

I sigh and call him. "Yes," I say, replying to his text message. "I heard, and I wasn't surprised. I told you. You don't embarrass a powerful man like him and not expect the same lashing you gave him and his reputation. The good news in this is that those idiots are out of the picture. I was given the authority to claim jurisdiction of the local murders or walk away."

"And?" he prods.

"And we'll talk, but not on the phone and not now. I have important shit I'm doing."

"Now, Lilah."

"Not going to happen, big brother, but I love you. Call you in a few hours." I hang up.

"I love you?" Lucas asks incredulously.

"He expected 'fuck you' so every time I say 'I love you,' he gets all flustered."

"You're evil."

"Yeah, but *I do* love him."

My phone buzzes with a text, and I read it with a laugh before rereading it to Lucas: Fuck you, Lilah, and I love you, too, but you are not escaping this today. I will hunt you down and lock you in a cell until this is done if I have to. I glance at Lucas. "See. He loves me, too."

"Yeah," he says. "Love. Overflowing." He changes the subject. "Check your personal e-mail. I just sent you a list of every book bought in Barnes & Noble in the past forty-eight hours. I know you said twenty-four, but I'm an overachiever."

"You rock," I say, pulling up my e-mail. A few minutes later I've imported the list into a spreadsheet and sorted alphabetically. And there it is: my mother's biography, purchased yesterday afternoon. As if the killer expected me and was just waiting for my arrival.

I roll my chair to face Lucas. "Did the bookstore have active security cameras?"

He hands me a flash drive, and I slip it into my Mac. I tab to the time stamp I need, and a man in sunglasses and a baseball cap catches my attention. He walks to the register and checks out, but it's impossible to tell what he's purchasing from this camera angle, but I check the time. That transaction is exactly when my mother's biography was purchased. It's not absolute confirmation that this is Suthers's killer. However, outside of who bought the book and killed Suthers, the timing of the book purchase tells me that my move had been anticipated and he was being killed.

That sends my mind to my call to the DMV, and damn it, I hate the idea that after all I did to protect Suthers, I may well have triggered some kind of alarm. But the book was purchased before that call. Suthers was already marked to die. "Don't let it fuck with your head, Lilah," I murmur, repeating Kane's words.

"What?" Lucas asks.

"Nothing," I say. "I talk to myself. You didn't know that?"

"No. Thus far until now, when you're with me, you talk to me, not yourself. But don't talk to me or you right now. I'm focusing." He turns back to his work.

I screenshot the photo and text it to Kane: Have you ever seen him before?

No, he replies. Who is he?

I reply with: Someone I picked up on a security feed at Barnes & Noble by Suthers's house. He may be no one. He may be the killer. I'll explain later.

Because you're with Lucas, he says, and I can almost hear the disapproval in his voice through that typed message.

I purse my lips and type: Who's a hacking genius.

So genius you had to save his ass from jail.

I could remind him that Lucas was set up by a rival hacker, but I'm not sure that helps his case in Kane's eyes, or really in mine either. And since I don't like to fight battles I'll lose, I just don't reply. I return my gaze to the security footage and expand the image, and freeze-frame the man's face, a large scar now visible down his cheek. This is the killer, and as I hunt him he taunts me, only now the taunts are turning bloody. My gaze jerks to Lucas with a bad thought. What happens when the taunts get bloody and personal, too? And that leads me to follow that question with another: Is hanging out here with him putting him on the radar of the wrong people?

CHAPTER TWENTY-ONE

I dial Kane. "I need something."

"I'm available. When and where?"

"Stop."

"It sounds like you just told me to start."

"I need you to put a man on Lucas and make sure he stays safe."

"Let me get this straight. You want me to protect a man who I dislike and who wants to fuck you?"

"Yes. I'll explain later."

"At my house."

"Kane, damn it—"

"I'll do it and you owe me, Lilah Love."

I hang up on the asshole and his "owe me" shit.

"Lunch is served," Lucas declares from the doorway, walking toward me with a paper bag in his hand, the smell of food traveling with him, but nothing my nose can identify, which must mean it's not pizza, Cheetos, or chocolate. I doubt that I'm going to approve. "Lunch is served," he says again, reclaiming his seat and handing me a bottle of water, followed by a Styrofoam box.

I set the water down and move my MacBook over to open the box and glance inside. "Grilled fish and vegetables? Really?"

"Really," he says, opening his lid, too. "You eat like shit. This is brain food."

"Chocolate and coffee is brain food."

"Eat it anyway."

I grimace but take a bite of the fish, which is edible and hopefully forgettable. I pull back up the security footage, and by the time I'm done eating, I've decided the dude with the scar is my man. I glance over at Lucas. "Do you have the ability to access facial recognition software?"

He glances over at me. "You're out of luck on that one." He returns to his work.

"How is it going?"

"Better if you weren't talking."

I return to my computer screen and decide this man could be the assassin. I have to find out who he is before he kills again. I log into the FBI message system, where I direct a message to Tic Tac: Hello?

He replies right away: Hello.

I load the photo into a message and type: I need you to run facial recognition on this photo.

Give me fifteen minutes, he replies.

I downsize the screen and reload the photos I took at my father's house, looking at personal investment statements, various town documents that amount to nothing but lawn care and a Christmas parade. Page after page, I dig for anything out of the ordinary, but this was a long shot anyway. My father is too smart to keep anything compromising in a place that might be searched. It hits me that he hasn't called me to bitch me out for taking his booze, but it's coming. Of course it's coming. My messages buzz, and I pull up the direct-message box to read: No hit. His face is not visible enough.

"Damn it," I murmur, downsizing the screen and glancing at a text message from Rich:

Just got to LaGuardia airport in NYC but won't be back until late.

I need to reply, but with Rich it's a delicate balance of leading him on, being civil, and being a bitch. I settle on keeping it simple: Let me know when you land in LA.

He replies with: Will do and be careful, Lilah.

"Jackpot over here," Lucas say, drawing my attention. "I'm in the Suffolk County database and pulling the Rick Suthers file now." He glances over at me. "Two of these cases are from Los Angeles. You can't get those files on your own?"

"I don't know who is dirty or what data they might keep from me. So no. I can't get it on my own." I scoot close to him to watch him work. He stops keying and looks over his shoulder. "Go away."

"Okay. Fine. I will be right over here." I scoot back to the spot in front of my computer. "Right here." He ignores me. I tab through more of my father's documents and stop on a few random scribbled numbers on a piece of paper. I dial the first one. "Pizza Jacks."

"Fuck me! Oh." I hang up and ignore Lucas's glare.

I dial the next number and it's a female. "Hello."

"Hello," I say. "I'm calling on behalf of Lucas Davenport about your investments."

Lucas rolls his chair around to face me. "What are you doing?" he whispers fiercely.

I turn to face him and hold up a hand. "Is there a problem?" the woman asks.

"No problem," I say. "I just need to confirm some numbers." I reach over and grab papers and flop around by the phone. "Oh, hmm. I can't seem to find your last name. I just had it."

"Becker. Sue Becker."

"Right. Huh. Well, Sue, you aren't the person I meant to call at all. I feel like a fool."

"Oh, don't worry about it. We all have those moments. What was your name again?"

"Roberta," I say. "I'm new, so please, if you don't mind, don't tell Lucas I screwed up."

"Of course. Not a problem. Have a better day now, Roberta."

I hang up and look at Lucas, who is glaring at me. "Tell me about Sue."

"How and why did you just call her?" he demands.

"I found her number on my father's desk, but there was no name. You invest for this entire stinking-rich town. It was a good gamble that you invest for her. Who is she?"

"Thirty-five. Pretty. Fake nice. The kind you know will turn into a bitch once you date her. She's the new town manager under your father and the daughter of Martin Becker, a New York senator."

"That sounds positively uninteresting," I say.

He hands me a new document drive. "There's your file, but it doesn't look fully updated yet."

"The murder was last night."

"The murder was last night," he repeats. "You say that like it's, 'Oh, the dinner party was last night.'"

"Dead bodies are my thing," I say.

"You are a freak, Lilah."

"Okay, but can you actually cross-reference all these cases to look for matching names and data, or do I have to manually do it all? Because I just did a project that way last night, and it was hell."

"I can," he says, "but I need to build a program to do it. Which cases do you want next?"

"New York City."

"Which will be the most well protected. This is going to take a while."

"On television they just punch keys and pull it up."

"So you can either get one of those actors to do this for you, or I can build a back door and protect us before I go in."

I tilt my head and frown. "Why are you so testy? You're never like this. I'm the bitch. You're the nice guy."

"Because I am," he says, turning away from me.

I study his profile for a moment, or more like ten, frowning as I turn away. Hacking must be messing with his head, and his nerves are making me nervous. I force myself to refocus on my work, inserting the document drive. For the next few hours, I study that file and the ones that follow, looking for clues and scribbling down notes, researching every book, movie, record album, and CD listed as a potential clue, but I end up in a corner of dead ends.

Lucas has finally moved on to creating a database for me when Kane sends me a text: Walk away from Lucas and call me.

That doesn't sound good, I think. I stand up. "I need to call my boss and get some fresh air."

Lucas nods but doesn't look up. Anxious to find out what this is about, I hurry out of the room and down the stairs, then make my way to the backyard. Once I've shut myself outside and plopped down on the diving board, I call Kane. "What's wrong?"

"My guy connected the overseas money from Ying Entertainment back to Wilkens Capital, a big hedge fund group out of New York City."

"Have you pulled the client list?"

"Yes, but the owner, Red Wilkens, is known to do off-books deals. He was even investigated by the FBI last year and came out of it squeaky clean."

"And I have reason to believe that the FBI is covering for Pocher's political recruits."

"They are," he says. "Which is why I'm going to have to have a friendly chat with Red, one-on-one, in the near future."

"I assume rope and a chair are involved," I say. "And don't reply to that. I don't want to know."

"We do what we have to, beautiful."

"Jesus, Kane. Shut up. I can't hear that shit. And at this point, I don't have to be a profiler to look to Pocher as the person pulling the assassin's strings. He has one political agenda after another and a connection to my mother, and Laney Suthers had a client list of powerful men that could have included him or any of the politicians he supports."

"Pocher is too smart to pull the strings himself. He'd work through someone else who might not even know it's him."

"There's a way to get to him, and I'm going to find it. Have you seen the actual client list for the hedge fund? Do we know if he's on it?"

"I have it and he's not, but as I said, Red goes off books, and often."

"I need to see that list."

"That's why I'm calling. Lucas is on that list. He does business with Red."

"Of course he does," I say. "He's the go-to guy in all of the Hamptons."

"I don't like the connection."

"What are you suggesting he's involved in? Laney's and Rick's murders? My attacks? Hiring an assassin? The blood tattoo says they're all connected."

"He's connected, Lilah."

"Then he can help us find out the link between the hedge fund and Ying Entertainment."

"Hold back until I do more research."

"I'll think about it. Right now, I need to wrap up here and go see my brother. And thanks to you and your legal action, claim jurisdiction. And with it send a message. I'm here. I'm not leaving, and come and get me. I'll be ready." I start to hang up, then add, "Protect Lucas." That's when I disconnect and intend to check the time, but the photos from my father's office are on my phone.

I start tabbing through them again and land on the page that had three phone numbers, one that I have yet to call. I punch it in, and a male voice answers, "This is Greg."

"Greg," I snap, shoving off the diving board and standing.

"Lilah," he says, sounding as surprised as I am pissed.

"What the hell is this? You have a strange number I don't know that my father has been calling?"

"Easy, Lilah."

"Don't fucking 'easy Lilah' me," I say. "What the hell is this, Greg?"

"This is my new number for the security job," he says, his voice dipping in random places and then lifting. "I didn't have cards yet at the party. Your father wanted it for some political fund-raiser."

That dip and lift is what he does when he's undercover and lying, which is why I hated for him to go undercover. "You're lying. I know when you're lying."

"I'm not lying. You're attacking me."

"What are you into, Greg?"

"You know me. I'm one of the good guys."

"Good guys go bad and not always because they want to. We need to meet."

"I'm on that book tour, which means Chicago right now and on to Washington." There are voices in the background. "I have to go. I'll be back in a week. Will you be there?"

It feels like a trick question, an information grab. I don't trust him. "Call me when you get back." I hit the End button and glance up to find Lucas leaning on the doorway with the glass door now open. Feeling really damn sick of everyone around me being dirty, rotten criminals, I walk toward him.

"That didn't sound good," Lucas comments, and I join him. "Want to talk about it?"

"No," I say, folding my arms in front of me. "I do not want to talk about it. In fact, the last thing I want to do is talk about it." I start to walk past him, through the gap in the door, but stop and back up, facing him again. "Aside from hacking at my request, are you dirty, dishonest, or a freak in any way that it's my business to know?"

"I've invited you to find out how freaky I am, but aside from that, you know my dirty secret. And I'm living it right now."

"Hacking is your only dirty secret?"

"Isn't that enough?"

"Yes," I say. "It is. And it feels good?"

"Yeah, Lilah. It feels good. It's an addiction, a high, an adrenaline rush that drags me to the dark side, and I don't want to come back." His lips thin. "Proof that sometimes what feels good isn't what's good for you."

He sounds angry. I'm glad he's angry. That means he has a conscience. And that conscience is exactly why I can't ask him to look into Red Wilkens. Because he has to do business with him, and if Red is dirty, and his guilt shows, *that* really could be dangerous.

"But you know all about things that are dangerous addictions," he says. "Don't you, Lilah?"

By *things* he means Kane, which I don't intend to discuss with him. Instead, I give him a half smile, but I don't say anything. Little smiles like that fuck with people. They don't know what to make of them. His brow furrows as if to prove my point, and with my success, I walk past him and head back upstairs, where I start packing up. "You're leaving?" he asks, appearing just inside the doorway.

"My brother will be hunting me down if I don't go deal with some legal issues," I say, sliding my field bag back onto my shoulder as I walk to stand in front of him. "And that would just piss me off, and you know that never ends pretty."

"I should have the program built and be able to cross-reference cases in the next few hours. You gonna come back by?"

"Based on the shit I'm about to stir up, I wouldn't count on it. But if you get any hits, text me. I might not be able to answer my phone. And if you do, I'll steal you another bottle of forty-year." I walk past him and head down the stairs.

"If you father asks me about it, I'm telling him you gave it to Kane."

Smart man, I think. Because even my father won't cross Kane.

I exit and head to the car, and once I'm inside, I start the engine, the war to claim jurisdiction I'm about to have with my brother on my mind, right along with the case files I've spent hours studying. Lucas's words replay in my mind: *It's an addiction, a high, an adrenaline rush that drags me to the dark side, and I don't want to come back.* The assassin is methodical. Practiced. This is a job to him. It doesn't even feel like a high, but it has to be done and done perfectly. After all, that's his reputation. He has shown that skill with every kill.

But the person who hired him, who ordered every victim to be undressed and humiliated, enjoys every kill. That person is emotional. That person will make mistakes, expose themselves if the right buttons are pushed. Maybe that person is Pocher. Maybe it's not. Whatever the case, that person hates me enough to taunt me or fears me enough to try to scare me away; either way, it's clear: I'm the button. I'm the bait in a trap I need to set.

CHAPTER TWENTY-TWO

It's six o'clock when I park in front of the police station and kill the engine. I reach for the door, but my gaze catches on my front window, where days ago I could easily expect to find a note from Junior. Junior's taunts lead me to another darker place: the growing body count. As of now it stands at two in Los Angeles, one here in East Hampton, one in New York, Woods, and—if this is all connected, and it is—Laney and Rick Suthers as well. Maybe even the two Romanos who had their heads chopped off. That's nine dead, but I can't connect those cases for my brother as they connect for me without circling back to my attack. In other words, I won't be connecting those dots for Andrew.

I pocket my keys and exit the car, walking to my trunk and opening it before tossing my field bag inside. It has too much of the data Lucas provided me with to risk it being picked up or nosed around in. I shut the trunk, glance down at my pink silk blouse, and decide I actually like it even though pink really isn't my thing. But it's girlie, sweet, and should remind my brother that I'm his little sister in need of love and support. And his understanding. The black slacks and jacket say I'm a professional. It's a good combination. I snort. Who am I kidding? He doesn't believe I'm sweet and in need of love; we're going to duke it out.

I hurry forward and enter the front door of the building to find the lobby the same as I remember it: a row of cushioned waiting chairs to the left and right, with a couple of tables set randomly here and there. The now receptionist-free front desk sits center stage, already cleared for the day. I walk past it and to the right, passing several closed offices on my way to the corner office, its door open and a male voice lifting from inside.

I step inside the archway to find my brother's asshole married-to-my-ex–best friend, pretending-to-be-family-when-he's-fucking-not second-in-charge, Eddie, leaning on the wall beside my brother's desk. My brother is behind his desk, feet kicked up on top. "Lilah," Andrew says, lowering his feet and straightening.

"Ready to go home?" Eddie asks.

I decide I'm not in the mood for an argument or a fight. This just needs to be over. "I'm claiming jurisdiction," I say, ignoring the asshole and focusing on my brother. "I've linked two LA murders, one New York murder, and your case together. Consider this official FBI notification, and there will be paperwork submitted through the LA office by morning." I turn away, but before I take a step, Eddie spouts off.

"Your power trip is going to fuck this town," he declares. "Make Woods the guy or fuck your town and your family."

I turn around to face him. "I can't 'make Woods the guy' if he's not the guy. And we all know he's not. Do your duty, uphold our oath for justice to be served, no injustice for convenience." I look at Andrew. "Be the man I know you to be, not the one you're being made into." This time when I turn away, I don't stop walking. I charge down the hallway, and I don't stop until I'm at my car door.

"Running again?"

At the sound of Eddie's voice, I laugh and face him. "More like giving you room to lick your wounds before I give you another lashing."

By the time I finish that statement, he's standing in front of me. "Go back to LA, Lilah."

"When I catch my killer, I will, so I suggest you start cooperating and help me."

"Don't be a bitch and a fool. Stick to being just a bitch."

I narrow my eyes on him, his agitation outside what is reasonable. I lower my voice, soften it. "Talk to me, Eddie. What are you afraid of?"

"I'm not afraid, but you should be."

"And now you threaten me. Okay. Go on back to your office." I turn away, and he grabs my arm. I whirl around, lift my arm, and shove my elbow to his face, stopping short of knocking the shit out of him. "That could have hurt. Let go of me and don't touch me again."

"Eddie!"

At the sound of my brother's voice, Eddie glares at me but releases me. He backs up and turns away, walking toward his fancy bright-blue sports car that he no doubt bought with Alexandra's money. My brother heads down the steps and joins me, leaning on the car, his booted feet crossed at the ankle, his arms folded in front of him. Relaxed because it's me but guarded because he's a part of this cover-up. And that makes me sick to my stomach.

I turn and mimic his position, and we both watch Eddie pull out of the parking lot. "He's afraid of something," I say. "Are you?"

He glances over at me. "The Love family isn't known for fear."

I push off the car and face him. "Letting Woods fall for this is wrong. And the brother I know would never let that happen. What aren't you telling me?"

"I have political pressure. I admit that." He unfolds his arms and presses his hands to the car on either side of him. "And if you don't understand that, talk to your boss. He will."

"Politics isn't what law enforcement is about."

"Again. Talk to your boss. Make that statement to him and see if he agrees. And do you have any leads on someone other than Woods?"

My lips thin with my unwillingness to share details with him, my own brother, someone I have always trusted. "Is Dad the reason why you're doing this? Is he the one pressuring you?"

"So you don't have a lead outside of Woods. Walk away, Lilah."

"In other words, let a killer kill again. I don't even know you." I walk to my door and open it.

He is immediately at the window on the other side, holding it open. "You do know me," he says, "and that's why I'm asking you to trust me and do this."

"And what happens when another body shows up?" I ask him and not for the first time.

"There won't be another body."

"And you know this how?"

"Because Woods is dead."

"The cover-up is done, you mean." I settle into the car and yank at the door. He holds it against my will at first, but with my second tug, he releases it. I start my engine and back up, heading out of the parking lot, more determined than ever to stop the corrupt sickness overtaking this town and my family.

Once I pull onto the road, I head toward Kane's rental house, where the local victim died, and dial Murphy. "It's done," I say when he answers. "Do I need to make contact with the NYPD, or do the politics of this require you make contact?"

"They were put on notice this morning after my conference call. I'll have paperwork faxed to them and your brother. How did he take it?"

"Like a regular champ," I say.

"That bad, huh?"

"It's handled."

"Any regrets about sending your backup back to me?"

"None. Rich is better off there. And I'm better off with him there."

"Where are you in the investigation?"

"Do you know of an assassin with a scar down his face?"

"Doesn't sound familiar. Have you had Tic Tac run a search?"

"Not yet."

"I'll have him do it. Where did that question come from?"

"Anonymous tip," I lie.

"Interesting," he says. "Someone knew to call you. That means they're close enough to this to know you're involved."

"Yes. Interesting." But the call goes nowhere else interesting, except for a few more worthless comments and a skipped goodbye when it ends.

And just in time. I pull into the driveway of Kane's rental house and park, the yellow crime scene tape still on display across the door. I exit the car and walk to the porch, intent on doing what I didn't do the night of the murder: search every inch of this place myself. I start right where I stand, walking over the porch, looking for scrapes or footsteps, before searching the outdoor furniture and even the exterior wood panels. Looking for something, anything that might have been missed by the crew, intentionally or unintentionally.

I head back down the steps and do a slow walk around the front bushes, and then do both sides of the house, which leads me to the backyard, which is now cast in the shadows of dusk. The back door is my ultimate destination, and I rip more crime scene tape away before trying the knob, which is, of course, locked. A problem I should have anticipated, but I'm here now, I need to catch a killer, and I'm going with the flow. And since that flow does not include having my brother or Eddie swoop in and breathe down my neck while I work, I'm not calling them for a key. I grab a brick lining the base of a funky-looking bush and break the glass panel beside the door. I toss the brick and then reach inside, unlock the door, and open it. Kane can buy a new window.

Entering what is, of course, a stunning kitchen, since Kane owns the property, I glance around the room that is teal and gray with a stainless steel–topped island that is rather industrial. The crime scene is processed, and gloves are not officially necessary, but I reach into my field bag and grab a pair anyway. Once I've pulled them on, I relock the door, my intent being to slow down anyone who might want to surprise me and force them to reach through the broken window to enter. My phone buzzes with a text, but for now I ignore it out of caution. I do a quick sweep of the entire house, including the garage, to ensure I'm alone. The good news is that aside from the items taken in the first search, which from the paperwork I reviewed today amounted to not much, everything is intact. I return to the kitchen, double-check the door, and then grab my phone and look at the message, which is from Tic Tac: Nothing in our database about a known assassin with a scar on his face, but I'm going to dive into closed chat rooms on the dark net. See what I can find.

I don't reply. I'm gloved and focused on searching every inch of everything, with an agenda: Why was this woman on the hit list of the assassin? Who did she cross? What does she have in common with the other victims? Does she have any connection to Pocher at all? I look in canisters. I look in drawers. I look in the freezer, which is a remarkably common hiding place, as are cereal boxes. Once I've declared it a room useless to my goal, the house is fading into darkness, and I have no choice but to turn on lights that could be noticed by someone else. I don't want to do that at this point, but I'm here. I'm going to get this done.

I walk into the living room and to the table where Cynthia was found lying naked, dead, and with a bullet between her eyes. The room is draped in shadows, and my desire to turn on a light and announce my presence to a killer or an asshole like Eddie, who will surely get in the way of my work, is pretty close to zero. I glance at the heavy, closed curtains and decide my risk of being discovered is low, but I choose a small lamp as my lighting. I spend the next fifteen minutes moving about the room, standing in the exact spot where the body was found. And for the first time since these murders began, I'm alone, on the scene, and able to dig deeper into what took place.

I return to the table and stare down at it, picturing her body, the bullet hole. Cynthia was a pretty woman who could have tempted a criminal to use her for pleasure before she was killed. But the autopsy concluded that the killer didn't rape her, at least not physically, suggesting a person of methodical control. He made her undress, though, since we know she didn't have her clothes on when she was killed. So he watched her undress. She would have thought that she was going to be raped. I wonder if she cried, if she begged? Or was she defiant, as I would be? I think back to my attack, to that man on top of me, and I can almost feel his hands on my breasts. I couldn't be defiant. I was too drugged. I don't even remember how I got undressed. I pant out a breath and open my eyes. "Damn it."

I refocus on the table and walk to the spot I believe she was standing when she fell. The spot where she undressed, and I wonder if the killer took a video of it all for the person, or persons, who hired him. I walk to the location where I believe he would have stood to watch her, to shoot her. I search the surrounding area but find nothing of interest before standing in his spot again. Would he have used his phone to record her fear? No. I don't think so. That would be too easily documented. He'd use a separate device and deliver the footage without an electronic fingerprint. He's proven from the cleanness of the crime scenes that he's too good to do anything else. I consider recent purchases of cameras and recorders, but the murders are spread out, and the camera most likely traveled with him.

I finish in this room, flip out the light, and use the flashlight in my bag to guide me to the most personal space in any house: the master bedroom. The curtains are equally heavy in this room, and I flip on a bedside light. I search the room, up one side and down the other. Drawers, jacket pockets, jewelry box, bathroom cabinets. I'm about to give up when my gaze catches on the lamp on the far nightstand that I've left dark. Something is dangling beside the cord used to turn it on. I walk to it and catch the pendant in my hand, opening my palm to stare down at the Virgin Mary. And there it is, the proof that links Rick Suthers's murder to two of the assassin's victims: two with a necklace and one with a tattoo of the Virgin Mary. It also connects these murders to my attacker.

"Holy Mother of Jesus," I murmur, my certainty that I'm dealing with a cult of some sort officially solidified.

I grab the necklace and drop it into a baggie before sticking it in my field bag. My cell phone rings, and I pull it from my pocket and glance at my brother's number. I hit Decline and stick my phone back in my pocket. It buzzes with another call. I grimace and grab it again, and this time it's my father. I decline again at the same moment my brother sends me a text: Answer. It's important. I will keep calling.

My phone rings again, and I believe him. He'll keep calling. And so I accept the damn call. "I answered," I say. "Now what?"

"Dad needs to see you."

"I don't—"

"It's important. You need to hear what he has to say. This is necessary, Lilah."

Necessary. It's an odd choice of word. "At the house?"

"No. He's at Mom's grave."

CHAPTER TWENTY-THREE

Dread isn't my thing. I don't find it to be a useful emotion, any more than I do fear. Both lead to over-the-top, irrational reactions to situations and people. Irrationality leads to mistakes, and mistakes get you killed. But as I pull up to the cemetery and park next to my father's silver Mercedes, dread is a beast that refuses to be ignored, settling hard in my gut. Maybe there is even some fear. I suspect my mother was killed, and my father wants to meet at her gravesite to talk.

I kill the engine and exit the car, pocketing my keys. The cemetery is well lit, poles with lanternlike tops placed in random locations. My father is standing with his back to me, looking down at my mother's grave. A willow tree, my mother's favorite, is draped above him, shading the plot when there is sun rather than newly minted stars and a half moon. I walk toward him and he doesn't turn, but of course he knows I'm here, and I wonder if he's fighting that same beast of dread that I am. That's all the more reason to get this the hell out of the way.

That thought steps up my pace, and I claim a spot next to him. "She was the sunshine in every room she entered," he says.

"Yes," I say. "She was." But as hard as I try to picture her smile and her laugh with those words, I cannot, and it's moments like these that do indeed create fear. So really, I lied to myself when I said I have no use for fear. I clearly do. Just not about things that go bump in the night or monsters who live under the bed or on the next street corner.

"She knew I had political aspirations beyond this town," he continues, the jump from sentiment to his drive for power proof that the sentiment was all about manipulation. "She supported me," he adds, turning to face me.

"I have no doubt that she supported you," I say, facing him, my gaze flicking over his neatly groomed salt-and-pepper hair and the navy-blue pinstripe suit that is no doubt worth a cool ten grand, money that he inherited from my mother.

"She would have told you to support me," he adds.

"She would never have supported an innocent man taking the fall for these murders. And that's what this is about, right? Me keeping this case open and hurting your record?"

A muscle in his jaw flexes. "The stakes are far higher than your little FBI job and a few murders."

"A few murders?" I demand. "Five assassinations. Five lives taken."

"There is a bigger picture," he bites out. "I was selected, and subsequently groomed, for this run for office years ago by what some call the Deep State or the Society. They are the real rulers of the world. And yes, I said *world*. Our government, and many across the world, are set up to be the face of those who are really in power."

"Who are they?" I ask, now faced with a version of a cult as I'd suspected. I just didn't think my damn father would be involved.

"I can't tell you that," he replies. "I won't ever tell you that. You don't expose these people. And you don't ignore their wishes without paying a price. I cannot dirty my record or they will not be pleased."

"What the hell are you spouting, Father? This is insanity."

"Call it what you will, but this is how it is, Lilah. They control all of us, but some of us know they have that control. *We* know because I am part of that inner circle."

"Is Andrew in that circle?"

"He knows enough not to cross them."

"That's not an answer. Did Mom know about this Society?"

"Yes. They are deeply rooted in Hollywood. They are deeply rooted with anyone who has the kind of money that equates to power."

"And Pocher heads this Society?"

"There is no one person who heads the Society, though there are heads of counsel."

"But Pocher is involved," I press.

"I'm involved," he says. "That's all you need to know. And you will not speak about this to anyone. Do not look for the Society, or they will kill you. And do not become a problem for them, or they will come for you."

I know then. I know who attacked me. "They already came for me. They had me raped."

His eyes flicker with something I cannot name, but rather than the fury I expect to follow, he simply asks, "When?"

"When? *When?* Right before I left for LA. I was raped. That is what you're endorsing. People who do bad things to people you love."

That something in his eyes flares again before his jaw sets hard and his spine straightens. "You don't know it was them."

"That's what you're going to say to me?" I demand incredulously. "I don't know it's them? I just told you I was attacked and raped."

He steps to me and grabs my arm, pulling me to him. "Rape doesn't kill you, little girl. That is what you need to understand. These are dangerous people. They *will* kill you. I'm trying to keep you alive."

"Like they killed my mother."

"Your mother died in a plane crash. Don't start creating conspiracy theories that will get you killed. Shut the damn case and then go back to LA before you piss someone off other than me." He releases me and starts walking, calling out, "And you owe me a forty-year single malt."

I owe him a bottle of booze. I told him I was raped, and that's how he ends this conversation. I watch him settle into his car and drive away. I stand there, watching long after he's gone, and I can feel myself trembling, a surge of anger just beneath the surface. I whirl around to my mother's grave and stare at the headstone, her absence in this moment cutting me to the point that I might just bleed. I am about to drop to my knees in front of the plot when the sensation of being watched overcomes me.

My gaze lifts to the cemetery and reaches wide, landing on the road that divides parts of the grassy area to find him: the man with the scar is standing next to a pickup truck. The idea that he is here to support my father and threaten me is a trigger. I snap. I pull my gun and start walking toward him, navigating a path of headstones and graves. He stands there as if he might actually let me confront him for a good sixty seconds before he moves abruptly, gets in his truck, and leaves. I run after the truck, trying to catch a glimpse of the plate, but he's already too far ahead.

I turn away and start along another path through the sea of dead-and-buried bodies and return to my mother's grave. I stand above it, thinking about my father's claim that she knew about the Society. She couldn't have been a part of this Society. Or maybe she knew and she got in the way, just like me. Everyone in my life is corrupt. Everyone. Even Kane, but at least I knew that, at least I understand who and what he is, unless . . . *Oh God.* Is Kane a part of it? I shake my head: no. He can't be. Pocher is his enemy, but I have to know for sure, and when I look into that man's eyes, I'll know.

And if he's betrayed me, too, the snap of moments before will be nothing. Adrenaline surges through me, and I dial Kane. "Where are you?" I demand when he answers.

"At home."

"I'm coming there," I say, hanging up and dialing Murphy.

"Agent Love," he greets.

"You need to know that I'm going to Kane Mendez's house, and I'm either going to kill him, fuck him, or arrest him. This stands as my confession if I kill him." He starts laughing, and I snarl back at him, "Are you seriously laughing?"

"Yes," he says. "I am. For the record, I don't believe you will kill Kane, I don't care who you fuck, and don't arrest him. He's too big of a resource, which you'll figure out at some point. Just remember. Your enemy's enemy is your friend, and everyone is Kane's enemy but you."

I have no idea what nonsense this man is spouting. "I'm hanging up on you," I say, "and I'm only giving you the courtesy of telling you because you're my boss." I disconnect and walk to the car, climbing inside before cranking the engine and heading toward Kane's house.

CHAPTER TWENTY-FOUR

Within fifteen minutes of leaving the cemetery, I'm at Kane's house, and before I can key in the gate code, it opens, which tells me that Kane is watching for me. I park in the driveway, and when I get out of the car, I remove my jacket and toss it inside. My gun and my badge stay on my waistband. I walk to the front door, and it opens. Kane is standing there in faded jeans and a black T-shirt, looking like a tall, dark drink of that forty-year whiskey I will never replace for my father and that I could easily get drunk on. Or a tall, dark drink of deception that is going to hurt before this is over. We're both about to find out which.

I walk toward him, and he backs up to allow me to enter, but I crowd him, pressing my hand to his chest, and he lets me walk him backward to shove him against the wall. I kick the door shut, and my fingers curl around his shirt. "Did you know?" I demand.

"Know what, Lilah?"

"*Did you* know?"

"Explain what the hell you're talking about."

"Because you aren't going to admit anything you don't have to admit, right?"

"I don't lie to you, Lilah. Tell me—"

"The Society," I bite out. "Did you know about the Society?"

His eyes flicker ever so slightly, and it tells me all I need to know. I pull my gun and point it at him. "I told you that the next time I pulled this on you I would shoot you, and this is that time."

"Okay, beautiful. Easy."

"Easy is like 'calm down,' and for a smart man, you are once again proving you're not so smart. You don't tell an angry person to calm the fuck down. You betrayed me."

"No," he says. "I would not, and have not, betrayed you. I know about the Society. *Of course* I know about the Society. And yes, I have suspected they were involved in your attack but failed to prove that to be the case."

"Well, they are. My father is a part of it. He knows who they are. He knows what they are and he doesn't care."

"How do you know this, Lilah?"

"He told me, and I told him they raped me, and he said it's better than killing me."

"Fuck," he breathes out, reaching for the gun and covering it with his hand. "Let me have it."

"No. I will not." My hand trembles, and Kane uses that sign of weakness to take my gun, but I let him.

And in true Kane form, he doesn't keep it. He shoves it into my holster, and then cups the back of my head, pulling me to him. "You can shoot me later."

"But I want to shoot somebody," I confess.

"I'd prefer it not be me," he says. "And I'd kiss you right now, but I told you that the next time—"

I push to my toes and press my lips to his, and that is all the encouragement he needs. His mouth slants over mine, his tongue licking against mine, and I moan and sink into the kiss. Let it consume me the way he consumes me. It's what I need. The escape, the inability to see and feel anything but the moment and this man. I don't even care if it's right or wrong. And when he pulls back, breathing with me, I don't want to breathe. I want that feeling of not being able to breathe, and I press my lips back to his, my hand sliding under his shirt, shoving up his body until his mouth parts mine again and he yanks the shirt over his head. I do the same, pulling the damn pink silk blouse over my head and tossing it, followed by my bra.

Kane's gaze darkens, and he gives me one of those animalistic once-overs that tells me I've affected him. That I have control, not him, and that's what I fucking need right along with the escape. Control. He drags me to him, fingers tangling in my hair, hand on my breast, even as his mouth is back on mine. There is this wildness between us, and I could say it's forbidden, but it's not. It's just how we are together, but this time there is a desperation that doesn't feel like it's all me.

He lifts me, and my legs wrap his hips, my fingers diving into his hair, but when he starts toward the stairs and his bedroom, I pull back. "Not the bedroom."

"Sorry, beautiful. I'm not stopping. Punish me if you like, but wait until you're naked."

I pant out a breath, my fingers digging into his shoulders, my awareness of what he's trying to do more than certain. He wants me in his bed, which I know he equates to some sort of ownership. But he keeps charging upward, and I just want out of my own head. My cell phone rings, and that is enough to have my lips press to his again. I want out of the world that I'm living inside and into the one I used to live inside with Kane. He enters his bedroom, walking across the gray-tiled floor and up the steps that lead to his bed. I release my legs, forcing him to let go of me, and when I would step back, he shackles my hips.

"To be clear, Lilah," he says. "No one else has been in my bed since you left."

"So you fucked Samantha downstairs."

His hand is suddenly behind my neck, and he drags my mouth to his. "Samantha—"

"Was a fuck," I say. "Or ten. Or however many. I get it. Stop talking and just fuck me already." I reach for his pants, and while he kisses me, I touch him in every way I know he wants to be touched, in all those ways that makes me the one in control.

"Undress," he orders, setting me away from him.

"You first," I order, and when my damn phone rings again, I pull it from my pocket and throw it across the room. I look at him again, and suddenly there is no "him first" or "me first." There is just now. I need us both naked *now*. "I'm tired of waiting," I say. "Together."

He gives a nod, and that is exactly what we do. We strip together and I finish first, waiting on him, and when I have the opportunity, I shove him back onto the mattress. But I don't get the upper hand on Kane. He pulls me with him, and when I fully intend to climb on him and ride him, he rolls me over and settles on top of me. "Do you hate me now, Lilah?"

"At present, the potential of an orgasm exists, so no. I do not. If you fail in that department, yes. I will fucking hate you all over again."

"I didn't ask last week, but you can't—"

"I'm not going to have a baby, Kane. I still get a shot, and come on, you and me and a baby would be about as fucked up as—"

He kisses me and slides inside me, and I'm there in that place where there is nothing but him. He brushes hair from my face and whispers, "I wouldn't want you to hate me." And then he rolls us to our sides, no longer taking control but not giving it either. What he does is every little trick he ever learned about what turns me on. And that's the thing about Kane: he actually cares what turns me on. He actually knows.

It's not fast, this encounter between us. It's slow, alternated with frenzy, and then slow again, the way I need it to be. That way I stay out of my own head for as long as I possibly can, but finally, and yet too soon, I shudder to that place that is always so damn perfect just before the end. Neither of us moves for a full minute, or two, or longer. I don't know. Kane finally squeezes my ass and pulls me to him. "Now you can't hate me."

The many reasons I can't be with Kane hit me hard: He's a criminal. I'm an FBI agent. He buried a damn body without asking me. And yet

I still fucking love him. And on a day like today, I know love cuts. I need air. I need space.

"I don't hate you, Kane," I say, because that's the easiest way to explain what I feel. "Not all of the time." I roll away from him and scoot to the edge of the bed, grabbing tissues because us girls get all the mess. That's how it is. Men fuck. Women get fucking messy. I've just tossed the tissues when my phone rings again, the sound like a punch that drags me fully back into the hell that brought me here. I need out of here. I need to leave.

And that's what I say. "I need to go." But as I try to stand, Kane grabs me, and suddenly he is sitting beside me.

"You don't want to leave. I don't want you to leave. Who are you trying to please, Lilah?" He doesn't give me time to answer, adding, "And you want the answers I can now give you."

Not the one I need most right now. "I need to talk to my brother, Kane," I say, pulling against him.

He holds on. "Not now. Not in your current state of mind."

"I need to know where he stands. I need—"

"Not now. Wait until you come down from the anger and the shock."

I start to get up again.

"Lilah," Kane warns.

"I'm not going to leave." I look over at him. "But I want to get dressed."

He pulls me to him and kisses me before letting me go.

"I swore you'd never kiss me for the hell of it ever again."

"And now?"

"And now, I just want to get dressed." He inhales and lets me go, but I sense his frustration, even his anger, as if I've used him when I have not. I wish it were that simple with Kane, but it's not.

I lean in and kiss him, my lips lingering on his for a moment before I say, "And now—that." I pull back then and stand up, walking to the foot of the bed to start dressing. Kane does the same, and by the time I'm awkwardly aware that I have a badge, gun, pants, and boots on with no bra or blouse, Kane has left the room shirtless and returned, fully dressed, with my clothes in hand.

I accept them without looking at him and finish dressing, while my phone once again rings. Kane grabs it but doesn't look at the number, and when he offers it to me, he catches my hand. "Facts before conversation. There is much I can tell you about the Society that you now need to know."

"Are you part of it?"

"Absolutely not."

"Why?"

"Because I don't follow anyone else's lead. Because no one owns me, just like no one owns you, and that makes us problems for the Society. Let's go talk."

I nod. I don't ask where he wants to talk. I know.

Together we walk out of the bedroom and up another level of stairs to Kane's attic, which he had converted into an office for me: my Purgatory when I was staying with him, which before my attack was often. I enter the room, taking in the giant gray wooden desk, the chairs in a corner, whiteboards and bulletin boards covering the walls. Memories slam into me, all those nights and days I stayed in here, working, chasing killers. All the times that Kane listened to me talk through my thoughts and gave me the perspective of a man who grew up in the center of a crime family. Murphy's words come back to me: *He's a resource.* I know this. I just don't understand why Murphy knows it. What don't I know?

I walk to the desk and sit down behind it. Kane walks to one of the corner chairs and sits down. I roll around and face him. "You said you have friends in law enforcement outside of me."

"Yes," he confirms. "I do."

"Who?"

"Why?"

"Is my boss one of them?"

"No," he says. "Your boss is not one of those people."

"He knows I'm here."

He arches a brow. "Really?"

"Yes."

"And?"

"He says that the enemy of my enemies is my friend, and that you're an enemy to everyone but me. Why would he say that to me, Kane?"

"Aside from the fact that it's true, you'll have to ask him that question."

"Why didn't you tell me about the Society?"

"I told you. You don't get to die, and I know you, Lilah. You're dogmatic in an in-your-face kind of way about what you want. And I fucking love it. It works for you. It works for me, but you can't approach the Society that way."

"I don't need you to make my fucking decisions for me, Kane."

He leans forward and rests his elbows on his knees. "This isn't one killer you're going head-to-head with. This is a massive group of killers, far more powerful than me. And you ask me why I allow myself to stay aligned with the cartel? Because that cartel gives them pause. It gives me the power to punch them in the throat, even if I can't destroy them. And there are those whispers on the borders about me ordering mass killings. They work for me, and for you, because they give me a level of control and power."

I don't let myself think about the implications of what he just confessed. I focus on the enemy in front of me, against me. "My father said that they rule the world. That they are that powerful. Is that true?"

"Yes. That is true."

"And they've tried to recruit you?"

"Yes." He offers nothing more.

"Is Pocher one of them?"

"Yes."

"Damn it, Kane. He's backing my father, and you didn't tell me?"

"If you would have gone after them, and if you go after them now in the wrong way, not only will we never prove they ordered your attack, you will end up dead. So no. I did not tell you. The time was not right."

"Would you have told me?"

"Yes. I would have."

"When?"

"When you trusted me enough again to listen and not get killed."

"All right. I'll accept that answer even if I don't like it. Now tell me about the tattoo."

"I didn't lie to you, Lilah. The Blood Assassins are as provable as UFOs."

"Is there any known attachment to the Society?"

"That's what I've been trying to find out since your attack. And that brings me to Romano and what I couldn't tell you before you knew about the Society: that lead came from him directly. He was working for the Society—Pocher, he believes, though he's not a hundred percent sure. The communications were guarded. They started pressing him, taking over his operation. He pushed back."

"And?"

"And one of his men came head-to-head with a Blood Assassin. Romano's man cornered him in an attempt to make him talk. The assassin killed himself. A day later, that Romano was dead. And that Romano was the nephew of the old man."

"Holy fuck," I breathe out.

"Yes. Holy fuck. Shortly after, that anonymous tip came his way, and he needed to distance himself from it until the heat was off."

"So he gave it to me."

"Yes."

"Did he leave the clue at the beheading?"

"I asked him that and he said no, which means whoever gave him the tip must have given it to you."

"It has to be someone who really wants the Society taken down if they came to us both."

"I would agree. And if you need more to prove how low the Society will go, it's unconfirmed, but the old man believes they killed his men to cause a turf war between his people and mine, to distract us both."

"I don't know if I buy that," I say. "I believe it was the Society, but I believe it was about Woods and making the murders go away. About pushing me out to allow that to happen."

"A two-for-one, perhaps," he suggests.

"Obviously, the Virgin Mary is attached to the Society: the tattoos. The necklace in Suthers's suit, and I was just at your rental property and found a Virgin Mary necklace on Cynthia's lampshade. What do you know about that connection? Because there is one."

"Until now, there wasn't one, or I would have already connected the Blood Assassins to the Society long ago, but yes, I agree. There is a connection, but it seems too careless to be approved by the leadership. I don't believe the upper-level management would allow themselves a method of identification."

Kane's cell phone rings, and he pulls it from his pocket, frowning slightly before he answers the call. "Mendez," he says. There is a pause and he says, "When?" Another pause and, "Where?"

He says nothing else before hanging up.

"You wanted Ghost. You're about to get him. He's ready to meet."

CHAPTER TWENTY-FIVE

It's finally time to meet Ghost. Maybe, just maybe, that means I will catch myself an assassin. And maybe, just maybe, that means I can take down Pocher. "He actually agreed to meet us?"

"With conditions," Kane says.

"What conditions?"

"He's not the guy you're looking for, but he's willing to provide information. But you cannot arrest him or kill him."

"Are you one hundred percent certain he's not our guy?"

"Yes."

"Why?"

"Ghost doesn't deny his work. He's too proud of it."

"When?" I ask.

"Now," he says.

"Where?"

"Agree to the terms, Lilah," Kane presses.

"I'm going to want to kill him more than I want to arrest him," I admit, because I can with Kane. And because it's true.

"We don't always get what we want. Agree or this ends now."

"This time," I bite out.

"*Say* it."

"Jesus, Kane, you are being a prick. I won't kill him unless he's trying to kill one or both of us, and I won't arrest him." And just to be clear, I repeat, "*This time.*"

He studies me for two beats and then says, "There's a chopper waiting for us at the airport, as long as we're there in the next forty-five minutes. Otherwise it leaves without us."

"And you think getting on a chopper that Ghost provides for us is safe?"

"Ghost and I share a mutual respect, but we won't get on that chopper unarmed."

"You and an assassin have mutual respect?"

"Your enemy's enemies are your friends, Lilah. There is the Society and the rest of us, and I make damn sure to align myself with people who can be useful if needed."

"And you're not going to apologize for that, right?"

"No, Lilah, I won't. And if you'd stop judging me, we'd both be a hell of a lot happier. Because we both know every time you judge me, you're judging yourself and us."

He stands up and heads for the door. I stand up and call after him. "My badge judges us, Kane."

He turns around and faces me. "You know how to fix that."

"So it has to be me getting rid of my badge, not you getting rid of the cartel?"

"Start counting bodies. Eventually you'll decide you can't live by the rules of that badge. Until then, and after that, I'll be here. But don't wait too long, because the Society will still be here, too." He exits the room.

I follow him, intent on replying, but he's already on the phone, and it's clear he's talking to one of his men and instructing them to follow us when we leave. And now isn't the time to debate right and wrong, anyway. Right now is about staying alive and catching a killer. Maybe that's his point, though. That's what this is always about.

He enters the bedroom, with me on his heels, both of us crossing through it to enter the massive closet that is lined with his clothes, with a table and chair in the center. He reaches under the table and hits the button I know from experience is there. The mirrored back wall immediately parts, displaying a separate room.

He walks inside it, and again, I follow him to a room equally as large and lined with weapons, many of which I am certain are illegal. And yet I've always known they were here. I've always accepted they exist. He grabs a shoulder holster and buckles it into place before inserting a Glock. I'm about to reach for an ankle holster when he hands me a knife already attached to an ankle strap. "I believe you know how to use this," he says.

"Bastard," I say, accepting it.

"It's time to stop hiding from it."

"I'm going to walk away before I punch you." I turn and head for the door.

"It's okay to have enjoyed it, Lilah."

Stunned that he knows what I didn't think even he knew, I stop walking and grip the doorframe as he adds, "He deserved it."

I turn to face him, and I don't even try to deny the truth. "I know. I know he deserved it."

"Then what's the problem?"

"Have you ever enjoyed killing someone?"

"Yes. Because they *deserved it*. And you know how much guilt I feel over any of those kills? None. And do you know what I feel when I think of you shoving that knife into that man's chest? Regret because it was over so fast."

I stand there for several beats, absorbing those words, trying to justify my crime with another crime. The very thing I've just sat in another room and judged him for. I inhale and turn away from him, walking toward the bedroom, but my gaze catches on the wall of clothing to my right. *My* clothing that I had left here, that he's *kept* here. I set the knife on the table, and my gun, badge, and phone follow before I yank off my boots, then pull off the damn sweet pink blouse that feels as fake as my badge right now. I toss it to the floor and quickly change into a black T-shirt and jeans, both of which will fade into darkness if needed. I slip my small hip purse back in place, the inclusion of money, ID, and credit cards one of necessity. I've just attached the blade and holster and pulled on a pair of low-heeled boots when my cell phone rings.

I stand up and glance at the number to find Lucas calling. I answer on speaker and set it on the table. "Lucas," I say, opening a drawer under the table, and sure enough, my backup shoulder holster is still here.

"I finished the program," he says.

"And?" I prod, shrugging into the holster, glancing up to find Kane standing in the archway dividing the closet from the weapons room, listening in on the conversation.

"I came up with the hits you predicted," Lucas says. "You and Beth were on multiple cases, but there was also a lab tech with a double hit. He was on the Laney Suthers case and the recent New York City murder."

"Can you text me a name, data, and the person?"

"I can," he says, "but just so you know, he dropped dead of a heart attack three nights ago."

My gaze meets Kane's, and we share a look of understanding: the man was murdered. "All right," I say. "Text me the information anyway. What about Greg Harrison? Did you pull his file?"

Kane arches a brow at that.

"Shit," Lucas says. "I was ready to get wasted on that forty-year single malt scotch you brought me. Give me a half hour."

"If I don't answer, leave me a detailed message." I pick up the phone and end the call.

Kane is in front of me by the time I've set it back down, tugging my holster fully into place and connecting the buckle. And I let him. "A forty-year scotch?" he asks, his hands settling on his hips. "That's an expensive showing of gratitude."

"I stopped by my father's house and took it."

He laughs. "Sounds like you and serves the bastard right." He pulls a small handgun from the back of his pants and shows it to me.

"My favorite flavor of Ruger," I say of the brand, accepting it.

"And unlike your service weapon," he says, offering me another ankle holster, "it won't track back to me or you."

"Right," I say, accepting the strap. I start to turn away, and he catches my hip.

"Lilah—"

"Whatever you're going to say, don't. I get it. I'm in your world tonight, not mine."

"My world is your world."

His cell phone buzzes and his jaw flexes. "We aren't done with this conversation." He pulls his phone from his pocket and glances at the text. "My men are ready to shadow us to the airport."

I nod and squat down, strapping on the ankle holster under my boot and inserting the gun. When I stand, Kane is two feet away, shrugging into a thin brown leather jacket that, while stylish, serves a purpose. It covers his holster. I grab an equally presentable but effective thin black leather jacket and pull it on over my holster. That's when my gaze catches on my badge that I have yet to return to my belt, and Kane's words come back to me: *Your world is my world.*

Since the moment I met him, that is true, right or wrong, good or bad. I can't deny that. I've tried for two years, and here we are, which means I need to control what that means. I pick up my badge and walk to Kane. "Do I influence your actions?" I hold up the badge. "Do you think about my badge before you make decisions?"

"All the fucking time."

"Did you think about it when I was gone?"

"Yes. Because I didn't plan on staying away from you or you from me."

"Then I'm keeping the damn badge. Because you don't get to be your fucking father. I won't let you." I turn and start walking toward the door, grabbing my phone and sticking it in my pocket on the way past the table. And I can feel him wanting to pull me back, but he doesn't. He can't right now. We have an assassin waiting on us.

~

A few minutes later, Kane and I are on the road in his black Mercedes Roadster, which is a new addition to his garage. "Expensive," I say as we settle into a steady speed on the highway, "but not too expensive." I glance over at him. "Smart. A man who knows he draws attention and settles in the middle."

"I have my extravagant moments," he says. "You know that I've never cared for the spotlight. That hasn't changed."

"But you do enjoy power and control."

"I won't deny that as a truth."

"And in contrast, my father craves the spotlight. That made him a target for those people, didn't it?"

"Yes. And because of that hunger in him, like many political figures, he will look like he has power and control, but he will be controlled, submissive even."

"I can't save him, can I?"

"No. You can't save him."

"Could you have? At any point, could you have saved him?"

"You could theorize that I could have, had I found out before he dived in headfirst, but as you said, he wants the spotlight, and to some, that's a drug that makes them addicts."

"I searched his office at his house. I found a number with no name. I called it and Greg answered."

"And?"

"He said he's doing contract security right now and he gave his new number to my father for potential work."

"Sounds like a bad lie to me."

"A lie that he stumbled over," I say. "And I told you, I all but saw him spoon a Romano, when a Romano bust is what supposedly got him in trouble. I'd like to think he's just trying to clear his name, but the connection to my father has me thinking he's one big fucking lying, cheating loser." That thought pisses me off, and I grab my phone and dial Lucas on speaker again.

"Fuck, Lilah," he groans, and then slurs his words. "You're an impatient hussy bitch."

"Yeah. I know you love me. What about Greg Harrison?"

"He has an open IA case, but the record is blank."

My brow furrows. "Blank?"

"Yes. Blank. As in there is a record, but it's blank."

"Smart-ass," I snap. "Obviously you're too drunk to do this now. Call me tomorrow."

"I could hack the United States of America ten times more sloshed than I am right now. The record is blank. I'm not going to call you tomorrow to tell you the same thing."

"When did he leave his job?" I ask.

"No documented resignation or termination."

And yet Greg told me he quit. I'd have Lucas check for an update tomorrow, but it's too dangerous, and I can find out this part of the equation through Murphy. Kane pulls us into the airport. "Go drink, Lucas. Celebrate your greatness. Call a woman who isn't me and get drunk with her. The booze is on my father."

"What? Oh fuck. Is this your father's booze?"

He's drunk and can't remember shit. I hang up on him.

"Sounds like Greg made a deal," Kane says, parking us near the door and under a light, no accident I am certain.

"The question is with who?"

"I know how to find out," he offers.

"How?"

"A chair and some rope."

"If you were anyone else, I'd think that was a joke. But you're you, so I'm saying this as if it needs to be said because apparently it does. No chair. No rope."

"For him or for you?"

"Kane—"

"You can think about both or give me a wink and I'll think about it." He glances at his watch. "Time to go meet Ghost." He reaches for his door, and I do the same, and together we walk into the building.

"Now what?" I ask.

He indicates a blank sign by a door, and we walk that direction, exiting to a private strip of the airway at the same moment that a chopper appears in the near distance, heading our direction. "You're sure about this?" I ask.

"If I wasn't, you wouldn't be going with me."

"And yet you had me arm myself with an unregistered gun and a knife."

"If I wasn't cautious, you wouldn't be with me either."

I don't really want to think about what kind of deal Kane has made with an assassin to feel safe with him. Or how much business he might have done with him to create loyalty, and now isn't the time to ask for details that might piss me off. The chopper comes in for landing, the sound roaring in my ears, the blades lifting my hair from my neck. The minute the blades hover just above pavement, Kane's hand settles at my spine and urges me forward. We hurry toward the small industrial aircraft, and there won't be staff or steps to aid our boarding.

Kane opens the door and holds up a finger, indicating he wants me to wait, and once he has my nod, he climbs inside, and I watch him move to the front where he leans toward the pilot. Thirty seconds later, he's offering me a hand, and I'm jumping on board. We head to the snug bucket seats and buckle in. "Where?" I mouth.

Kane grabs me and presses his lips to my ear. "Forty-five minutes is all he would say." He pulls back, and we're already lifting off. I glance at my watch. It's ten thirty. I start my timer. We're officially headed into the dark unknown to meet a man who kills for money. My arm flexes over my weapon at my rib cage: technically, I kill for money, too. When I'm given cause. And if Ghost gives me cause, I will kill him tonight. And I might even enjoy it.

CHAPTER TWENTY-SIX

As soon as the chopper is in the air, the pilot begins a weave and circle that ensures Kane and I have no opportunity to gauge our travel direction, be it north, south, east, or west. The darkness and absence of city lights that soon follow don't help matters. Fifteen minutes into the flight, I accept the inevitability of being blind and dumb until our arrival. Leaning into the seat, my leg and hip align with Kane's and not because either of us is suddenly trying to play the lovey-dovey couple that we've never been nor will ever become. Kane and I do this hate/ love, throw-a-fist, fuck-to-make-up thing too damn well to screw it up with fluffy bullshit.

No. Right now, our legs are melded together because we're crammed inside this hellhole of a chopper that is loud, rough, and sporting only one tiny-ass double seat. I suspect the uncomfortable ride is meant to keep us on edge, anticipating the meeting with Ghost, maybe even fearing him. Or maybe he's just a cheap-ass bitch. That's probably it, since Kane's known to Ghost, and fear for Kane is like fear for me. It works about as well as Eddie and I did at my father's house for dinner.

At forty minutes into the expected forty-five-minute ride, the chopper begins a descent. Kane doesn't visibly react to our arrival, nor do I, but I can feel the slight tensing of his body, the readiness that wasn't there moments before. Once again, I attempt a look out the window, but still, I find nothing but darkness. No city lights. Confirmation that we're headed to a secluded location.

Five minutes later, the chopper officially touches down in what appears to be a field, and the pilot stays in his seat, a silent message for us to get the fuck out of his chopper. Kane unbuckles his belt and moves to the door, opening it and scanning outside. I am behind him by the time he leaps to the ground, and I don't look for his hand, nor does he offer it. He's focused on the horizon that includes a farmhouse of some sort. I, too, jump to the ground. Already, my eyes are adjusting to the darkness, the clear night, the full moon and heavy star-speckled sky, the rows of trees circling the large grassy field where we stand.

The chopper's engine roars, and it lifts off behind us. Kane and I back up and turn to watch it depart. "It's going to be one hell of a walk back to your place." I glance left to what looks like crops and another silhouetted structure. "Hurd Family Farm," I say. "The trees are apple trees. I remember being here years ago."

"And known to accept chopper landings," he says. "Which places us in Modena, New York, on the edge of the small town Plattekill." He pulls his phone from his pocket and makes a call. "Chopper. Hurd's Farm. North side of the farmhouse. Now." That's it. He ends the call and looks at me. "'Now' translates to an hour to get us out of here."

"Or for me to get standby agents here to arrest him if that had been my plan." The lights in the farmhouse flicker and go dark.

"He obviously wants us to come to him."

"Wonderful," I murmur. "A bossy assassin with a flair for horror-movie dramatics."

We start the short walk, and as our feet hit the dirt leading to the open farmhouse door, the lights inside the structure turn on. Kane catches my arm. "If we play this right, he'll help us fuck the Society and their assassin. But if he crosses us, shoot to kill. There won't be a do-over."

"That doesn't sound like you're confident in that mutual respect," I comment.

"I'm cautious and realistic. When a man feels trapped, he will always lean on instincts and what he does best. In his case, that means kill and move on."

"And what's your instinct, Kane?"

"Kill or be killed."

I have a momentary flashback to me driving a knife through my attacker's chest, a man who Kane restrained with the intent of talking to him. Because apparently, my motto is "Kill because they deserve it." I can't blame the Society for making me who I am, but they damn sure woke that part of me up, apparently after they'd already pulled my family into hell. I want them to pay. I'm *going* to make them pay. And if Ghost can help me do that, I'll shake the monster's hand if I have to tonight and come back for him later.

I give Kane a nod, and we move together, closing the short space to the farmhouse that is actually a barn. We step into the doorway to discover two horses, one left and one right, each enclosed by wooden fences, a narrow walkway beyond leading to more gated stalls. A man—Ghost, I assume—is sitting on the fenced area to our left, his hands balancing his position. His dark brown hair is short but not short enough to read as military, as Murphy seems to believe is his background. His temples are streaked gray, but I don't believe him to be more than a few years older than Kane, perhaps thirty-six or -seven.

It feels like an easy trap, and Kane's flat-footed stance says he's of the same mindset. We don't move. We make Ghost come to us. His lips curve as if he's amused by our hesitation, which he sees as intimidation. Or that's what he wants us to think to lure us to him. We stand our ground, and he jumps down from the fence, his clothing like mine—all black. No logos that might tell a story about his character. But as he moves toward us, he is tall, muscular, and confident, his grace that of a practiced soldier.

Kane and I meet him halfway in the center of the barn, a decision we make in unison, the way Greg and I had once played off each other.

We halt, as he does, with two feet between us. He gives Kane a nod. "The notorious Kane Mendez."

"Ghost," Kane greets. "You're looking like the killer that you are."

"If only more people knew how to give a compliment," he says, glancing at me, his pale-green eyes strikingly cold. "Do you like horses, Lilah Love?"

"They're a hell of a lot better than most humans," I say dryly. "Especially those who make their living as assassins."

His lips quirk with amusement, his gaze boring into me.

"If staring at me is supposed to fluster me," I say, "it won't work."

"You sure about that?" he challenges.

"Unfortunately, yes."

He arches a thick dark brow. "Unfortunately?"

"There is something wrong with a person who can look into the eyes of a killer and feel no fear. Don't you think?"

"If you don't feel fear, what do you feel?"

"Irritated that I can't kill you today."

"You can't kill me period, little girl."

"You sure about that?"

He gives me a flat two-second stare, his cheekbones high, nose straight, expression carved into stone before he says, "I'm going to help you get your assassin," he says.

"Why help me?" I ask.

"I'm not helping you," he says. "You're helping me."

"How are we helping you?" Kane interjects.

He shifts his attention to Kane. "I turned down this job, and in the wake of my withdrawal, they chose to copycat me. I want this little prick taken down."

"Why'd you turn down the job?" Kane asks.

"I didn't at first," he says. "The payout made it worth considering."

"But you got spooked," Kane assumes.

"I don't get spooked," Ghost says. "I stay smart. They presented me the job, which was cut-and-dry. A list of Society members who were planning a coup of their leadership. And don't ask for details. I didn't care to ask myself and don't have them to give."

"If it was cut-and-dry," I say, "why did you pull out?"

"They wanted me to sign on as their exclusive agent, with a price tag of fifty million a year. I refused the broader offer but accepted the contract job. I'd taken a down payment, agreed to terms, even started planning, and then they fucked me."

"That doesn't seem smart on their behalf," Kane comments, echoing my own thoughts.

"Smarter than you might think," he says. "At least in the short term. Word got back to me that I was being buzzed about as the new assassin for the Society, as if I'd taken the job."

"And with a coup," I say, "that buzz intimidated Society members."

"Exactly," he says. "An especially effective strategy on their behalf, considering I killed a key Society leader years ago, and when they then sent a half dozen Blood Assassins after me, I lived. They died."

Confirmation, I think, that the Blood Assassins exist and that they work for the Society. Additional confirmation, as well, that the Society was behind my attack.

"It made the Society look bad," he says. "But hiring me makes it look like they ordered the murder of their own people, then and now."

"Which is why the assassin who took the job is copying you," Kane says.

"Yes," he confirms, that one word like a blade cutting through the air. "And that's where they pushed me too far. I don't like being copied."

"Who do you deal with at the Society?" I ask.

"Pocher," he says. "It's always Pocher."

"Is he the leader?" I ask.

"He's like the guard dog for the United States division," he says, "but no. He's not the leader, and no, before you ask, I don't know who is. But they know you."

"What does that mean?" Kane asks.

"It means your woman is a bigger part of this than you know," he replies, but he's still looking at me.

"What does that mean?" I ask, brilliantly repeating what Kane just asked.

"There were two hits on the list that were in LA. I was told to kill the assassin outside your territory. Not outside your city, outside *your reach*, specifically."

"Obviously those instructions were ignored," Kane says.

"That's what happens when you hire second-best," Ghost comments dryly, his attention still on me even as he adds, "Obviously Pocher believed you could identify a Blood Assassin and become a problem."

My fingers curl into my hands by my sides. "Did he tell you why?"

"No." He offers nothing more.

"I want the assassin."

His cold-as-ice eyes meet mine. "You mean the man with the scar who you chased at the cemetery?"

"What the hell is he talking about, Lilah?" Kane demands.

"I handled it," I say, never looking away from Ghost. "Who is he?"

"They call him the Gamer. He likes to taunt his victims, and since he's taunting you, that must mean that you're now on the list."

"And yet you were obviously there, too, watching us."

"Sizing you up. That's what I do."

There is a threat in those words that I welcome. Bring it the fuck on. I will kill him, but right now, I want the man who I can now assume is both Junior and the Gamer. "What's the Gamer's real name?"

"Ask a better question," he says.

"*Where* do I find him?"

"You can wait for him to come to you, as he clearly will soon, or catch him before his next and last kill. Which, by the way, will not look like one of his kills any more than Suthers did. That's why Woods died when he did. He was no longer needed."

"They wanted Suthers to look like he copied his sister," I say. "But what about this one? Why is it different?"

"Suthers wasn't planned, but since you were involved in his sister's case, I assume your return triged that."

"Did you kill Laney?"

"I never kill and tell unless I want to, and I don't."

That's close enough to a confession for me, and my fingers itch to pull my gun as he adds, "As for the upcoming hit, he's a member of law enforcement, and when a member of law enforcement commits suicide, that person can become a fall guy for a slew of shit for years to come."

Suddenly, I'm not thinking about Laney. Greg. *Fuck.* He crossed the Society. "Who?" I ask, my throat tightening.

"Eddie Rivera," he says, stunning me with the unexpected. "A man so close to your father that any dirt that might surface during his campaign can land on him."

"Is Eddie part of the Society or just a fall guy?" Kane asks.

"He's one of the Society members creating the coup," Ghost says, looking at him and then back at me.

"What about his wife?" I ask, looking for confirmation that Alexandra set me up the night of my attack.

"Not on the kill list I was given," he says. "That's all I have to offer."

"Is the coup made up of people who wanted out of the Society?" I ask.

"Yes."

"Then why was Eddie pushing so damn hard to let Woods fall for the murders?" I press.

"Sounds like a man desperate to cover up his coup activity," Ghost says.

That was the fear I sensed in him. "When will he be killed?" I ask.

"Should have already happened. Could have already happened."

"How do we get to the Gamer before he kills him?" I ask.

"You don't. You wait until he comes for Eddie and grab him. Be warned, though: you won't get to the Society through him. He'll claim the killings are personal vendettas. He'll be killed in custody to ensure he doesn't change his mind and talk. But you close your case, and I get rid of the Gamer."

The sound of a chopper approaching fills the air. "That will be my ride." He looks at Kane. "If she takes the Gamer down, I'll owe you." He walks around Kane toward the door.

I turn around and call out. "You'll owe me," I say. "But I don't want a favor. I want you next."

He faces me. "You're Kane's woman. There are rules of engagement, and those rules make you off-limits. But if you come at me, you break the rule, not me. And you'll go down, not me."

He gives me his back and walks toward the door. My mind conjures an image of Laney tangled in a sheet, her face pale, her life gone, and anger burns inside me. I'm done talking to Ghost. I have what I need, except for justice for Laney. I take a step toward him, and Kane pulls me around to face him. "The Society is the enemy you need to battle right now. Not Ghost. And he'll be ready for anything you do right now."

Kane's right. I'll wait to go after Ghost. But not for long.

CHAPTER TWENTY-SEVEN

Kane and I lift off in his plush private chopper without warning Eddie that he will be dead soon if he doesn't protect himself. I don't have his number or address. My brother wouldn't answer his phone, and Lucas is apparently drunk and mute. I have to get to Eddie before he dies, because the reality here is that haters are gonna hate, and assholes are just assholes, but as an FBI agent, I protect everyone, *including* assholes like Eddie. And now that I know about Eddie's role in overthrowing the Society, I understand the fear I felt in him. I also respect him, despite his asshole-ness that has me thinking of him as a wounded dog protecting himself. And doing so from an organization that I am certain that he involved himself in by trying to impress my manipulative and self-serving father.

For forty-five minutes, we're in that chopper when I need to be on the ground saving Eddie and catching the Gamer. Instead, unable to call anyone, unable to find out what Kane's man is doing on the ground, I can't do anything but sit and wait for our landing. I remind myself that a murder that looks like suicide won't happen unless Eddie is alone. I'd feel comforted about this, but let's face it: Who the hell wants to be with that man? If Alexandra does—and I don't care if she calls him husband—I'd be shocked.

When Kane and I are finally close enough to the ground for my cell phone to work, it doesn't. I can't get a signal. Once we're on the ground, the minute we are in the airport, away from the roar of the chopper, he calls his man. I check my messages, of which there are no damn messages. I listen to Kane's clipped conversation as we exit the airport and make our way to his Roadster. Kane opens the door for me, a gentlemanly habit that I can't convince him isn't necessary no matter how many times I flash my badge or gun. I stop inside the door as he ends the call. "Eddie isn't at his house. His wife is. But they have yet to find Eddie."

"Fuck! I have to call my brother again." I slide into the seat, and Andrew's line has gone to voice mail again before Kane joins me and shuts the door.

"Nothing?" he asks.

"Nope. Nada. Nothing. I have to text a warning." I start typing, reading as I do: I have a lead on the assassin and an anonymous tip that Eddie is a target. I have to reach him. I glance at Kane before I hit Send. "Talk me out of it or I'm hitting Send."

"I have his address," he says, starting the engine. "We're going to him now. Someone is watching his house." He places us in reverse. "And you have no idea how irrational your brother or Eddie are, or how he might react to that kind of message."

"How far is the house?"

"Twenty minutes."

"But he's not there."

"But his wife will know where he is."

"Drive there, yes, but have your man go up to the door and try to get Alexandra on the phone."

"He doesn't speak English," he says. "But he can hand the phone to her."

"Holy hell, Kane. He doesn't speak English?"

"Every person on my staff has a special skill. His special skill is killing people. A far better skill than English with an assassin involved."

"I hate that you employ people who have that skill. What is your skill?"

"You know my skills, but I'll be happy to demonstrate again later tonight. And in the morning." He hits a number on his phone.

I dial my father. And damn it, his line goes to voice mail as well. "I need Eddie's number to discuss the case and potentially closing it," I lie. "It's urgent. Call me." I hang up. Kane is speaking in Spanish, with my name thrown into the conversation, before he places the phone on speaker.

"Eduardo is going to the door," he says. "He'll be there in about sixty seconds."

There is movement, footsteps and knocking. The sound of Alexandra calling out, "Who are you?"

A male, highly accented voice shouts, "Call. Lilah. Call. Lilah."

"Jesus, Kane. She's not going to open the door with a strange man who can't even speak English. Drive faster."

"Lilah!" the man shouts. "Call. Lilah!"

I hear the door open. "Lilah?" she asks. And he says again, "Call." I assume he shoves the phone at her, since I hear, "Lilah?" And this time it's Alexandra saying my name into the phone.

"Yes, Alexandra. It's me. I didn't have your number. I need to reach Eddie. It's about the case I'm on. He'll want to hear what I have to say. It's urgent."

"Obviously. He says he had some campaign meeting with your father and brother and a bunch of money men tonight."

That explains why no one is answering my calls. "Why aren't you there?"

"I'm not a part of whatever they do," she says.

"Where are they?"

"I have no idea."

This is odd. Everything about her and Eddie together is odd. "I need his number. Can you text it to me so I have yours and his?"

"Yes. What's your number?"

I give it to her.

"Got it," she says. "I'll send it when we hang up."

"I need you to call him and tell him it's urgent I talk to him in case he doesn't take my calls. And text him."

"His phone is off, but I'll try. Do you want to give me details?"

"No. I don't."

I hang up and dial Eddie once I receive Alexandra's text with his information. His line goes direct to voice mail. "Lucas is nearby," I say, glancing at Kane. "We have to go to his house. He'll find Eddie."

Without one bitchy word, Kane pulls a U-turn. That's the thing about Kane. He knows when to let things go, except me. And I thought he had. Maybe he did, and I showed back up and shook his world. I don't like where that leads me, and that path is not one I need to travel now, or perhaps ever.

My phone buzzes with a text message, and I glance down to read: Eddie's phone is off but I left him a message.

I could say thanks, but I guess it really isn't my thing, at least not with a woman who might well have set me up to be raped and murdered. And Lord help her and me if I find out that's true.

Kane and I pull up to Lucas's house and walk to the door. I ring the bell over and over, and he doesn't answer. I try the door. It's unlocked. It's one of the rare moments that people being stupid works in my favor. Kane and I walk inside and down the hallway and *holy shit*. There is a naked woman sitting on top of Lucas on the couch. Her gaze lifts to mine and she gasps. "Shit. Shit." She climbs off Lucas, who makes a pained noise that sounds a bit like a wounded animal.

"Baby, what is happening? We were fucking." He must see where her attention rests because he twists around.

"Oh fuck. He's finally going to kill me, isn't he?"

200

"Kill you?" The woman gasps and looks at us, pulling a dress over her head. "I didn't see or hear anything." She grabs her shoes and runs toward us and past me.

"Ellen!" Lucas shouts, standing up, as naked as the day he was born. The door opens and shuts.

"Jesus, Lucas," I spout. "Put some fucking clothes on."

"Do you know how to knock?" he demands. "I was fucking enjoying fucking."

"I need you to find Eddie Rivera," I say. "His phone is off and his life is on the line, but clearly you're too damn sloshed."

"I told you," he says. "I can hack the United States government shit-faced."

"Then do it now," I say.

"Hack the United States?" he asks, and he's so damn drunk that he's serious.

I walk to him and lean on the couch. "Unless you're trying to impress Kane with the size of your dick, get dressed."

He grabs his pants. "You're right. I need to get dressed before he realizes what a threat I really am."

"Don't taunt him, Lucas," I warn, turning to face Kane, my hand flattening on his chest, and while his expression is indiscernible, his eyes glint with the kind of hate that no man wants from Kane Mendez. "He's drunk."

"And stupid," Kane replies, his tone lethal. "More so than he realizes."

"Because," I repeat, "*he's drunk.*"

"I need his phone number," Lucas says from behind me. "Or do I have to get that myself, too?"

I rotate to find his drunk ass dressed and sitting on his coffee table facing us, his blond hair standing on end, with a laptop in his hands. "I have it," I say, fishing my phone from my pocket and reading him the number. He keys it into his laptop and, in about sixty seconds, says,

"The last GPS location was the docks down at Halsey's Marina." He presses a few more keys and adds, "He owns a boat that is parked at lot 11105 at the west end. Now what?"

Now I need to know if he's alone, I think. "Where are my brother and father right now?"

He doesn't ask for those phone numbers, keying them in from memory, and a few seconds later, he says, "Both phones are at your father's house, so one would assume the people who own them are as well."

"Oh shit," I breathe out, turning to face Kane. "Eddie isn't with them." I dash for the door, and Kane is immediately by my side.

"You're welcome!" Lucas shouts as we exit the house, but I can't think about his drunk attitude and anger now. Right now, I'm thinking about saving the family asshole, or at least one of them. If Eddie isn't already dead.

CHAPTER TWENTY-EIGHT

Kane is on the phone the instant we are outside Lucas's house. By the time we are inside his Roadster, he's hanging up. "I have men on the way to the marina now." He cranks the engine and pulls forward.

"How long will it take them to get there?"

"Twenty minutes longer than it will take us to get there, but we'll have backup."

I open my mouth to reply, and a horrible thought hits me. "Oh God." I face Kane. "What if this was all a setup? What if Ghost was planning to take out my father and brother? And getting us out of town and focused on Eddie when we returned was a diversion to ensure we don't interfere?" I don't give him time to reply. "Go to my father's house."

"Ghost was not taking out your family," he says. "He knows what kind of enemy that would make me on your behalf."

"I have to know they're okay."

"I'll go to your father's house," he says. "But that is twenty minutes out of the way. Those minutes may cost you Eddie and the Gamer."

"This is my father and brother we're talking about."

"I know that," he says. "And I wouldn't risk what is important to you, *ever*. Ghost is not coming after you or your family. The Gamer might come for you. We need to get to him before he does."

"My family—"

"Eddie lives close to your father. My man is still there. He can be to your father's ten minutes before we can."

"Send him," I say. "Send him now."

Kane punches a button on his phone and then speaks in Spanish to his man before hanging up. "He's going to walk to the door when he gets there and tell them to call you," he says. "Just like he did with Alexandra."

I nod and face forward, immediately dialing my brother, only to get his voice mail. I dial my father with the same result. "Damn it. Fuck. Damn it."

"Relax."

"Do not fucking tell me to relax, Kane, or I will slap you again but harder."

"Ghost is not going after your family, Lilah," he says. "You know me. My word should mean something to you. And I'm giving you my word that, under the present circumstances, Ghost will not go after your family."

"Is that a promise, Kane?"

"If you live by the words you speak, you shouldn't need to fluff it up with the word *promise*. And I mean the words I speak."

"You just don't always speak the words I want to hear."

"That's a trap that leads to lies, and if my word isn't enough for you—"

"Of course it is."

He glances over at me. "Because you trust me?"

"I trust you," I say, despite the fact that I know this pulls us closer when I have been trying desperately to keep him at a distance. "You're the only person I do trust right now."

"And yet you doubted my efforts to avenge your attack?"

"You kept things from me, Kane. And I know you. I knew what you were doing regardless of the reasons."

"The Society was the reason. I could not have you chase them and end up dead."

"So what? I should just forget my attack? I should just get over it because it was them?"

"Do you think, *do you really fucking think*, that is what I want or will accept? Don't you think I have a plan to make them pay?"

I press my hand to my temple. "Now is not the time for this."

"It's the perfect time for this," he says. "Anytime we finally talk about this is the right time."

"Fuck you, Kane."

"Anytime. Anywhere."

I look at him, and I'm about to blast him when I realize what he's doing. "Holy hell. You're distracting me from freaking out."

"That doesn't make this conversation any less important."

I turn away from him. "Damn opportunist."

"That's a mild statement for you, Lilah Love. Where are all the F-words I so love and expect?" His cell phone rings and he answers it, listening for a few beats before hanging up. My phone rings instantly. "That will be your brother," he says.

I let out a breath and answer the call. "Andrew."

"What the hell is going on, Lilah? Why do I have a man that I don't know who doesn't speak English at my door saying 'Call Lilah'?"

"The assassin is real. Buckle down and protect Dad until I call you back. I'll explain the rest later."

"Explain now. What the hell does that mean? Is Dad a target?"

"I'm being cautious. Eddie isn't with you, is he?"

"No. Why?"

"*Was* he with you?" I ask.

"Yes," he says. "He left about an hour and a half ago. He said he was going home."

"Is Pocher with you?"

"Yes. Again, why? And I repeat, what the hell is going on, Lilah?"

"I have a tip that the assassin is coming for Eddie. I also believe that Pocher's organization is behind it, but that's a conversation your punk ass is going to have with me later. Watch your back. And Eddie is not at home and his phone is off."

"He and Alexandra have been fighting a lot. He'll go to his boat at Halsey's Marina. That's where he goes when she kicks him out. I'll meet you there."

"No," I say as Kane pulls into the dark parking lot of the marina where Eddie's boat is parked. "Stay with Dad," I say. "Protect him. Lock down." And I say the words again. "Promise me."

"If I stay here, I'm going to send two patrol cars to the docks."

"No," I say. "Don't trust anyone."

"I trust my men."

"Trust *no one*, Andrew."

"You can't go after an assassin alone."

"I'm not alone."

"Kane," he says.

"Yes, and that's better than your patrol cars." I hang up before he argues, but I do so with the realization that he didn't ask why anyone would want to kill Eddie. I don't like where that thought could take me, but Kane pulls us into a parking spot and I set it aside for now.

Neither of us speaks. We scan the harbor, which houses at least forty boats and is well lit with lantern-style lights in some places and dark in others. Kane and I look at each other. "The Gamer has already shown interest in you. You're a target. He's not the average asshole. He's not even the exceptional asshole. He's a hundred times better. We're better together."

"Agreed," I say, and we share a quick nod before exiting the vehicle.

We meet in front of the hood, both of us doing another scan of the area. The night is eerily quiet. The signs of life, invisible. The moon and stars are now covered with clouds, and there's muffled thunder in the distance. Kane motions us forward, but I hold up a hand and then squat down, removing the knife inside my boot, along with the leather case, but leaving the ankle strap in place. Standing, I shove the knife under my jacket and into the waistband of my jeans.

I nod, and Kane and I start walking, following a sidewalk to a boardwalk. My gaze lands on a sign with dock numbers, and I point to it and then to the right. We cut in that direction, and side by side, we walk through the path of boats, some small but most medium and large yachts. Since Alexandra did not have a boat when I lived here, I assume that it's a toy she bought for her boy, and that is as manly a term as Eddie gets from me. The walk is long, the dock numbers passing us by until we are at the very end of the row of boats. And *The Rivera* turns out to be a rather large yacht with the lights in the enclosed lower level glowing through the glass.

Kane and I both pull our guns and we climb onto the deck, weapons aimed in front of us. The glass door leading to the main cabin is tinted too dark to see beyond it. I motion to the right and Kane points left, and we sweep the top of the yacht, returning to the door to stand in front of it. He points to himself and the door to tell me he's going first. I've learned that no matter how kick-ass I am, no matter how big my badge or attitude, men do this macho thing. And later, when I save their asses, they are really damn glad I do it just as well.

So I let him go first, but I'm a gentlewoman—I open the door for him.

He enters and curses. I follow him inside and do the same, stepping to his side, both of us holding our weapons in front of us, while Eddie is facedown on a glossy wood-laminate table, blood all around him. Both hands are positioned with palms facing up, wrists slit. "I'll clear the cabin," Kane says, moving forward, while I do the same, but I head straight for Eddie and press my fingers to his neck. There is no pulse.

Kane returns from the back room, weapon lowered. "We're clear."

"And he's dead," I say, "and aside from that sucky news, the Gamer got away." It's at that moment that there is a loud plop on the outer deck. Like someone jumping from the top of the boat, where Kane and I did not check.

"It could be a trick," Kane says. "Lock the door." He heads toward it and I follow. I'm not letting him walk into a trap without backup.

Weapon ready, he exits the door, and I am right behind him. As soon as I'm outside, by his side, the sound of footsteps running catches our attention. "Lock yourself inside," Kane shouts at me, and he launches himself off the boat and onto the walkway. He takes off running, and nothing about this feels right. I turn around and study the exterior of the boat, listening for any movement. There is nothing but the soft swish of water and a few creaks of the boat. I consider searching the boat again, but while I go left, someone could go right or underneath. And I need to protect myself and the crime scene.

I open the door and enter the cabin again, looking for a lock. It's broken, and it looks to me to have been shot off the door. I harness my weapon and move toward Eddie. Maybe I'll feel emotion later. Maybe I won't. But I feel none now. I am in that place I go: the Otherworld, where bodies are just part of the crime scene. I am not bothered by the body, even Eddie's, but I am not fond of blood, and right now, red and thickening, it's dripping off the table onto the tan-colored carpet.

I walk toward him, my shoes squishing with the blood that has spread even closer than I suspected. I don't react. I focus on the body. I do not have my field bag with me, and that limits my ability to touch anything, but I need the proof that this is a murder. My instinct is to study the scene from directly in front of the body, but I cannot risk my back to the door. I walk around him, placing Eddie's back to my front, and I look at the scene as if I were him. There is an open, empty bottle of pills by his head, which will be blamed for his decision to kill himself, as will the fight with Alexandra. Suddenly, that fight appears really damn well timed. And knowing that Eddie was a part of a coup, remembering the fear I sensed in him, I now wonder if Alexandra is really as removed from the Society as I was starting to assume. After all, she was with me the night of my attack.

For now, I set her and her potential guilt aside. Eddie has my attention more now than he ever did in life. Perhaps I should have pulled him aside, talked to him. Tried to get him to talk. But guilt and self-doubt are as useless as fear. I don't need them. I don't use them. They don't get to use and abuse me.

Eddie is dressed in the short-sleeve version of his tan uniform. I stare at his arms, his wrists both faceup. I imagine him cutting his wrists, and unfortunately, I can also imagine a drugged version of Eddie holding them as they are now, to watch himself bleed out. I squat down and scan the floor, looking for a clue. The door suddenly bursts open and footsteps rush toward me. I yank out my weapon, and the moment I have it in front of me, the Gamer is there, too. He's close, behind the desk with me, and his gun is pointed at my head.

CHAPTER TWENTY-NINE

I want to take the Gamer alive, to force him to confess to the murders, to show the Society they cannot hide. He holds his gun on me, his hand steady, his stare just as steady. He expects to intimidate me. He fails, and he can thank his employer for his failure. Thanks to the Society, I've been here, done this, with a Blood Assassin. I know how to get to the other side.

I'll arrest him if I can, but he dies before I die.

"Put the gun down and come to me, Lilah Love," he says, his voice a low purr meant to be seductive, which shows he's a really fucking sick bastard.

"Let me think about it," I say. I pause for two seconds. "Okay. I thought about it. Fuck you."

"Give me the gun," he orders, his purr more a growl now.

"You want my gun?" I challenge. "Come and get it, but word of advice: pray really hard before you do."

"I can kill you before you ever get a shot off," he says. "That's how good I am."

"People who are good don't need to tell you they are good. They show you. And we both know that you aren't that good. We also both know that you got greedy. You wanted a two-for-one night with a big payoff, but you didn't think it through. If you kill me here, Eddie's death won't look like a suicide."

"You're right. It will look like you did it."

"To blame me, I'd have to be dead," I say. "And I can't kill myself from where you stand, and you aren't getting any closer."

"I paid a guy living in his boat down the way to say he heard a scuffle and walked in on you killing Eddie. Of course, he shot you."

I laugh. "Really? You did that in the five minutes after I showed up? We both know you didn't expect me, so that is some skill you got there. And Kane is here. He'll be back. He'll know what really happened."

"Kane is dead."

I blink with the shock and pain of those three words, and it's the blink that gives the Gamer an advantage. He moves toward me, but at that same moment, a thud hits the boat as someone jumps onto the yacht. The Gamer blinks this time, and I shoot him in the shoulder. The bastard must be drugged up or just crazy, because that bleeding hole in his body doesn't stop him. He turns toward the door, gun aimed at whoever has entered the cabin. I step in to him and somehow retain the sense to try to keep him alive. I ram a hard knee into his groin, and he gives a guttural groan and starts to fall, but damn it, he drapes himself on top of me.

"Lilah!"

The sound of my brother's voice reaches my ears a moment before I'm on my back, the bloody, wet carpet soaking me, the weight of my would-be assassin on top of me. Andrew shouts my name again, and a wet stickiness soaks my face. The Gamer's blood is pouring all over me, while his breathing is shallow and rough. *Kane is dead,* I think, and that thought delivers anger. Deep, uncontrollable anger, a rage like I have felt only one time before: when I knifed a man to death. It's in that moment of absolute fury that history repeats itself. Someone lifts the Gamer off me, but the Gamer finds a surge of energy and elbows the person at his back and then rolls, taking me with him and placing me on top of him. Using me as a shield.

I reach for my knife at my back, and even before I see the gun in the Gamer's hand, I drive it into his chest. His eyes shut on a pant of heavy air and he drops his gun. I roll off him and fall backward, squishing in the carpet as I do. Suddenly, Kane is by my side, kneeling.

"I see you still know how to use a knife."

Relief washes through me. "You're not dead. He said you were dead."

"I can't die before we finish that conversation we started in the car. But now you have to agree to have it with me."

"Are you really negotiating with me now? You really are an opportunistic bastard. You are—"

He stands up and takes me with him, blood dripping off me, the heavy, sticky dampness of my clothes making me crazy. "Punish me when we're alone." He softens his voice. "Are you okay?"

"Right now. Yes." And that's the truth. Right now.

Suddenly I have EMS techs surrounding me, checking for injuries, while my brother steps in front of me. "He confessed," I say as a blanket is placed around me. "He killed Eddie," I add, "and intended to make it look like I did it. And he killed the victims you pinned on Woods. All of them."

"All of that matters but not now. You first. Let the techs fully look you over."

"I'm fine. Move on."

He gives me a hard stare and then cuts a look at Kane. "We need a moment, and you outside the crime scene."

Kane looks at me. "I'll be above deck," he says.

I nod, and as relieved as I was that he is alive and here, I am just as relieved that he is leaving. He knows me too well, and I connect with those things when he's here. I can't be that human right now. I have to be Agent Love.

Kane walks away. A number of official staff enter the room to collect evidence. Chaos erupts, and Andrew is drawn into questions that I let him answer.

I need to call Murphy. I head for the door, and right when I step onto the upper deck, Beth is doing the same. "What are you doing here?" I ask.

She gives me a once-over. "Holy wow. You look—"

"Bloody good," I say. "I know," and again, I ask, "why are you here?"

"Apparently I can't use this town to escape reality and have it really be an escape anymore. What do I need to know?"

What do you know already and won't ever tell me? is the real question. But it's the question I have for just about everyone in this town. It seems like my world is infested with the Society. "Double homicide. I killed the one on the floor." I step around her, take off my bloody shoes, and then jump off the boat and right into a gaggle of official staff. They clutter the boardwalk and part like I'm a horror-movie version of a goddess when I walk in their direction.

I walk left toward the end of the pier and hop onto some random person's boat before digging my phone from my pocket, shocked that it's still inside after I rolled around and played in a couple of people's blood.

It rings in my red-stained hand, and the minute I note Rich's number, I'm reminded of the errands I sent him on, and I answer. "Rich."

"The woman you wanted me to talk to committed suicide."

No, I think. She was murdered to shut her up, but I need to get him out of this. "It's over anyway," is a well-intended lie, meant to get him out of this before he "commits suicide" as well. Protect him when I should never have involved him in the first place. "The corruption points to Eddie, and now he's dead, so it's over."

"What? Eddie is . . . he's *dead?*"

"Yes. So is the assassin who killed him. I got in the way and he got in the way. I lived. He died."

"When? How? Fuck, Lilah. Are you okay?"

"Like I said. I'm alive and he's dead. End of story. I'm at the crime scene, though. I need to go."

"Call me when you get out of there."

"I'll try," I say, and hang up.

I'm about to call Murphy when I think about Pocher and his financial connections, not just to Laney but to my mother. I have to prove he killed her. And Lord help my father if I find out he was a part of it. I walk to a seat on the side of the boat, and since no one, me included, wants to see my butt imprint in blood, I decide against sitting after all.

I dial Murphy. "Agent Love."

"I caught the assassin," I announce. "I shot the assassin. He kept coming at me. I drove a knife through his chest."

"He's dead, I assume?" he asks, all casual and matter-of-fact as if I've just shared my grocery list. I don't actually dislike this response. It's better than, "Are you okay?"

"Dead and never coming back. And so is Eddie Rivera from the local police department."

"Are you okay?"

"I hate that question," I say. "I was just loving you for not asking it. I'm alive. He's dead. I'm good."

"First, it's really damn nice to finally get some love instead of hate from Lilah Love herself. It's okay to be human. You know that, right?"

"What I know is too much now to go back to LA."

"You're keeping the case open," he assumes.

"No." And then I add a necessary lie, to appease the Society while I rip them open and watch them bleed. "The assassin confessed."

"Why would he do that?"

"I got the impression when he told me that he was going to kill me that he didn't plan on letting me live to tell."

"Smart-ass. Who hired him?"

"I don't know," I lie.

"What were the motives?"

"I don't know," I lie again.

"What do you know?"

"They called him the Gamer."

"You killed *the Gamer*?" he asks incredulously.

"It was him or me."

"And you came out on top."

I flash back to exactly that: me on top of the Gamer, *Junior*, driving the knife into his chest. I squeeze my eyes shut. "Yes. I won."

"*We* won. He is a very big feather in your cap, Agent Love. And your success is my success."

"Well congratu-fucking-lations."

"I'm back to: Who hired him?"

"I don't know," I repeat.

"Then how are we closing this case?"

"It's a dead end."

"What aren't you telling me?"

"I can't go back to LA," I say, rather than tell another lie.

"If the reasons you're staying relate to the corruption you suspect within your family, working for that New York City bureau could be a problem for you."

"If they're dirty, I'm a problem for them."

"I'm not going to approve that transfer."

"Then I guess I quit."

"No. You work for me. You don't get to walk away that easily."

"I'm not going back to LA," I repeat. "You can't keep me if I don't want to stay."

"Don't bet on that."

He hangs up.

"Asshole," I murmur, and turn to stare out at the darkness, where the water stretches into a sea of eternity and my mind replays the feeling of driving that knife into yet another man's chest. I want it to freak me out. I want it to make me melt down. Instead, I think back to the night on the beach, my attack. My knife driving over and over into that Blood Assassin's chest. Kane's words play in my mind next: *It's okay to enjoy it.*

"No," I whisper. "It's not." I toss the bloody blanket still draped over me over the edge and watch it sink into the water, washing away the blood as it does. I grab my badge, remove the photo I have inside it, and then toss it as well, watching it sink. And with it, the rules it represents.

CHAPTER THIRTY

"I could ticket you for pollution."

At the sound of my brother's voice, I turn to find him joining me on the boat. "I was just ridding myself of some dirt. I would think you'd want to do the same."

"We're back to this?"

"We never left *this*."

"Then let me repeat what I told you before. Whatever you think you know, Lilah, you don't."

"Why was your phone off?"

"I was in a meeting."

"Vibrate works just fine."

"Pocher takes our phones. He's that paranoid."

"What? He's afraid someone will know he gets off on the vibrations or what?"

"Can you *ever* not be a smart-ass?"

"Yes," I say, though that quite possibly might be a lie. "Just not on the days I'm covered in the blood of two dead men after one of them came close to killing me. Back to you. Your phone. *You* are the police chief. You can't just turn it off."

"Eddie was on call."

"Yeah, well, that worked great. His phone was off."

"Yeah, well, forgive me if I don't fire him, sister. In case you didn't notice, he's dead right fucking now."

"Stop cursing at me!"

"You curse at me all the *fucking* time. He was my friend. He's dead, and you came damn close to joining him. Now is not the time to throw daggers at each other."

"You scared me. And for more than one reason, so yes. I will throw daggers and keep throwing them until you feel them enough to get your shit straight."

"I have my shit straight. And you scared me, too. I couldn't get that asshole off you."

"But you did, and I killed him. Right after you wouldn't answer your phone and I thought he was going to kill you. Don't do that again."

We stare at each other, and he scrubs his jaw. "Damn it. I don't want us to fight."

"Me either."

"You see monsters where there are no monsters."

"Are you sure about that?"

"Yes, Lilah. I *am* sure."

"Okay."

"Okay?"

"What else do I say? I hate fucking blood and I'm wearing it. Nothing about this conversation is going to improve at this very moment."

"You're right. You need to go clean up and rest. Unless you have an objection as lead on this case, I'll run the crime scene."

I want to control it myself. I want back on that boat. I want to look for clues, but to what end? The only place they could lead is the Society, and I need room to breathe to figure out how to hurt them. I need them to think that I backed out. "Take the scene," I say. "I'll make a statement tomorrow and follow up on the details as they unfold."

"That works, but give me something to go on. What do you know about the killer?"

"They call him the Gamer. And my boss says he's known, but not beyond the nickname. He was—is—a big deal. This was a win, he said."

"You believe he killed them all?"

"Yes. Including Woods."

He paused a beat, two at the most. "And this closes the case?"

Closing the case is all he cares about. Nothing else. I want to shake him. I want him to care about something other than covering for Pocher. I want to tell him that Pocher killed Mom, but now isn't the time for that either. "He confessed," I say, and then I add a willing lie I intend to get back to the Society. And I do so because it leads me to an open field where the Society will roam and graze, and I will poison them. Destroy them. Hurt them first. "He said it was personal," I continue. "I have no proof if it was or was not, so yes. I'm closing it."

"Who gave you the tip to come here tonight?"

"I told you. It was anonymous."

"Delivered by who and how?"

The push makes me feel like he's asking this for someone else. "A stranger on the street," I say, offering him a method that is impossible to check when I add, "a kid. A teen. He ran off before I could get more from him."

"Then it's over?"

"Yes."

"Good. We need this behind us. I'll have a patrol car take you home."

"Work the scene. Use your people to take care of your people."

"Because you're leaving with Kane."

"With my boss's blessing," I assure him.

"Really?" he asks, sounding less than convinced, but then I had about the same reaction.

"No. I lied because I want to fuck him all night long."

"Jesus, Lilah. Give me a break for just one night. I'll call you when this is done."

"It's got to be midnight. Call me in the morning."

He nods and starts to turn and then hesitates. "Your boss is right. This is a big win. It's over and you're alive." He walks away, leaving me with a million ways to take that statement, and I don't like the similarities to my father's earlier tone. But if I analyze that thought now, I could lose my shit and go after his. I need sleep. I need a shower. I need to think. And my wet clothes are a constant chill on my mind and body.

I step off the boat and work my way through the busy walkway, and this time I don't stop. I hurry toward the yellow tape with the intent of continuing on to the parking lot, where I am certain Kane will be waiting for me. Another moment where I realize that the only person I'm ever certain of is Kane. And Rich. I know I can predict Rich's actions, because he is an honorable man. I duck under the tape, and I've traveled all of two steps when Alexandra is in front of me, halting my progress. Next thing I know, she's sobbing and throwing her arms around me, seemingly oblivious to the blood all over me. She starts this frantic mumbling of things I can't even understand before she pulls back, her eyes and nose red. Her cheeks are tear-streaked, yet this emotional display feels fake to me. And sure enough, she now has blood on her cheek and probably more hidden in the black of her T-shirt.

"Eddie and I were fighting," she says. "The last words I said to him were not nice."

Not nice.

That's her version of cussing him out.

It reads like a woman putting the finishing touches on the stage set. Did she do exactly what it seems, to me, she did? Set a stage and let someone else attack?

"I have to see him," she says, starting to pass me. "I have to—"

I grab her arm. "No. You can't go past the tape."

"I have to see him!"

"Alexandra."

At my brother's voice, I whirl around as he catches her shoulders. "You need to calm down," he brilliantly tells her, like that won't set her off all over again. "And you shouldn't be here or driving."

"I am going to see him!" she shouts, proving my point and not even slightly calmed down. "Move out of my way."

Two officers step to Andrew's side, and Alexandra just gets bigger and louder in their presence. A few minutes of chaos follow that end with Andrew on this side of the tape, his arms around her, before he picks her up and starts walking. I watch them depart, heading toward the parking lot, two officers shadowing them, and I don't like the place my mind goes. My brother is a good man, but he's involved in this mess. Maybe more than I want to believe, and I have to change that before he ends up as fucked as Eddie.

I wait until they disappear around the corner, then start walking toward Kane's car. Once it's in view, so is he. I find him leaning on his Roadster, ankles crossed, hands at his sides. Waiting on me, and as Murphy declared, he's an enemy to everyone but me. I don't know if that is ultimately true, but I know that Kane would bury a body for me. For a woman covered in blood who just killed a man, that's damn romantic.

He watches me approach, and he doesn't come to me or coddle me, thank God. I stop in front of him. "I threw away my badge."

"When?"

"A few minutes ago. I also killed for you."

"What does that mean, Lilah?"

"The Gamer told me he killed you, and there was no coming back for him after that." It's a truth I admit to myself only in this moment. "He was going to die after he made that declaration."

"And you blame me for your actions?"

"No. Not at all. But that badge keeps me sane. You make me *in*sane."

"Which do you prefer?"

"It's not about which one I prefer, because insane wins. You know you win. But it's about what is right and wrong."

"And where does that statement leave you and us?"

"I'll let you know when I decide." I walk to his passenger door, and when he unlocks it and joins me in the V of the open door, I turn to him. "I'm going to make a mess of your car."

He grabs me, pulls me to him, and kisses me hard and fast before he pulls back.

"You have blood on your face," I say.

"A little blood doesn't bother me," he says, "unless it's yours." He turns away, toward the car, and it hits me that Kane is with blood as I am with bodies: he really isn't even slightly bothered by it. Therein lies our difference, which feels significant. Bodies to me are shells of the living. Blood is the magic of life. I can remove my badge from between Kane and me but not the blood. And yet, I still get into the car.

CHAPTER THIRTY-ONE

Kane and I have one exchange once we're both sealed inside his car. Technically it's not even an exchange. I'm the one who speaks. "Your place," I say.

He looks over at me, his strong features drenched in shadows, and he says nothing. I like this about Kane. He doesn't waste words. He doesn't create a need for explanations and chitchat. In this case, he simply starts the engine, places the car in gear, and gets us the hell away from the marina. The rest of the drive is silence. It's an easy silence, which says much about our comfort level with each other, and that leads to what I most need to be doing right now: sleeping.

It's been one hell of a long day, with hardly a blink of sleep the night before, and I lay my head on the leather seat, close my eyes, and I'm out. I don't even dream. There are no flashbacks of blood, knives, and murder. I don't even know I've fallen asleep until the sound of Kane's garage opening wakes me. I sit up and stare at the door opening, and it's a welcome sight. This place is an escape to me, an oasis with a wall around it, the one place where I don't have to pull out a weapon and start shooting or cutting my way through the sea of sharks surrounding me.

I don't even wait for the engine to be shut off. I exit the car and walk into the house through the kitchen. Beyond it, I pass through the living room and don't even hesitate to start up the stairs. I enter his bedroom and walk straight to his luxurious and masculine bathroom of gray stone and tiles. I also don't hesitate to strip away my clothes, start the shower, and step under the hot water.

It's then that I watch the blood pool at my feet. So much blood. Images flash in my mind, the memory of falling backward into the blood-soaked carpet. The blood is what is fucking with me. The damn blood. I shake my head and press my hands to my face. The shower door opens and Kane, still fully dressed, appears.

He hands me a glass of whiskey. I down it and glance at his cheek. "Fuck, Kane. You have blood all over you." I hand him the glass. "Get it off."

He narrows his eyes on me but doesn't say what I know he is thinking: *You still aren't over the blood.* He takes the glass and gets rid of it, I don't know or care where, before he undresses and joins me. I grab a bottle of soap and spray it on him. It's not about romance. I want the blood gone.

He rinses off, water splaying all over his muscles as he flexes here and there. He looks good. That fact, and his money and power, and every Hollywood freaking starlet in this town wants to win his favor. That's not me. "I'm not having sex with you, even though you look like that naked," I announce.

"I know," he says, palming his hair back over his head.

"How do you know?"

"Because that's not what you need from me tonight."

"What do I need?"

"To talk."

"About what?"

"Your badge. The one we both know you can't get rid of."

I'm not a big scowl person, but it happens here and there when I feel extra inspired. I'm extra inspired by his mixed messages. I scowl. "It's what you wanted."

"Not for the reasons you chose to do it right now."

"Really? What are my reasons?"

"To take off your own cuffs and mine. And that doesn't work."

"What the hell are you talking about, Kane?"

"I do the dirty work so you don't have to."

"Not anymore. That's the point. My freedom and yours."

"That's the point that doesn't work. I pull you a little bit over here with me. You pull me a little bit over there with you. And we meet in the middle. That's why we work."

"You said you wanted this," I repeat.

"You can leave and still be you, but if you leave right now, in your present state of mind, it will change you. And I might be able to live with that, but you can't."

"I want to slap you again."

"As long as my palm gets your cheek afterward, I'll let you."

"*You'll let me.* I'm done." I move for the door. He pulls me to him and kisses me. "What happened to talking?"

"Things change. It's not what you need anymore." His mouth closes back down on mine, and I don't fight him. He's right. Things change, which is the entire point of me throwing my badge in the water. I need a change.

I wake up in Kane's bed, draped in sheets so divine they must be a million thread count, sunlight beaming through a nearby window. I roll over and find him on his back staring at the ceiling. I do the same. "First three thoughts that come to your mind," he says.

"I'm in your bed. These sheets are really soft and must cost a fucking fortune. I don't have my badge. Your turn."

"You're in my bed. These sheets do cost a fucking fortune. And you don't have your badge." He gets up and pulls on pajama bottoms. "I'll make coffee."

"You're wrong," I say, knowing what he's thinking. "I don't want it back."

"No," he agrees. "But you *need* it back." He heads for the door, and I watch him exit.

"You're fucking wrong, Kane Mendez."

"Tell me that after you've had your fucking coffee," he calls out, his voice growing farther away.

I inhale and blow it out, biting back another shout. I will have my words with him over that coffee. I throw away the blankets, and naked as the day I was born, I walk into the bathroom. I pee. On my way to the sink to brush my teeth, I realize that my horror-movie clothes are missing. Kane took care of them. When he's not being the definition of an asshole, he really knows how to be a non-asshole.

I brush my teeth and pull on one of Kane's T-shirts before walking into the bedroom, my gaze landing on the nightstand where I charged my phone last night. I grab it and note the missed call from my father. I sit on the bed and listen to the message: *Your boss was right. This was a win. You're alive and this is over.*

Not: *I'm worried about you, Lilah. How are you, Lilah?* And yes, I hate that question, but a father should care enough to ask it. Last night, not this morning. Instead, he repeats the same statement Andrew had made to me. It feels like a threat from my father and, in the morning light, a warning from my brother. This drives home one point: the Gamer might be dead, but the people who hired him to kill me are not. I hurry toward the door and down the stairs. Kane stands at the coffeepot and turns to face me as I pause on the opposite side of the island, set my phone down, and press my hands to the counter.

"What keeps the Society from sending Ghost or someone else after me again?"

Kane walks to the island and mimics my position, his hands pressed to the counter as well. "Me and Pocher."

"Pocher? Why would Pocher stop them?"

"I promised you that I'd make the person responsible for your attack pay. I meant it. And the minute I found out that was Pocher, I began making that happen."

"What does that mean?"

"He'll come to you soon for a favor. He'll need you. You'll know what to do when he does."

"I repeat. What does that mean?"

"Deniability, Lilah. Once again, it's my gift to you."

I want to push him, but I know him. It's wasted breath. "Pocher is one man in the Society. How can he offer me any protection?"

"He's powerful. And he'll be motivated to make your interests his interests."

"What happens when he makes destroying you his interest?"

"You underestimate me, Lilah. He won't, I promise you."

"I don't underestimate you, Kane."

My cell phone rings, and I glance down to find Murphy's number. "My boss or ex-boss or whatever the hell he now is."

I answer the line. "Director."

"I'm here."

My gaze meets Kane's, and his brow lifts at my obvious shock. "Here as in where?"

"In East Hampton. We need to have a one-on-one talk."

"Where and when?"

"Since I know you're with Kane, I'll give you time to make lovey-dovey and get some clothes on. Thirty minutes. The cemetery. Your mother's grave."

He hangs up. I look at Kane. "He's at my mother's grave."

"Your mother's grave. Where is that headed?"

"He's an asshole but a smart one. It's a play to make sure I show up."

"You believe she was murdered. He chose her grave. There are no coincidences, Lilah. Your own words."

He's right. "I need to get dressed." I hurry upstairs, take a quick shower, clip my hair to the top of my head, and throw on light-blue jeans and a black T-shirt. I have my gun, attached at my waistband. I have a knife, which I decide is my new lucky charm, and I have my purse. I do not have my badge. I pull on a black blazer and call it done. Kane has dressed right alongside me, and when I'm ready to leave, he meets me at the bottom of the steps and offers me his keys. "Unless you want me to drive you," he says.

I don't remind him that I have a rental parked here at his house. There is just something so immensely satisfying about picturing Kane Mendez in that piece of shit, and driving his car delivers a message I want to deliver. I take his keys and head for the door, my answer in my actions. Once I'm inside and I've started the engine, Kane's words come back to me, my words: *There are no coincidences.*

Last night, everyone's phones being turned off was a perfect storm. I hope like hell my brother wasn't involved in setting up Eddie last night. That thought cranks up my cranky. Murphy with his meeting at the graveyard better not be part of this, too, or I swear I'm on a roll: I might just cut the man.

CHAPTER THIRTY-TWO

I arrive at the cemetery to find a nondescript white rental car, a twin of the one I left with Kane, parked close to my mother's gravesite. Murphy is leaning on the hood, and gone is his standard suit, replaced by dark jeans and a collared shirt that I suspect has some sort of FBI logo on it. I park next to his rental, real close, and I do so to drive home a point: I've traded in the FBI for Roadsters and revenge. Sanity for sweet insanity of the best kind. I no longer have boundaries.

Exiting Kane's Roadster, I round the hood, noting absently that the day is cooler than most, telling of a winter soon to approach. The month is September. I think. Who cares, really. I stop in front of Murphy, and it turns out that I'm right: his shirt is navy blue and the logo is a yellow FBI emblem. His hair is thick and salt and pepper, more salt than pepper. His build is fit and his eyes an intelligent cool gray. "Nice car, Agent Love," he says.

"Just Lilah. I quit, remember?"

"I won't let you quit. Remember?"

"Why are we here?"

"I knew your mother."

I blanch. "What?"

"Before your father and you. She was already famous. And once upon a time, she had a stalker. I was actually in private security and her personal bodyguard."

"Are you telling me you fucked my mother?"

"I had a relationship with your mother, yes," he says, unfazed in his demeanor.

"You did fuck my mother. You. My boss. *Ex-boss.*"

"I cared about your mother."

"And yet you were not together. Why?"

"It was complicated, as are most relationships, but we stayed close friends. Right up until her death."

Up until her death.

"Why haven't you ever told me this?"

"Knowing would have impaired your objectivity about why I hired you. And then some other lucky bastard would have snagged you and your skills instead of me. And I'm also arrogant enough to believe that your talent is better developed under me than someone else."

"So let me get this straight: I'm skilled. You wanted me on your team. But still, you felt that I was so small-minded and stupid enough that I would have had *impaired* thinking if I had known you fucked my mother?"

His jaw tenses. "Stop referring to my relationship with your mother that way."

"She was a movie star and a notch on any man's belt."

"Your father's, yes. Not mine."

"My father married her," I argue. "You did not."

"I'm not going to give you the private, intimate details of my relationship with your mother."

"Then why are we at her grave?" I ask. "And why did you tell me at all?"

"Reverse order on those questions with answers. Why did I tell you at all? I don't like lies or secrets, while sometimes, as you know, they are necessary. Going forward, you and I cannot afford such things between us. As for why we're at her grave: to make a point. And that point is that people die. You can die just like her if you go off the deep end."

"You really are ridiculously arrogant to believe that if I choose not to work for you, I'm going off the deep end."

"You think that transferring to the New York division under a director you know is not only corrupt and dangerous but tied closely to your family is smart? It's not. It's a good way to get killed."

"So is this job in general, and who says the New York director is tied to my family?"

"Stupid doesn't suit you, Agent Love. But if that is how you want to play this, I can tell you that he's tied to Pocher. And Pocher is tied to your father. You are not working for him."

"Block me. I don't need the job." I start to turn away.

"I want what you want."

I face him again. "Which is what?"

"The wrong people, who are in power, out of power."

"You have a problem with the New York director."

"You'll work for me but live in Manhattan. You'll be part of a task force that I'm being assigned to head up. Together we'll solve cold cases around the country, but you'll be assigned to the New York State region, since it's your home turf. You'll consult locally and still travel to aid other regions if your skills are needed."

"And this does what for me and you?"

"In time, that will be clear. For now, you keep your badge and my protection, but you'll reside and work in New York State."

"You mean the badge I threw away?"

"You mean the badge you lost during your physical altercation with the Gamer?"

"Right," I say dryly. "That one."

"I'll handle the badge. And I'll be sending you three cases to look at next week. As part of your new role, you'll have the unique ability to review all cold cases across the entire country. I'm sure you will find corruption is often buried until the right person looks. And now, I'm going to the city to have dinner with my counterpart there."

"The one you hate and want to take down?"

"Yes. Him. Keep your friends close and your enemies closer. An old saying but a good one. Remember it. Make the local director feel that you are on his side. Make them all feel that you are on their side. Your family included. And you tell me everything. You listen to me. I will guide you and keep you alive."

I tilt my head with that statement. "Enemies closer," I repeat. "You said Kane is everyone's enemy but mine."

"His enemies want to control him, but only you can. That makes you a very powerful person."

"I won't lie to Kane, and I won't use him."

"Good. Make sure you hold me in the same regard."

"I won't tell you everything. Not yet. I don't trust you enough."

"Good again. You shouldn't. I haven't earned it. But then, neither have you, Agent Love. It will be interesting to see where this new relationship goes, once we clear the trust barriers." He pushes off the car. "Communicate." He walks toward his driver's side door.

I glance at my mother's tombstone and then back to him. "You think she was killed, don't you?"

He turns to me, looking at me over the open car door now. "Did I say that?"

"You just did," I say, smart enough to know what that reply infers: she was murdered.

"Time will tell a story, Agent Love. Time has a way of doing that." He starts to get into his car and pauses. "Rich is working a task force in Paris. He's radio silent."

He doesn't explain his sudden turnaround on Rich. He simply gets in his car, and I have the distinct impression that Rich was an unknowing part of some test Murphy was giving me.

I watch his car pull out of the lot, and once he's disappeared, I walk to my mother's grave and stare down at it. "I'm going to find out your story, Mom. That's a promise."

I dial Kane. "Come here." I hang up and I sit down under the willow tree and replay the conversation with Murphy, and each time I do, little tidbits of the conversation lead me to new conclusions. I'm on my fourth replay when Kane pulls up, and somehow the man makes my rental car look like a Roadster. It's carriage. It's style. It's confidence. And it's a lesson to me about myself. I have to own my next moves. I have to convince everyone that I am here and committed to my father's campaign. Maybe even that I was scared into submission. Okay. No. Never mind. No one would believe that. Not for a minute.

But I have my own story to tell. And it begins now.

Kane sits down next to me and rests his wrists on his jean-clad legs. He doesn't ask questions. He waits for me to talk. I enjoy the silence. The cool breeze. The willow tree limbs swaying around us. The calm before the storm that is coming. But finally, I tell him everything.

"You're staying and you're keeping your badge," he concludes.

"Yes. I'm staying. I'm keeping my badge and I'm going to find a place in New York City to rent."

He glances over at me. "You can stay with me."

"You know I can't do that and create the trust I need to create with the New York bureau."

He stares at me for several beats, his expression indiscernible before his gaze shifts forward again. "Sanity, not insanity," he says.

I think he's more relieved than he wants to admit. I think Kane needs me to pull him to the middle. Even if it means that the badge is now, once again, between us.

CHAPTER THIRTY-THREE

Kane and I head to the police station to give our statements after we leave the cemetery. Kane doesn't hang around after we finish up, leaving at my urging to allow me time for a brother-sister hate/love fest. I begin that process by joining Andrew in his office. "My boss is in town. He knows I'm closing the case, but there's more."

My brother stands up and walks to his door and shuts it before he sits down on the arm of the visitor's chair beside me. "What now, Lilah?"

"I'm moving to New York City. I'm going to be working on a cold-case task force for my boss. I'll still be reporting to the LA bureau, but I'll be focusing on New York State. And I took the job because Mom's grave reminds me that we will all be dead one day. I need to be with you guys. I want to help Dad with his campaign. I want to fight with you in person, all the fucking time."

We talk for an hour, and this time I get my doughnuts with him. And today, my brother feels like my brother, and that is not a person who would involve himself with the Society if he knew they existed. But for now, it's better that I leave that topic alone. What he doesn't know can't kill him. I hope.

"Have you told Dad?" he asks before I leave.

"We had a fight yesterday," I say. "I just need to get over that first, but I will. That's the entire point of being home. Family."

"Family," he says. "Remember that. We protect each other."

And Dad's version of that is that I get raped and not killed, but I don't say that. I give a reply of, "Don't fuck with the Love family," and leave.

~

I stay with Kane that night. Murphy lets me know that he's aware of my sleeping arrangement by express-mailing a new badge to me at Kane's house. It's not long after I've opened that package that Kane announces he's leaving on a business trip. The kind of business he doesn't discuss, and just like old times, I know my badge is the reason. I stay at my cottage, despite his insistence that I stay at his place here or in the city. Of course, I'm certain someone is watching me. I'm still a target for the Society, but even Kane agrees that Eddie will be well buried before they come for me. They have no option. My death, this close to Eddie's, would bring unwanted attention to them and to my father.

I spend the rest of the day in leggings and a T-shirt, pinpointing rentals in New York City online, and I decide I'm not going to live the way I lived in LA. That isn't how you fit in, in East Hampton or even in New York City. I rent a place without visiting. I don't have time for that chitchat, check-things-out-with-the-Realtor shit. I know the locations. I've seen the photos.

I've just DocuSigned the lease when there is a knock on my door. To my shock, Pocher is standing on my step. I open the door. "If you're recruiting me to put out flyers for the campaign, I suck at that stuff. I end up cussing people out for blowing me off at their own house. But I can deliver doughnuts to the men in blue and do the whole 'my father supports law enforcement' spiel while trying not to eat them."

"Can I come in?" he asks, his expression and tone troubled, as if he was a real human. Even his dress pants and white button-down appear rumpled and out of order.

I don't have my gun on me, but he's a delicate man, and I'm pretty sure I could take him with a knee to the groin. I offer him space to enter and wave him forward, pointing toward the kitchen while unwilling to give him my back. Once we're in the kitchen, I stop at the island and put it between me and him, and the only refreshments I plan to offer him are my knee and my knee again, not that I have anything else in the house to offer, anyway.

I have to play a little nice. I am, after all, supposed to be playing the part of the cooperative daughter. "I guess you heard that I'm staying."

"My brother was kidnapped. There is a sizable ransom."

"Oh," I say, because that's about as brilliant as I ever get. "I'll call the local FBI bureau and—"

"The kidnappers are the rival to the Mendez cartel in Mexico. I need to talk to Kane."

Murphy's words come back to me: *You are the only one who can control Kane.* And that's power. But I also remember Kane's vow to make Pocher pay for my attack and force him to turn to me.

"He won't take my calls," he says. "Call him."

"You're going to have better luck with the FBI. I can take the lead."

"Call Kane," he all but shouts at me. "Please," he adds, softening his voice.

Man, that *please* must have hurt like a bitch-slap. I pull my phone from the hoodie I have on and dial Kane. He answers immediately. "You've decided to move in with me," he says. "Or Pocher is standing there."

"Pocher is here. His brother has been kidnapped by a rival cartel, and he seems to believe you can help."

"Put him on speaker after asking me to do this for you."

"He's quite distraught, Kane. Please talk to him for me."

"Please," Kane says. "Aren't you submissive and sweet, Lilah Love. When I get back—"

I hit the speaker button. "Kane is on the line," I say. "Kane. Pocher is standing here with me."

"You have my ear, Pocher," Kane says. "One of them. I have a meeting to get to, so make it fast."

"My brother was kidnapped by the Rodriguez cartel," he says. "They want fifty million dollars. I need him back alive."

"Rodriguez is my enemy."

"Can you get my brother back?" he asks.

"What's in it for me?" Kane asks.

"You get the fifty million," he says. "I'll wire it to you now."

"I don't need or want your money," Kane says. "The kingpin, Luis Rodriguez, owes me a personal favor that extends beyond the war between our cartels. To call in that favor comes at a price to me. You know what I want in return."

Pocher looks at me. "She has my protection."

"You're getting there," Kane says. "Go further. Dig deeper."

"I will ensure that no one from our organization hurts her, but I can't save her from her own stupidity," he snaps. "And she stays away from our organization. Agree to that now, or I can't make this deal."

"Who are you talking to?" I ask. "Because it sounds like a third party, and if it were me, surely you'd look me in the eyes and speak to *me*."

"Give him what he wants, Lilah," Kane says.

"I'll stay away from the organization," I say, already thinking through the creative ways to spin that statement.

"If I get your brother back," Kane says, "and you break your word, Pocher, I will personally deliver your brother back to the kingpin himself. Do you understand?"

"I get it, Mendez. Get him back."

"I'll see what I can do," Kane says. And proving he still has someone watching me, he adds, "Now leave her house. Pick up, Lilah."

Pocher gives me a hard look and then turns and walks away. I pick up the phone and disconnect the speaker. "I'm here," I say, placing the phone to my ear.

"I have to go, but know this, Lilah Love. He will pay for your attack ten times over. This is just the beginning." He disconnects.

~

The day of Eddie's funeral, I start my morning with yet another call from Pocher, and I give him the same answer I did yesterday: *I have not heard from Kane.* And it's the truth, but not a surprising one for me. Kane's business trips to Mexico are usually in what he calls "dark territory" for cell service. And so I dress in a black dress and black knee-high boots.

I arrive at the funeral home to a roomful of uniforms that do not include Greg, who leaves me a voice mail that goes something like "I'll be in touch" or some crap like that. From there I decide the rain is the best part of the day. There is my brother with Samantha hanging on his arm, casting me gloating looks. Then there is the encounter with my father just before the service starts. "When were you going to tell me you were staying?"

"At least by Christmas," I say, and that is pretty much the best part of the exchange before he joins Pocher in the front row of the church. The very fact that Pocher is here proves that the devil does not burn when he steps inside a place of worship.

I claim a seat in the back row, and the service begins, tears and sobs beside me, in front of me, all around me. I've never done well with other people's tears. I don't like public displays of emotion. I withdraw, clam up. I didn't even cry at my mother's funeral, and it wasn't about an absence of grief. It was about too much of everyone else's grief suffocating me. Which is why when Pocher gets up and walks to the back of the church, I rotate and watch him leave, then seize the opportunity to leave early and follow him.

I exit the service room, and the front door that has been opened shuts. I follow him, and as soon as I step outside, I find Kane, dressed in a perfectly fitted black suit, standing beside his Roadster with Pocher in front of him. Kane opens his back seat, and a man about ten years younger than Pocher gets out and throws his arms around Pocher. A black sedan pulls up, and Pocher and the man I assume to be his brother get in the back seat. Kane's gaze lifts and finds mine, and I quickly weave between cars to join him.

"It's over?" I ask.

"No," Kane assures me. "It's just begun."

I don't ask what he means. I know. We're now at war with the Society. Maybe we always were, but now I know. My eyes are wide open.

∼

Raindrops begin to pummel us. Kane clicks his locks and we quickly take shelter in his car. "Cemetery or inside?" he asks as it slows.

"Cemetery."

He nods and places us in gear. We arrive a short time later and before everyone else, and as the storm becomes a near monsoon, the canopy above Eddie's plot blows away. His goodbye is as brutal as his murder. "I have to go back out of town," Kane announces.

"Cartel business or otherwise?" I ask, thinking how much I hate his announcement. How much I want him to say the right thing, the thing that he can't say. He's Kane Mendez. I know what that means.

"Lilah," he says, his voice a soft prod, willing me to look at him.

"I know. Don't ask. Plausible deniability, right? You do the dirty work so I don't have to, right?"

"Yes," he says. "I do. What I just made happen with Pocher did not come without a price. You have to understand that."

I face him. "I don't want to be the reason you do bad things. I'll do my own bad things. I'll save myself."

"I pulled a man off you after you were raped, Lilah. Don't expect me to even think about limits when it comes to making those responsible pay. There are none. And if that pisses you off, be pissed off. I can live with that."

"And if I can't?"

"I'm still doing it." He faces forward and starts the engine.

I'm furious with him, so fucking furious, and I don't even know why. But then the stupid tarp to Eddie's grave blows in front of the car, almost as if Eddie is telling us something. And I flash back to the Gamer saying, *Kane is dead*, as Eddie's body bled out a foot away. "You don't get to be your father and be with me, not because of me. *Especially* not because of me."

He sits there a minute. He doesn't look at me, but suddenly the tarp blows out of our path and we drive away. I glance down and find the photo of Kane and me, which had been in my bloodied clothes, in his cup holder. I pick it up and turn it over, looking at the marks on the back. The number of cases I've solved to avenge a murder I let Kane cover up.

He buried one body for me. He'd do it again. He goes to that dark, dirty place too easily. I can't let him go there again. And I can't let myself go there with him.

CHAPTER THIRTY-FOUR

By the time Kane and I stop by my house and I change into jeans and a T-shirt, pack a few small things, and we chopper our way to New York City, it's nearly nine at night. Kane has a private jet waiting on him, and he is forced by his "business" to see me off in an Uber rather than seeing me to my apartment. He kisses me, of course. I let him kiss me. Okay. I don't *let* him. I enjoy the damn kiss. I like the fucking kiss. I'm crazy in love with a man who may be the drug that kills me, which is exactly why his trip and my new apartment are well timed.

I arrive to the Central Park high-rise at ten and discover a package from Murphy waiting on me. Since I haven't given him my new address, I consider assigning him the title of my new stalker, but I decide he's not quite worthy of that title just yet. I grab the package from the security post, and my keys, before I head to the fifteenth floor. Entering my new apartment, I flip on the lights. The windows are floor-to-ceiling and wrap the living room that is to the left, while the kitchen is to the right. The furniture I'd picked online is cream colored, as is the rug, while the floor is a medium shade of shiny brown hardwood. I walk to the couch and sit down, opening the envelope, and I find three case files. There is also a file on the Gamer with a handwritten note that reads: PROFILE FOR THE PROFILER—MURPHY. I open the file and discover a man who was a Yale law school graduate like Kane, with a five-year difference, never married, hunter for sport, no living family. Not much else. For now, I move on and look through the case files, but I gravitate toward a series of call-girl murders that were never solved that remind me of Laney Suthers. I know who killed Laney, don't I?

"There are no coincidences," I murmur, which means Murphy gave me this case for a reason, and he quite possibly—most definitely, actually—is a part of a bigger picture I don't yet understand. I flip through the crime scene photos—four, total—gruesome stabbing murders that don't match Laney's faked suicide at all. But that doesn't mean the killer wasn't the Gamer, perhaps hired by Pocher?

Intrigued by this idea, I walk to the kitchen to make coffee and dig into my work, but I realize I have no food. I grab my briefcase and pull up a grocery store I know nearby on my phone, but it's too late to order and have a delivery arranged. "Pizza it is," I murmur, and this is no hardship. I love me some New-York-fucking-pizza-pie.

I dial up a local spot I love and order my old favorite, and since I still owe Nicolas at the DMV one as well, I arrange a delivery for him tomorrow. Once the pizza is all set, my need for chocolate, soda, and coffee has me hurrying to the door. I'm on the sidewalk in a flash and cutting through back streets that lead me to a corner store. I'm a block from my destination, about to turn a corner, when a man steps from a side alleyway into my path. Close. So close that under a glowing moon and streetlights I can trace every line of his hard, familiar features.

"Ghost," I say, standing my ground. "What are you doing here?"

"Why aren't you pulling your gun?"

He knows I'm unarmed. That's why he chose here and now. "Do I need to pull my gun?"

"I'm not here to kill you," he says. "Or you'd be dead."

"I don't die easily," I say, sizing him up again, everything about him controlled, calculated. Military trained.

"Careful now," he warns. "I love a challenge."

"You love a payday."

His lips quirk. "That's true, but I do enjoy a little sport as well."

"Why are you here?" I repeat.

"I owed you a thank-you."

"For what?"

"You not only got rid of the Gamer for me, you killed him yourself."

He shouldn't know this. I don't ask him how he does. He steps to me, right in front of me, and he stares down at me. "Bang," he says. "I owe you one. But just one."

I'm fairly certain he's just told me he'll kill someone for me for free, before he turns away and heads back down the alleyway. "I'm still coming for you; you know that, right?" I call after him.

He stops and turns to look at me. "You intrigue me, Lilah Love. Not one time did you pull the Kane Mendez card. Not one time did you use him as a shield."

"Kane is not my protector. I am. And I'm damn good at it. You could ask the Gamer, but as you said. I killed him."

His lips quirk again and he says, "And as I said. You intrigue me, Lilah Love. We'll see each other again." He grabs the fire-escape ladder on the wall and is up it in a flash, and I watch him disappear onto the top of the building. I let out a breath I've apparently been holding so long I might have to consider a career shift to Olympic swimmer, except I hate swimming.

I start walking, but I do so slowly, certain he is watching. I grab my supplies at the store and throw a few extra chocolate bars into the mix. I eat one on the way back to my apartment. A Mr. Goodbar, which has me telling dirty jokes in my head. A couple dozen of those dirty and also very bad jokes later, I reach my door at the same time as my pizza. I tip the guy with a twenty and hold up the candy bar in my hand. "Give this to her. Then she can't say you didn't give her a really good Goodbar tonight." I deliver the words with remarkable earnestness.

He responds with a look that is incredulous bordering on indignant. Maybe that's because the joke sounded better in my head, as most usually do. Or maybe it's because he's about sixty and is no longer a Goodbar kind of man. Either way, he lets me keep my Goodbar, which I intend to enjoy this very night.

I shut and lock my door and walk to my kitchen, where I set down the pizza box and stick my sodas and ground coffee in the fridge. The coffee doesn't belong in the fridge, but I realize now that I don't actually have a coffeepot, so I don't think it matters where it is. I walk to the island. It's stainless steel, which I'm pretty much digging. I do good Internet shopping. I open my box and grab a slice of pie and take a bite. That's when I freeze. There's a note. A *Junior* note.

I toss down my slice and read it without touching it:

M is for Miss me? I missed you.
D is for Disappointed. He's not for you. This city is not for you.
S is for sorry. You are going to be so so so so so so so sorry.
W is for warning. Don't say I didn't warn you.

Junior was not the Gamer. I grab a slice of pizza and finish it. My cell phone rings and it's Murphy. "I got the case files," I say. "The call girls—"

"Later, Love. The locals requested our help."

"Really? Already? Is it some sort of power trip?"

"No. Unfortunately, they have three dead women and what they believe to be a serial killer. They're desperate to solve the case before it goes public. They want you to profile."

"They have one of the best profilers in the freaking world," I say, thinking of my old mentor for the first time since I took this new role in the task force. My mentor *is here.* Why did I not think about this before now?

"Yes," Murphy confirmed. "Roger Griffin. And he's the one who asked for your input. Go, now. I'll text you the address. And Agent

Love, remember the lesson you've learned. *Communicate.*" He hangs up and leaves me with a personal problem to solve.

My mentor, the man who sees monsters and killers where other people see ballerinas, school teachers, and Lilah Love, is about to look me in the eyes. And I have already misstepped by coming here, by giving him the chance to see the monster I fear is inside me. But it's too late now. I can't run and I can't hide.

ABOUT THE AUTHOR

Photo © 2014 Teresa Lee

Lisa Renee Jones is the *New York Times* and *USA Today* bestselling author of the highly acclaimed Inside Out series; the Dirty Money series; the White Lies duet; the Tall, Dark, and Deadly series; The Secret Life of Amy Bensen series; and *Murder Notes*. *Murder Girl* is the second book in the Lilah Love series. Visit her at www.lisareneejones.com.